BLACK ICE

by

Cyan Brodie

Enjoy the read

C/Brodie

First published February 2017

2nd edition January 2018

ISBN-13: 978-1543218817

ISBN-10: 1543218814

Cover Image © Phil Jones

For Karen

who knows all the reasons why

A falling body accelerates at a constant rate of 9.8 metres per second per second regardless of its weight.

That means after the first second it will have already attained a velocity of 9.8 metres per second. After the next its velocity will have increased to 19.6 metres per second, and so on. . .

From a 45 metre-high building, disregarding air resistance, it will take a body approximately three seconds to reach the ground. The body's velocity on impact will be approximately 29.4 metres per second or 105 Km per hour.

BLACK ICE

JULY

1

ALEX dropped Paulina off at the railway station at the back of eight. The air smelt of dust and diesel fumes, and she could already feel herself wilting under the residual heat of the day as she headed off in search of a taxi.

"Xpro Hotel please."

The driver swung across the line of slow-moving traffic and headed towards the airport. "You travelling far?"

"I'm meeting someone. A dinner date."

"Lucky guy."

She leant back against the seat, closed her eyes and let the air conditioning caress her brow.

This one was Theo. That was the name Jonno had given her. But the chances were this was another made-up name. Another lie. Most punters lied.

When she arrived at Reception, she didn't bother asking the front desk to telephone and let Theo know she was there. She took the elevator to the fourth floor then tapped on the door of room 414. He kissed her cheek as soon as he let her into the room. She could smell aftershave. Peppery. A hint of lavender maybe.

"Polly, yeah? And on time."

Mid- to late-forties, Theo appeared to be well-mannered and attentive - a charmer by the look of it - but a real gentleman compared to some of the *dupki* she had to deal with. He helped her slip off her coat, draped it across the back of the chair next to the bed and offered her a drink.

"Vodka?" he said. "Or I have gin if you'd prefer?"

"After we have supper."

"Shall I put your bag here for now?" Theo placed it on the same chair as her coat then took out an envelope. "What did we agree? Two fifty?"

"For the night," Paulina replied as she surveyed the room. A slim-line laptop sat open on the low table in the centre of the bedroom along with a silver phone, one of the latest iPhones. A half-empty glass of clear liquid and an unopened bottle, mini-bar size, stood next to them.

Theo checked his watch. "So if you'd like to freshen up first. I have one or two emails to send before close of business in the States."

"That's fine. Thank you."

Paulina folded the envelope in half, picked up her bag and retreated into the bathroom. She knew from bitter experience how some punters hated her contacting the outside world while they were together. Especially if they were paying for her services by the hour rather than the full night. But she realised if she didn't text Jonno to tell him she'd arrived and all was well, he would become concerned. He'd made it clear this guy was one of their special clients. 'Whatever Theo wants, he gets.'

Paulina would decide for herself what Theo got. She tore open the envelope and checked its contents. Five £50 notes as agreed.

On the glass shelf above the washbasin Paulina noticed a fancy canister next to the tube of shaving gel. Dunhill London ICON. Not cheap. It meant she'd get a big tip, if she played along. There were things even Jonno did not need to know. She took out the single wrap from her bag, sprinkled its contents onto the glass shelf, rolled up one of the crisp new banknotes and snorted half a line of coke up each nostril.

Then she dabbed her face with a dampened tissue, applied fresh mascara and tidied up her lipstick. She studied her face in the mirror one more time to make sure everything was perfect. Her cheeks bore a natural scatter of freckles, intensified by the July heatwave that had caught everyone unawares. A splash of SJP NYC at the throat and behind each ear and she was done.

Her mother would have approved. 'A blossom without scent is like a man without a soul.'

Paulina's friend, Ania, had helped choose the dress for tonight. A cocoon-style, draped wrap in midnight blue with low neckline and ruched sleeves. Jonno had passed on a request from the client that she not wear a bra for their date. All she wore underneath the dress was a pair of flesh-coloured silk stockings, complete with maroon suspender belt and matching panties. Some clients weren't as choosy, but in her experience most men despised tights.

When Paulina came back out of the bathroom, Theo gave an admiring nod. "You look amazing."

"Thank you so much."

"I have to say, I didn't realise there were such pretty girls in Aberdeen. I'm honoured."

She detected an accent when he said 'such pretty girls' - maybe Scandinavian or Dutch.

Theo straightened his tie and put on the suit jacket laid out on top of the bed, then he picked up his mobile phone and took her hand.

"Shall we go down?"

The hotel restaurant had been quiet. Mostly businessmen,

dining alone on their expense accounts no doubt. Theo seemed more than happy to walk in with her on his arm. He ordered a martini, without the olive, then once the food arrived he worked his way through a bottle of expensive Riesling. Paulina stuck with bottled water. They both selected seafood starters. Then Theo asked for steak, filet mignon, medium-rare. Paulina chose a salmon salad.

Theo checked his watch again. "There's time for a malt, then we go upstairs. Will you join me?"

"You mean a drink? Maybe later."

Finally, after another glass of Laphroaig, Paulina helped steer him to the elevator, and once he figured out how the electronic lock operated they were back inside his room.

"I get undressed now, if you are ready," Paulina said. "Let me take this off."

Theo placed his phone on the table, shrugged off his jacket and watched as Paulina unzipped her dress.

"You eat like a bird. Do you have to look after your figure all the time?"

"Not so much, but it's expected," she said. "It's part of, how do you call it? The job description?"

His smile broadened as she rolled down her stockings to below her knees then sat on the bed and released each foot like a magician performing a trick.

"Leave your panties on for now."

"Of course." She stood once more and folded her dress across the back of the chair.

"I'm guessing that means you work out as well?"

"I do yoga sometimes, that's all. But I watch my diet."

"Well, it's worth it. That's all I can say." Theo grabbed one of her hands and pulled her closer until she was pressing against him. Whisky on his breath. "Stand still and let me look at you properly."

His gaze covered every inch of her body, like a caress, and Paulina felt her skin grow flushed under such intense scrutiny. "I take a drink now. You say you have vodka?"

She stepped aside and crossed her arms against her bare chest while he opened the mini-bar bottle and poured them each a measure.

"Do you take juice with that? There is orange or lime."

She shook her head, took the glass and drained it in a single swallow.

"Wow," he said as he checked the time on his watch once more. "Somebody's in a hurry. It's not even eleven thirty."

"Not really. It is how we drink vodka in my country. It is customary in Poland." Flustered for the first time that evening, she placed the glass back on the table and reached for his left arm. Noting the black watch-face and stainless steel bracelet - simple but expensive-looking - she unclasped it from his wrist. "You're not paying for my company by the hour. Forget all this and come to bed."

"Let me look at you again, properly," he said. "Turn around. Slowly."

Paulina turned her back on him, finally expecting a response. But, when she faced him again, he'd still not moved a muscle.

"You like?" she said.

He put down his own glass, stepped closer, placed one hand on her shoulder and nuzzled her neck. "I like very much."

Eventually, Paulina pulled away from Theo, and once he'd kicked off his shoes she helped unbutton his shirt. Dense, black hair covered his pale chest, but he smelled clean and fresh. She ran a finger down as far as his navel. Belt and trousers next. Then she let him remove his socks and underwear while she unfurled the sheet and lay down.

He stepped closer, and Paulina could tell he was ready. She hooked her fingers either side of her pants and raised her bottom off the bed.

"No wait. I want to do that for you." He knelt next to her and began to stroke her bare skin before taking hold of her hips. Theo was more laid-back than most clients - patient and keen to let her control the pace.

The air inside the room had grown stuffy from the lingering heat of the day, and when it was all over Paulina sat up in bed and asked for a cigarette.

"I don't smoke. Not that it matters," he said. "But it is not allowed, unless you go down to the main entrance. They have alarms in every room."

"I wasn't thinking," she said. "I don't know why they give away books of matches at the hotel bar if you can't smoke inside their bedrooms."

He smiled and pointed to the heavy drapes hiding one entire wall. "There's a balcony through there. We could let in some fresh air at the same time."

A set of French windows stood behind the curtains. The coral sky was fading and a full moon, almost close enough to touch, added to the magical effect. A fainter, duplicate image hung in the same sky trapped between the double glazing. In a perverse way, it reminded Paulina of the night they'd crossed over from Ireland. Her and Ania and the three other girls.

There had been talk of a party. She'd put on her best dress. They drank champagne at one of the bars and giggled like schoolgirls as they were escorted onto the large motor boat. She didn't notice they had set sail until the receding lights of Portrush disappeared below the horizon. The sea remained calm during the crossing, but Paulina grew increasingly nervous as all signs of land disappeared. The dream of a better life might well prove to be another false hope. Another broken promise.

Sometime later, the boat's motor grew quiet and the five girls were herded one by one into a tiny dinghy. Ania had complained until a familiar voice barked at her to be silent. And as they approached the desolate shore of this unfamiliar land, Paulina had marvelled at the tranquillity of their surroundings. No motorways, with endless flares of red and yellow ribbon trailing into the distance and the constant buzz of traffic whatever the hour; day or night. No city centre blocks, with squares of light that never seemed to dim. Just a moon floating above the waves and a canopy of dark sky, filled with nothing but stars. So many stars.

She slipped into her pants, then inched open one of the glass doors and gasped as a breath of cooler air caressed her skin.

"Take my jacket if you're cold," Theo called out.

She wasn't. Her body felt as if it was glowing. But there was something intensely erotic about slipping a man's suit jacket over her naked shoulders, with next to nothing underneath, then stepping outside where anyone might see. Its silk lining felt colder than the night air but Paulina didn't care. She could smell him inside its folds.

She shielded the flame of the match as she lit her cigarette. The fourth floor balcony was barely deep enough to stand on, and the low glass partition surrounding all three sides gave a wonderful sense of being suspended in space. The distant horizon had already dissolved to haze as the sultry afterglow colouring the sky changed from pink to grey. An aircraft, way in the distance, tugged itself free of the runway then climbed steeply towards her right before disappearing. The roar seemed to follow long after take-off. And closer at hand, she could make out the bright landing lights of

15

another plane approaching the airport. It appeared like a beacon through the mass of street lights from the direction of Dyce.

Turning her back on the view, she rested her bottom against the top of the handrail and peered into the bedroom. Theo looked to be asleep. She took out the wallet from his jacket pocket and flipped through its contents. One Handelsbanken account card and two credit cards - Amex and Statoil. All three bore the name Theo Gunvaldsson, so he'd given Jonno his real name and she'd been right about the accent. Various business cards were wedged inside the zippered pocket. Most bore the details of engineering consultants representing the oil industry. His wallet also held a number of glossy membership cards for men's clubs: Seventh Heaven, Club Rouge, O-NYX, Diamond Dogs. But apart from a dog-eared €10 note there was no cash in sight. No cash meant no tip.

Skurwiel.

Theo's iPhone and wristwatch sat in plain view on the table. His laptop would be too bulky to fit in her bag. No matter. She stubbed out the cigarette and let it drop over the edge.

As she turned back to face the bedroom, the sliding glass doors opened wider. "Hey! Were you going through my wallet?"

She froze, the sting of unwarranted guilt like a slap to the cheek. Then the breeze freshened momentarily, inflating the empty sleeves of Theo's jacket. Paulina reached out a hand, but too late. The garment was sliding from her shoulders. She twisted her torso to retrieve it and felt the world tilt. Balance lost. Light-headed. Swimming in forty-five metres of air then nothing.

2

09:15 and the station car park had grown quiet. Most hard-working commuters were already chained to their desks by now and the kids who didn't have the brains to wag it were at school. But Alex still felt out of place - his comfort zone crumbling all around him.

Shit. What the hell was keeping her?

Time to make the call.

"Aye?"

"Alex here. I'm still at the station and yer lassie's a no-show."

"Paulina? What time is it?"

"Well after nine. I've been here the best part of an hour. What do you want me to do?"

Every girl knew the routine. They were to text Jonno if there was an unexpected delay or a sudden change of plan, otherwise they were to meet the car at the pick-up point at the time arranged. Those girls who worked the airport hotels took a taxi to Dyce railway station where Alex would meet them and ferry them back to the flats. The station was close to the airport but far less conspicuous. Jonno had made it clear Alex was never to show his face within sight of where the girls had been working. You never knew who was watching.

Some mornings, especially at the weekend, there would be three or four girls to collect from Bucksburn or

Danestone as well as Dyce. The girls congregated inside the station's only bus shelter, rain or shine. Having a smoke and sharing the latest gossip, no doubt. Alex knew the Polish ones called him *kierowca autobusu* behind his back - 'the bus driver'. He didn't mind. He'd been called worse names back home in Bearsden.

Paulina was his only pick-up this morning and she was already well behind schedule.

"Let me think," Jonno said.

Alex transferred the phone to his other ear and fiddled in his pocket for a cigarette lighter. If Paulina didn't turn up there'd be shit flying in all directions and he realised he'd be the first to get splattered.

"It's the new Xpro," Jonno said. "Go round and see if there's any sign of her outside the front or in Reception."

"You sure?"

"Can't you listen to what I'm telling you for once in your life?"

"Yeah. Fine, fine. You're the boss. I'm on my way. But if anybody sees me. . ."

"Just keep your head down. Act like you're there to pick up a fare or something. And when you find out what's going on, let me know."

Most of the traffic was heading the other way into Wellheads. But as soon as Alex joined the airport road, he was forced to sit in the queue of stationary traffic blocking the main approaches to the terminal. He'd been tempted to pull over and get out. A fifteen-minute walk, tops, and he'd be at the Thistle Hotel. The Xpro couldn't be that far away.

Instead, he stayed inside the car and scanned the roadside for signs - half expecting to see Paulina hitch-hiking in the opposite direction, wearing her normal outfit. Grungy crop top and mini-skirt, six-inch heels, and fishnets torn at the knees. But there was no sign. And as

18

Alex's car inched closer to the steel arches at the airport entrance, the reason for the tailbacks became clearer. He could see blue lights in the distance - police cars parked at each of the access roads to the parking compounds. The chances were this was simply a terrorist incident. The airport on lockdown. At least it might explain why Paulina had been unable to take a taxi as arranged.

He signalled right and followed a red Volvo heading for one of the short stay car parks at the side of the terminal building. No joy. A policeman in a high-vis vest held up his hand to bar entry. Alex wound down his car window and listened as the uniformed officer explained they'd have to turn around and find somewhere else to leave their vehicles.

"I'm supposed to be picking somebody up," Alex said.

The officer pointed to a row of half-built industrial units away to his right. "There are spaces down there if you're not stopping for long. I can't let you any closer."

New buildings seemed to have sprouted up everywhere since Alex had last visited the airport. Hotels. Conference Centres. Every one looked the same. Every new factory calling itself Hi-tech something or other. In his side mirrors he could see a tall building directly opposite the car park. A flash of bright orange contrasting with the uniform grey and white - the outline of an aircraft replacing the letter X in the Xpro logo. He didn't stick around to admire the architecture. More uniformed policemen stood at the hotel's reception area and a group dressed in white overalls congregated outside a makeshift tent next to the restaurant frontage.

He'd seen his share of police dramas on TV. He headed away from the crime scene and thumbed in Jonno's number.

"Hi. I've been to the airport and there's no sign of her." He waited for a heartbeat to pass.

"Did you check at the desk?"

"I couldn't get near because there's coppers everywhere. At the hotel, I mean. It looks bad."

"What kind of bad?"

"Looks like somebody's checked out a little prematurely. There's a bunch of stabz in white onesies. You ken what I'm saying?" Alex explained about the forensics team on site and the police cars blocking off every road.

The line went dead and Alex could hear an aircraft's engines in the distance building up power for take-off. "You still there?" he said.

"Let me think. If they're not letting anyone leave, let's hope she had the good sense to keep her gob shut."

"So what do you want me to do? I'm sticking out like a dick in a fanny factory."

"I'll call you back."

3

IN the end there was no need to wait for another call. Alex turned on the car radio and heard the 10:30 bulletin. By the time he got back to Rosemount, the news had spread through the city like a virus. On-line, on the local radio, BBC Scotland, STV and Sky News.

So far the police statement remained predictably vague. The body of an unidentified woman had been found in the grounds of a hotel close to Aberdeen airport. Evidence pointed to accidental death but the investigation was ongoing. A number of people at the hotel were still helping police with their inquiries.

Jonno ran his fingers through his long, greasy hair.

"You don't think the wee bastard did anything to her, do you?" Alex asked.

"Why would he? Paulina's no choosy. Paying clients can do whatever the fuck they want with her when it comes to sex, so he's no reason to hurt her."

"I'm only saying."

"For Christ's sake, let me think. I mean, we don't even know for sure it's our girl they've found."

Theo Gunvaldsson was one of their regular clients. Alex knew him by sight. Whenever he visited Aberdeen on business, he'd always book a table at O-NYX. "D'you think he's still at the hotel? Perhaps you could make the call and ask the fucker what happened."

"Ring the client while the police are sniffing around?" Jonno asked. "Are you serious?"

"I'm thinking out loud here. The polis are going to be interviewing everybody. If our mannie's in the frame, he needs putting straight. If he tells them anything that connects the girl with this address. . ."

"Can you not stop talking for one fucking minute?"

This was nothing short of a shit-fest. Alex knew if they sat tight, the problem would not go away. The chances were, if the victim was Paulina, the police would be unable to identify her. All she ever carried was the throwaway phone with Jonno's private number locked in to the unregistered sim-card. Jonno had her passport and any other relevant documentation safely locked away. The same applied to all the girls. In most cases that meant no documentation at all.

Paulina and her friends were so far below the Border Control's radar that no one would ever know they'd been anywhere near Aberdeen even if one of them did turn up dead. But, if this Theo guy had been hauled in for questioning by the stabz, God knows what he'd be telling them.

The clock kept ticking. "So what about Paver?" Alex said finally. "You gonna make the call before he catches the lunchtime News?"

Jonno cursed before thumbing in Gordon Paver's number. "Let me do all the talking."

"Aye, right. But put it on speakerphone. I wanna hear what his majesty's gonna do about this one."

The telephone only rang three times at the other end before being picked up. "You're the one calling me, so there must be a problem in Aberdeen. Am I right?"

"Not a problem, per se."

"Per fucking se? Let's get to the point, why don't we?"

"There's a situation. Something I thought you should

know about. It's one of our Polish girls."

While Jonno explained, Alex waited for the explosion at the other end of the phone. But Gordon Paver barely raised his voice. "It's useful to be kept in the loop, but I've more important matters to worry about. I'm back in Scotland for the foreseeable future, but I'm not here to get my hands dirty. That's what I pay you for."

"Right," Jonno muttered under his breath.

"If she's dead, I don't see a problem. You say you're sure there's no ID on the body, so as far as everybody's concerned she's just another piece of Polish trash waiting to be picked up by the street cleaners."

"I thought. . ."

"I don't pay you to think. I pay you to fix things when they go wrong and keep my name out of it. Are we clear?"

Jonno held his breath for an instant. "That's what I'm trying to do. We don't even know if it's our girl yet, let alone how she died. I'm worried about this Gunvaldsson guy. Right? He's got a reputation to protect."

"So?"

"So. If he's forced to save his skin, there's no knowing what he'll tell the police."

"So get your arses in gear and find him. You and your junkie partner."

Jonno raised his hand before Alex had a chance to respond.

"I'm giving you both carte blanche to do whatever it takes. And don't call me next time you have a problem. Deal with it. OK?"

"What the fuck does that mean?" Alex asked as Jonno terminated the call.

"It means we do whatever it takes," Jonno said. "No holds barred. Because if we don't get this sorted, Paver's likely to bring in someone else to do the job for us."

4

LAST night I dreamt about Gordon Paver and his idiot son. They were chasing me along the hospital corridor, both intent on killing me. One held a hypodermic syringe - the other carried a rocket-launcher. I woke up whimpering and soaked in sweat sometime before dawn.

"Can I get you anything, Amy?"

I asked the nurse for another pain killer and my mind went blank. Cold reality retreated until it was out of reach. The next time I woke, Kay's name escaped my lips. I'd been calling out for her. But Kay never came.

Instead, Mum and Leanne sat at the side of my bed. Their selfless devotion only made my distress a hundred times worse. Mum had already asked the doctors if there was anything they could give me to reduce my distress. But all they did was double the dose of sedatives making me increasingly groggy and nauseous. More twitchy than chilled. Despite my pasted-on grin, I was a long way from happy on the happy chart.

The antiseptic smell that filled my private room gave the impression I was on the mend. Most of the damage no longer visible now my physical wounds had been cleaned and dressed - stitched, patched and covered up. Both knees had been sliced to the bone by the rocks guarding the White Shore as I fought to reach dry land. And my right shoulder held a constellation of tiny scars. Shrapnel from bits of scorching hot fibreglass rather than actual glass.

"No one will know what happens after everything is healed over," the young, red-headed nurse had assured me as she picked out pieces of boat from my body. Not a Scottish accent. Eastern European maybe.

Patches of gauze dressing had been attached to various parts of my body like post-it notes marking each cut and abrasion. There were also superficial burns to the back of my neck and scalp, but any marks would disappear in time.

My top lip was a different matter. I could feel the stitches inside my mouth each time I explored with my tongue. Mum's blatant attempt to lighten the mood wasn't helping. "It's amazing what a bit of make-up can do."

I had reason enough not to smile even if I'd been able to. I didn't care how I might look on the surface. The real damage ran much deeper. I felt dirty inside. Unclean. The underlying stench of shame curdled the air until I knew I'd gag if Mum or Leanne made any more attempts to cheer me up.

As the hours coalesced into days, everybody kept repeating the same mantra. It was over. I was safe. They would always be there if ever I needed to talk. No one mentioned Kay Jepson, other than to say she was fine. No need to worry. It was obvious there had been something going on between us. Most of the events leading to my hospitalisation had unfolded in Kay's flat. Kay had been discovered the following morning; hungover, but alive nonetheless. But it seemed the wounds pock-marking my flesh weren't enough to prove I was as much a victim as Kay.

The press had their own explanations why I ended up spending almost twenty four hours in the company of a deranged homicidal maniac. Mum and Leanne didn't believe a word of it, but they still needed to hear my version of events. And the police were naturally as desperate to discover the truth - begging permission to interview me as soon as I was able to speak. For the first week, the medical staff kept them at bay, but finally everybody got their wish.

"We'd like to begin piecing together a witness statement whenever you're ready to talk, Amy. Just a few questions, while everything's fresh in your mind."

Mum held onto my left hand - the hand without the intravenous drip - as the two officers pulled their chairs closer to my bed.

"I'm not sure Amy's up to answering your questions right now," she said. "The poor girl's been through so much."

"We'll not take long, Mrs Metcalf. But the sooner we gather the facts, the sooner we can close the investigation."

I was still doped to the eyeballs, and I'd barely uttered three consecutive sentences since having my disfigured mouth stitched up. "I'll try," I said. "But everything's still a blur. I'm remembering odd fragments, all jumbled inside my head."

"That's understandable. We're not here to pressurise you into trying to recall every single detail right away, Amy. But we see this all the time. It's like completing a jigsaw puzzle. If you tell us whatever comes to mind, right from when you went inside Miss Jepson's flat, we can maybe try to piece individual memories together. Getting things in focus and in the right order might help you come to terms with the situation. It might help you move on."

Except I didn't need their help to move on.

"So whenever you're ready, Amy."

5

I'D expected Mum to continue intervening on my behalf, to fight my corner and insist the two uniformed officers come back later when I was fully recovered. Perhaps ten years from now. But it was obvious she was as keen to hear my story.

Tears came easily as I fought to explain the sequence of events during the sixteen and a half hours between my leaving the Stag's Head and turning up, naked and bloodied, at the White Shore.

"I must have been sozzled. I don't know. I'd had a couple of gins when my shift finished at the pub."

"Amy's over eighteen," Mum offered. Not helping.

"But you didn't go home, even though someone offered to give you a lift," the interviewing officer said.

"No."

"Do you remember why, Amy?"

"It's all a bit hazy still."

Mum shook her head, as much in frustration as sympathy, I guessed. "Amy's been on medication the last few months - for her nerves. Something to help her sleep"

"Leave it, Mum."

"Maybe we should let Amy speak for herself," the officer said. "In your own time."

I gathered my thoughts. "When I got to Kay's flat the

living room was filled with lights. Candles."

"Did Kay let you in?"

"No. It was Peter Paver. There was loud music. I could hear it in the stairwell even before he let me in."

"So there was a party?"

I shook my head. "Not really. I remember someone handed me a glass of vodka," I said. "I don't normally drink vodka."

The officer recording my statement for posterity seemed to pause mid-sentence as he held the pen to his lips. "Do you remember who it was gave you the drink?"

"Must have been Peter again, I suppose." I began snivelling. "And I could smell weed. It turns my stomach thinking about it."

"OK. Take your time," the other uniform said. "So what made you cross the road and go up to Kay's flat in the first place?"

"I already said, I don't remember." I shook my head, trying to dislodge the memory. "I told Mum I was going to go straight home to bed."

"So why the change of plan?"

"I don't know."

The words were drying up. The officers sneaked a look in Mum's direction, as if pleading for her support. I'd already lost the train of thought.

"You were seen crossing the road and going in through the double doors at the bottom of the stairwell. Try and cast your mind back, Amy. Maybe you noticed something unusual. Or heard a sound. Someone calling your name perhaps."

"God, I don't know. There was Jimmy Jump's pick-up in the street," I said. "I probably wondered what it was doing there that time of night."

"Jimmy Jump?"

"The one who turned up dead in the chalet park," Mum

explained. "It's what the locals used to call Peter's uncle, James Paver."

"Peter had been using his truck," I continued.

"So you knew Peter would be there. Is that why you went up to the flat? To see Peter?"

"I honestly can't remember."

I knew exactly why I'd gone there.

"Did you have a thing going? You and Peter."

I shivered. "God, no. He made my skin crawl."

"But you still went inside Kay's flat, knowing Peter was there. Can you think why you might have done that?"

I let go of Mum's hand and wiped away a trail of snot from my top lip. "No."

"They found traces of drugs," the guy taking notes said. "Do you remember being given anything?"

One of the nurses had taken a sample of my blood as soon as I was admitted. I assumed hospitals were not allowed to pass on confidential medical information to the police without my permission, but none of that mattered for now.

I nodded and felt Mum take hold of my hand again. "I didn't ask for it, honest. That's not why I was there - to score. I kept telling him it was late. I was tired. But then he passed me a rolled up piece of silver foil. Said it was GBH or something. It would help me stay awake."

"Peter gave you this?"

No.

"Yeah." I nodded. "He said he'd already given Kay some. He told me to put it on my tongue. I remember it tasted salty."

"So what was Kay Jepson doing while Peter acted as host?"

Kay had been off her face. Drunk and high and already close to passing out naked on the couch.

"She was slumped on the sofa. I could tell she was past

29

caring what Peter did next."

Mum's hand squeezed tighter.

"Was there anyone else there with you, apart from Kay and Peter?"

I shook my head.

"It was dark inside - hard to see anything properly. The curtains were drawn closed and the music kind of filled the room. I could smell weed, so I knew they'd smoked a spliff or two. There were stubs in the ash tray."

"You're doing really well, Amy. We're starting to get a clearer picture of what exactly happened. So is there anything else you'd like to add?"

Nothing I was willing to share. They continued probing; finally asking if I'd voluntarily gone along with Peter Paver's orgy of destruction that ended so catastrophically. As if I'd admit to that.

Mum is probably the strongest person I know, but she looked broken by the end of the interview. I watched helplessly as the tears overflowed then ran down her cheeks, trailing to the wings of her nose then dripping off her chin.

"The doctor says Amy needs to get as much rest as possible," she whispered as the two uniforms stood and made to leave.

"You can go as well, Mum. If you don't mind." I pulled the sheet up to my chin. "I'm feeling sleepy now."

I could see the strain in her face as she glanced back before leaving the ward. Fifteen minutes later I managed to catch the young red-haired nurse's attention

"I need to speak to someone. It's urgent."

6

THE middle-aged woman sat at the edge of my bed and tried to reassure me there was no need to feel embarrassed or ashamed by her questions.

"We're here to give you the best treatment possible, Amy. We're not here to judge. I'll leave you some documentation to read through after I've gone. It explains everything about the screening process and our duty of care and confidentiality. We can test for a whole range of STDs, but unwanted pregnancies are the most frequent situations we come across."

Shit. A frigging baby? No way.

"I'm not pregnant," I said as I shoved the leaflets under my pillow. "I want to check I haven't caught anything. You know?"

"I understand. We'll run all the checks."

She uncapped her pen.

"So how long is it since you had intercourse?"

"Eight days ago," I muttered. "The night before they brought me in here."

"That was when? The 26th?"

"Yeah."

She made a note. "Was it vaginal, Amy?"

I bit back a sob. "Uh, no. I mean, we did other stuff as well. You know?"

31

"Anal or oral?"

"Oral." I began blushing more furiously than ever.

She continued jotting on her clipboard. "And your partner, he wore protection?"

"I think so. We were both pretty drunk and we'd taken something. He'd given me drugs."

She nodded and carried on writing.

"Have there been any symptoms? Any changes you've noticed such as an unusual discharge, itching or a stinging sensation when you pass water?"

I shook my head. "Nothing. But it's probably too soon. I don't know."

"You've actually left it a little late if intercourse took place more than three days ago. But let's see what we find," she said.

"I didn't want to say anything before now," I continued. "But it's been playing on my mind. I might have picked up something, you know?"

She lifted her head and pushed her glasses more firmly onto the bridge of her nose. "You're doing the sensible thing, Amy. Are you still in a relationship with this boy? Because we might need to speak with him as well."

I shook my head, barely able to hide the revulsion from my voice as I explained how it had been strictly one-off. I didn't elaborate on why there would never be any need to contact Peter Paver.

"You mention you were drunk and on drugs. I can see from your medical notes that the doctor who examined you on admission found bruising to the inner thighs as well as several other injuries. Chafing to the skin surrounding the entrance to the vulva often indicates forced intercourse. We see it all the time with date rape."

Jesus.

I swallowed the bile welling in my throat. "It was nothing like that," I said.

"That's fine. But I have to ask. It's more common than you'd think. Girls have a drink or two and the boy thinks that gives him permission. Or maybe they are too drunk to understand what they are agreeing to."

There was no way I was changing my story. As soon as I'd asked to be tested for STDs, the immediate assumption was that I'd been sexually assaulted. I'd assured them that hadn't been the case. The lies came so easily.

"I knew exactly what I was doing. Sorry if that sounds awful."

"That's fine," she said. "We already have your blood samples so the nurse here will just need to take a few swabs. Then we'll send everything off to the laboratory."

The red-haired nurse had already put on a pair of latex gloves.

"The police won't get to know about any of this, will they?" I said.

"Of course not. This examination isn't for forensic purposes. And besides, most of the physical evidence the police need for a rape prosecution disappears within the first twenty-four hours."

"Only they've already been to interview me about everything else that happened."

"We won't reveal anything to anyone without your permission."

I opened my mouth and held my breath as the nurse gently scraped the inside of my cheek. I'd always known doctors are supposed to keep your private business strictly private. Everyone's allowed their privacy. But paranoia has a sneaky habit of sneaking up on you. I'd die before telling anyone what really happened at Kay's flat that night.

"And I'd rather my family didn't find out. My mum."

"That's fine, Amy. Try not to let that worry you." The

woman got up from the chair and took off her spectacles to wipe the lenses clean. "We should have the results within the next forty-eight hours, then we can discuss what happens next. Prescribe treatment if necessary."

I nodded and turned to watch her leave as the nurse pulled back the bed sheet.

"It's better if you lift your knees slightly when you open your legs, if it doesn't hurt too much."

"No, it's OK," I said.

The air felt cold between my thighs and I flinched as I felt her touch. It felt like I was about to be penetrated all over again.

"That's my hand."

"Sorry."

"It's fine. And now I'm going to take two swabs to be sure. I'll tell you everything I'm going to do, once you're ready, Amy."

"That's fine."

I closed my eyes and wondered what she could work out for herself by looking at me down there. Would she know how many times we'd screwed? Would she know there had been two of them?

"And now the second one if you're comfortable for me to do it again right away."

"Yeah."

Then she pulled down my nightdress, folded the sheets back over me and tucked them in.

"Thank you." I turned onto my side and curled up into a ball.

I heard the nurse say something.

"What?"

"I said it still looks very tender down there. I can get you something to reduce the irritation if you'd like."

"There's no need."

"OK, but if anyone has tried to hurt you, Amy, you

shouldn't keep it to yourself. Talk to somebody. They can help."

I shook my head. "It's not what you think."

"If you're certain."

"Honest."

The events of the day had been emotionally draining. Time for some shut-eye. But I could hear the constant hum of traffic outside, and the chatter in the corridor increased as the nurses changed shift. One of them came into my room and checked my dressings. Then after taking my temperature she offered to get me a cup of tea.

"A nightcap, then I'll leave you in peace. You look like you could do with a good night's sleep."

But when she returned she had someone with her. "You've got a visitor, if you're feeling up to it. He says he's an old friend."

7

"HI, Ames. How's tricks?"

And for a moment it seemed as if the events of the past four months had never happened. The floodgates opened and I began to weep like a pathetic, snivelling schoolgirl.

"Hey, no need to get all emotional."

"Sorry," I sniffled. "I didn't expect to see you, that's all."

"No probs." Matt's left arm was strapped to his chest and in his right hand he cradled a bunch of flowers. A last-minute purchase from the hospital gift shop, by the look of it. He placed the bedraggled bouquet on my bedside table and sat at the foot of the bed, pulling the hem of his gown over his bare knees. "So how are you feeling?"

I wiped the tears from my face and tried to sit up. I was supposed to hate this guy. "Like shit, if you must know."

"I didn't know what to think, to be honest."

"Thanks for bothering to visit," I said.

"No. I mean, all that stuff in the papers. There was even a photo of you on the TV news. They'd wrapped you in some kind of tin-foil sheet before bringing you in here. You looked half dead."

I remembered the lifeboat crew, the paramedics, the clattering helicopter ride to Inverness.

"They wouldn't say much. None of your injuries were life-threatening, but they were keeping you in under observation. I didn't know what to expect."

"This is worse than it looks." I touched my torn lip with a finger and winced. "So what about you?"

Matt had also suffered the consequences of young Paver's vendetta. We'd both been in the wars since we'd last spoken - since we'd last fallen out.

"Two cracked ribs and a broken elbow. They put the dislocated shoulder back in place but, Christ, it fucking hurt. I'm supposed to keep it strapped up for another three or four weeks and they reckon I might need physio."

"Really?"

"It's OK. It means I can take things easy for the rest of the summer. Light duties."

"I take it you're moving back home?"

"For now," he said. "I don't have much choice."

"God, that's going to be a bummer," I said.

"I know. Dad's not going to be splashing the cash, so I'll be on the wagon unless I find some other way to pay my tab at the Caley. Maybe I should sell my story to the papers."

"Yeah. Sure. So when is it you're getting out?"

"The doctor reckons Tuesday. I've had a minor kidney infection as well. Their choice of words, not mine. My pee turned the colour of Buckfast. That's why I'm still stuck here."

"Shit. You caught a bug from this place?"

"No." He shook his head. "It was after being in the water for so long, you know? Out at the quarry. There's all kinds of crap in there."

"So have the police spoken to you?"

"We had a wee chat on Friday," he said. "But there wasn't much I could tell them."

"No."

37

"I didn't give any details. There was no point."

"Why not?"

"They'd only be asking more questions. Why I'd arranged to meet someone at the quarry in the first place."

"Right."

"They're assuming it was something to do with Slippy. It was his van I was driving when I was attacked, so it could be mistaken identity."

"Right."

"Don't worry. I'm not going to breathe a word. But we both know it was your wee pal. Right?"

"My wee pal?"

"You know who I mean," he said. "I should have listened to what you said when we bumped into each other outside Leanne's."

"If you mean Paver, he was never a pal of mine. So I don't know where you got that idea from."

"But you told me I was top of his hit list."

"Well, yeah. I heard he was out to get us both after what happened with his dad. But I didn't think he'd go that far. I didn't expect any of this." It went quiet and I could guess what was going through his mind.

"So, what did you expect?"

There was no way I was going to mention what I did know and what I didn't. I made my excuses. Drink. Drugs. Panic. Heat exhaustion. I told him the doctors had warned me once the memories came flooding back I'd maybe need to talk to somebody. Counselling.

"Everything's still a bit vague."

Matt patted the back of my hand and I could feel my eyes welling up again. "I've told you. I don't intend saying anything to the police about you or Peter. I'm curious, that's all."

Christ, I needed to grow a pair.

"I'm guessing the police have been giving you a hard time as well," he continued.

"Oh, yeah. I've already got two coppers on my case - Tweedle-fucking-Dum and Tweedle-fucking-Dee," I said. "They were round here grilling me earlier on. Getting me to tell them all the ins and outs."

"It must be tough. Not being able to remember, I mean."

I shrugged.

"What about you? Will you be moving back home once you're out of here?"

"It looks like it," I said. "But I'm not looking forward. I'm sick of everyone making such a fuss."

"Sympathy has its advantages. I'm going to get nothing but shit as soon as I get home. You know what Dad's like. He won't forgive and forget."

Matt feeling sorry for himself as usual. No change there.

"He'll come round."

"If you say so." I heard Matt clear his throat. "Anyway, I'm sorry things turned out the way they did - between you and me, I mean."

You and me?

"I'm over it," I said. That relationship had died months ago.

His face stiffened. "So how long were you and Paver seeing each other? Before he kicked off, I mean."

"We weren't seeing each other! It was never like that."

My sister, Leanne, had warned me about the rumours circulating on-line. She'd handed me her iPhone and let me read what people were saying. Perfect strangers who claimed to know exactly what happened. Some argued I couldn't be as innocent as my family were saying. A real-life Lady Macbeth with more blood on my hands than running through my veins.

"People are concerned, that's all. You know what the papers are like."

"And you believe the crap they print in there? Christ, Matt. Give me some credit. There was nothing going on, I'm telling you. I didn't even see him until I went to Kay's flat that night - wrong place, wrong time."

"That's what I thought." He got to his feet and leant over to plant a kiss on my forehead. "The papers make up half the stuff they print anyway, to sell more copies and keep the advertisers happy - trying to sensationalise everything if the facts themselves aren't juicy enough. You shouldn't let it bother you. It'll all be forgotten in a few months, Ames. Just like this Referendum."

That's what Mum and Leanne kept telling me, but I didn't react. If he believed the lies they plastered all over the front pages of the tabloids then he could fuck off like the rest of them. I wasn't looking for sympathy, least of all from Matt Neilson.

"Keep smiling," he said.

"I'll try."

I knew the scars would fade over time, but there was deeper damage Matt would spot a mile off if I let him get too close. In the old days I'd have told him anything and everything. But times change.

8

THEO'S solicitor met him at the railway station.

"How was your journey?"

No time for small talk. "I'm on time so why don't we get this over with?"

"The police have invited us to attend Queen Street at eleven-thirty. That gives us an hour to go over one or two matters before the interview."

"There's already a meeting in Bremen I've had to reschedule at short notice. It is not good enough that the police don't even allow me to leave your country."

"It's normal procedure, Mr Gunvaldsson. They're investigating a suspicious death and you were the last person to see the victim alive."

"Eleven days now and always wanting to ask the same questions. Always the same questions. How do you know this girl? How much did you both have to drink? Did you give her drugs? Did you maybe pay this young woman for sex? We know she has intercourse soon before she dies so can you explain your relationship with this young woman?"

"It's a formality, Mr Gunvaldsson. It's perfectly legal for someone to pay a female escort for their company and to share a drink with them. As long as you don't proposition her for sex, you're also free to sleep together like any consenting adults."

"That's what I am telling them. Do they think she has come back to my room to read me a bedtime story?"

Theo had surprised himself with how well he'd handled the situation. As soon as he realised exactly what had happened, he rang down to Reception, reported the incident and asked them to call for an ambulance and to inform the police. He'd been able to retrieve the envelope from Polly's bag and put the money inside the case of his laptop long before the police arrived. All he needed to do was to remain calm. Shock was often delayed in such circumstances.

"You were seen dining together in the hotel restaurant. The girl appeared to be relaxed in your company. And it's obvious you didn't pick her up off the streets."

"Of course not."

"There were no signs of violence, so it's likely her unfortunate death was an accident."

"That's what I keep telling them. And again and again I ask why do they want to keep asking me the same questions."

The solicitor threaded his vehicle through the heavy traffic entering the city. "There's the matter of identification," he said. "That's why they're keen to interview you again today."

"But I cannot help them with that also," Theo said. "I have not seen the girl before that night."

"Exactly. But at the initial interview, you kept calling her Polly. You said she was Polish. Yet she carried no ID. Nothing in her bag apart from traces of cocaine, an unregistered telephone, a small quantity of cash and some items of make-up. You told the police you had arranged to meet her for a dinner date - and a drink in your room afterwards."

"What does it matter why we were together?"

The solicitor swung the car into a private parking area

at the rear of his firm's offices. "There was barely enough money in her purse for a taxi ride home. So if you didn't pay her for dinner or whatever, who did you pay for her services?"

Theo patted his brief case. "Maybe I pay nothing."

"You'd never met her before, yet you managed to arrange a date - on-line maybe. So you must have Polly's contact details, even though she carried no ID. No house keys. No nothing."

He switched off the engine and reached into the back of the car for his briefcase. Theo decided silence might be in order, for the time being.

"They're getting desperate. There's been a television campaign and posters displayed around the city's Polish neighbourhood, but no one has telephoned the helpline with a name so far. It's like she appeared from nowhere and nobody cares."

"And how does that concern me?"

The solicitor nursed the case on his knees. "It's bad timing, that's all. The police are clamping down on prostitution in Aberdeen. A number of high profile arrests have already been made. Brothels have been closed down and young women held, pending further investigation under Immigration legislation. They're well within their rights to charge you under the 2003 Sexual Offences Act if they believe you caused or incited an act of prostitution. So if there's something you're not telling them - something that might shed light on where Polly comes from, or on who she works for - it might be in your best interests to disclose that information today."

Theo drummed his fingers on the dashboard of the car. "I have told you already. I have friends who I meet with at various clubs. Glasgow. Edinburgh. I pay membership fees, and a variety of personal services are made available to me when I travel from one city to another all over Europe. It would not be wise to reveal the names of the individuals involved even if I knew them."

"To be blunt, Mr Gunvaldsson, no one gives a shit what you get up to when you're abroad. They're only interested in the Aberdeen connection. If you know who Polly was working for, I advise you to inform the police. It always pays to be completely honest in these situations."

"They give me a telephone number," Theo said. "I leave my name, the name of the hotel and a date and time. All this I leave on an answering machine."

The solicitor opened the driver's door and signalled for Theo to follow him.

"The police take my mobile phone and my laptop," he continued. "They have proof I tell them only the truth. What more do you want me to say?"

"We'll discuss this in my office. If you cooperate, the chances are the police won't be bothering you any further. That's entirely up to you."

Theo glanced about him as the solicitor ushered him into building. "It is not only the police I have concerns over," he said. "My contacts rely on my discretion."

"If you explain all this to the police, tell them all you know, then they're unlikely to press charges."

Theo knew Jonno had covered his tracks, but he would be saying nothing more to the police today. Jonno's first step had been to have someone visit Theo at his place of work. It seemed discretion did not always matter. Theo had accused Paulina of being no better than a thieving whore, but the scrawny young man in track-suit bottoms and hoodie ran a finger across Theo's throat. He explained what would happen if anything was said to the police about the flat in Rosemount, or the O-NYX connection.

9

FOUR days after the all-clear from the hospital laboratory, the same two officers turned up again. By now I was over the worst. I'd been transferred into a communal ward and one of the policemen asked if they could speak with me somewhere more private. I put on my dressing gown and followed them into an empty consultation room.

"There's a few things we'd like to clear up, Amy. If you feel strong enough to go through everything with us one more time."

"I'm fine."

I realised if I gave them enough dirt they might stop hassling me.

Tea lights on the windowsill. Music. Silver foil. The taste of salt on my tongue. Dancing with Peter. Stripped down to my underwear with Kay Jepson already laid out on the sofa like a rag doll, lost to the world.

I folded my arms across my chest as soon as he produced the ziplock bag. Squeezing my rib cage. Tightening. Deep breaths. Steady.

He didn't need to open it.

"We found various items of clothing on the floor of Miss Jepson's flat. Track suit bottoms and a pair of flesh-coloured tights. A red vest top, navy blue sports bra, white blouse, and black trousers."

I said nothing.

"Can you confirm if any of these are yours, Amy?"

"Yeah," I said. "The trousers and blouse are mine. It's what I'd worn for work."

No response. He was wanting more. Maybe some kind of explanation why most of my clothes had been discarded on Kay Jepson's living room floor.

"It was roasting hot and I remember taking my blouse off," I said. "I had a t-shirt and bra on underneath."

"Is this your bra?"

I nodded. "I must have taken that off sometime during the night as well. Things got a little wild. I can remember Peter's hands were all over me, wanting to help, but I wouldn't let him touch me."

I pretended that my head was beginning to clear. "I'd asked him to turn down the music. I was trying to get comfortable."

"Comfortable?"

I sensed the interviewing officer tensing up as I tried to explain what I meant.

"So you got comfortable by stripping down to your underwear," he said.

"If you want to write that down then go ahead. Christ, Kay was already down to her knickers even before I got there."

I allowed him a moment to savour the image of Kay and me both half-naked.

"I already told you we were pissed. He'd given me drugs. He'd given Kay something as well. Paver was up for anything and was obviously expecting more than a dance or two. All I know is that I was still wearing my t-shirt and underpants when we went outside the next morning."

I caught the smirk on his face as he looked at his

colleague for confirmation maybe. "You remember getting undressed. So did anything of a sexual nature happen? Between you and Peter? Or Peter and Miss Jepson?"

"For God's sake, what do you want me to say? I can hear this voice telling us he wants to party. But then there's like a blank space inside my memory. I remember wandering outside the room and going for a wee. And I remember him helping me down the stairs when we left."

"But you didn't think to get dressed first."

I shook my head. "It's hopeless. I've seen the stuff on the News, but I can't believe I was there when Paver went on the rampage. It doesn't make sense."

"What about your time in the truck? Do you remember where he took you?"

"Things keep flashing in my head," I said. "Pictures. I honestly can't tell whether they happened, or whether it's something I've seen on TV."

"You're having flashbacks?"

"Bits and pieces - like the camera crews in the big lay-by at Inchnadamph reporting how they were trying to clear the Skiag Bridge road. Aerial photos of what's left of the chalet park where I used to work. They said on the news he used rocket launchers."

"Right."

I said a silent prayer of thanks to the media for covering the incidents in such detail. So much for not compromising eyewitness evidence.

"I know it was all down to Peter," I said. "He kept saying how he wanted to pay everybody back for what they did to him and his dad. He had these walkie-talkie radios. He'd planned everything in advance. Putting the bombs, or whatever they were, in place a few days before. I can't believe how much destruction he's caused."

"And what about the time you spent on the boat?"

47

I stared into his face. "I already told you. It's flashes. Fragments of recognition. I remember trying to get away. The deck was slippery under my bare feet and I ended up leaning against the handrail with my back to the water and then I'm falling."

"You're doing well, Amy," he said. "The more you can tell us, the sooner we can put this matter to rest."

"I'm trying. You have to believe me."

"I appreciate that. It's a case of connecting your individual memories so we get the full story, that's all. Would you like us to give you a little more time?"

I didn't need more time. Everything was as fresh in my mind as if it had happened this morning.

"The water was colder than I expected and the salt burnt my skin. I could taste it on my tongue as well as something else, chemical, while I was trying to swim towards the shore. I could smell burning, but if there was an explosion on the boat I don't know anything about that. Sorry. I didn't even hear the bang."

From the disappointed look on the officers' faces as they got up to leave, neither of them believed a word I'd told them. As if I cared.

AUGUST

10

I'D been home less than two weeks when we heard they were reopening the investigation into Caddy's murder. Seven months after I'd discovered her body, they were suddenly acting like proper policemen. Fresh evidence had come to light suggesting their chief suspect had been killed in circumstances suspiciously similar to those in which my best friend died.

There was no need to read the front pages. The buzz. The fabricated frenzy of unfounded gossip and lies. I'd already heard the real murderer confess everything. It seemed advisable to keep my head down and my mouth shut. I had my own guilt issues to deal with.

Then the weekend before our local Highland Games, Matt Neilson called round and suggested I attend the Games with him. But there was no way I could face the Lochinver public en masse. Leanne and Steve were sure to make a weekend of it. Steve's family from Aviemore usually came up to stay. There'd be drinks at the Caley Hotel followed by a meal if they could book somewhere, followed by the Games Night Dance. Everybody would then crash out at Mum's and wait for their hangovers to subside.

But I had other plans.

Things might have been different if Caddy had still been alive. She'd always loved Games Day. The crowds and the spectacle. The evening ceilidh when everyone let their hair down to celebrate one of the highlights of the year. With Caddy at my side, I'd not have felt so exposed - so isolated. She'd always believed in me, even when I let her down.

The day of Caddy's seventeenth birthday coincided with this year's Games Day. That would have given us another excuse to dress up and party with all our friends. But instead of all this she got a naff write-up in the local rag.

In Memoriam

CADDY NEILSON (August 8th)
Taken too soon.
Never a day goes by without me thinking of you - my baby girl. Sleep tight, darling.
Love always
MUM

Matt had cut out the piece from the Family Notices page of the Northern Times and brought it to show me when he called round.

"Keep it if you want," he said. "I don't think Dad and Steff have seen it, and I thought it best not to remind them."

Much as I missed Caddy, I felt like screwing it up. But like all my other mementoes, it would finish up in the shoe box at the bottom of my wardrobe.

"It's not Steff who's put this in the paper."

"God, no." He laughed. "It's Vanessa. You know what she's like."

Caddy had never got on with her step-mother, Steff. Yet her biological mother, Vanessa, barely gave her daughter a single day's consideration while the poor girl was alive, despite what she'd posted in the newspaper.

By the look of things Vanessa was feeling needy all of a sudden.

Or guilty.

Vanessa Neilson had left Lochinver years ago - walking out on Mike when Caddy and Matt were wee bairns. Until the day of his daughter's funeral, Mike hadn't seen Vanessa in years. Even at the graveyard, she'd been more concerned with taking photographs for her Facebook page than building bridges with her estranged family.

I couldn't begin to imagine how much being abandoned as a child must have hurt Matt and Caddy. Yet I was planning on doing the same: walking out on my own family for my own, selfish reasons. It was the only way I could prove to myself that I still had control of my wretched life.

11

MY uncle Brendan had suggested I could flat-sit for him the rest of the summer. Space wasn't an issue since he spent half his life working offshore. I needed somewhere to lie low, somewhere I might feel safe, so I welcomed the offer. Lochinver held too many memories. I needed to recharge my batteries, and the East coast was far enough away from my troubles for now.

No doubt, Mum had dropped several unsubtle hints of her own, pressurising Brendan into offering me a place to escape the publicity machine while I licked my wounds. I'd already told her how desperate I was to leave home. I'd have settled for a sleeping bag and a rolled-up blanket in a shop doorway as long as I was no longer within walking distance of the scene of the crime.

I'd only visited Aberdeen on a handful of occasions, even though Dad's family still lived there - a legion of aunts and cousins and various other distant relatives I'd never even heard of. But apart from a few, brief weekend trips to the grandparents when I was still a child, I'd only been there twice since my dad died. Once had been to visit Brendan, and the other had been with the school. We'd stayed for two nights in a Youth Hostel. The teachers took us on a tour of Dunnottar Castle and Stonehaven followed by an afternoon at the amusement park then a fish supper on the way back to our dorm. Scottish culture at its best.

For much of the journey from Inverness, the railway skirted the main towns as it passed through the rolling countryside. Countryside much greener than home. Much simpler. Flatter. Then, as we approached the city, we passed the airport on our right. A new skyline appeared in the distance, studded with increasingly impulsive evidence of offshore wealth and greed and ambition. The tide of new-builds grew until it seemed determined to swamp the entire landscape.

I staggered off the train, desperate for pure air and sunlight. Brendan was waiting outside the main concourse, ready to ambush me with a bear hug.

"You're still a bonnie lassie." He lifted me clear of the ground. Then came the usual crap - how much I'd grown.

Shit - what did he expect? He'd not set eyes on me for over seven years. From what little I recalled of Brendan, he'd always been built big. Not working-out-at-the-gym-five-days-a-week big. More like healthy-appetite-and-a-fondness-for-beer big. He scooped up my suitcase but I held onto my rucksack for dear life until we reached the car.

"I've moved most of my stuff into the guest room," he said as he bundled my luggage into the boot of his battered BMW. "You can take the master bedroom. There's an en-suite, so you'll have your privacy."

"There's no need to go to all this trouble."

"Ach, it's nae bother."

He told me to fasten my seat belt as we left the multi-storey car park.

"This will all be new to you," he said. "Union Square. You'll nae mind a great deal from the last time you were in Aberdeen."

I recognised bits here and there as we headed North out

of the city, but so much had changed.

"I remember the harbour and the huge boats," I said. There were fishing boats and offshore oil rig support vessels moored virtually alongside the main street.

"Aberdeen's an awful busy place. Busy people," he said.

"I can see."

I'd always thought rush hour at Inverness was mental, but this was in a different league. Most of the traffic seemed to be heading in the opposite direction as we followed the signs for Peterhead. I thought back to my trip to Peterhead Prison three months earlier. Matt Neilson had been serving time there. Funny how my life seems to move in circles.

"When do you go away again?" I said.

"Not until next Tuesday. There's things I have to do before I fly out, but I can show you around the neighbourhood. A wee jaunt if the weather's fine."

"I don't want to take up any of your time."

"It's nae bother. And it's the least I can do. God, how long is it since I saw you last?"

"I was eleven."

"Aye. That'd be not long after Davey's funeral. The time flies and I wish we'd kept in touch. But your ma, she's an independent so and so."

I didn't want to think about losing my dad right now, but seeing Brendan in the flesh brought it all back. They both shared the same cuddly bear look. The same sunken eyes that twinkled whenever they smiled.

"She's doing fine."

"Mum? Yeah. She seems settled enough. I don't think she'll ever come back here to live. She's got a good job and all her friends are in Lochinver now."

"And what about yourself?"

I shrugged my shoulders. I could see Codonas on our

right across the flat expanse of seafront. I recognised the big fairground wheel.

"I remember coming here with the school," I said.

"It's a bonnie place."

"So you're still staying in the same flat?"

"Aye. The maisonette. It's only twenty minutes by bus to the city centre, so you'll be able to get out and about nae problem."

Mum, Leanne and I had visited Brendan a couple of months after Dad died. Mum had some bits belonging to Dad she wanted Brendan to have. All I could remember about the flat was the smell of stale takeaways and dusty carpet in the shared stairwell and the depressing views out across the parking lot.

"Seaton Park is close by whenever you fancy stretching your legs," he continued. "I go there now and again, when I can't get out on the hill. But you're best not going near at night. They've put signs up."

I nodded. "Mum said you and Dad used to go hill-walking together a lot."

"Aye. A long time ago."

Next thing, we were driving alongside a blue-grey sheet of water with the horizon virtually invisible on our right. I wasn't used to so much sea without a single rocky island or headland to break the monotony.

"You'll mind the schemes," he pointed to the tower blocks beyond the golf links on our left. "Promenade Court. It makes the place sound like the fucking Riviera, excuse my French."

"That's OK."

"You're best keeping away from this end of the city as well. There's all sorts go on here. Drugs. Gang fights. It's nae place for a young lassie on her own, if you ken what I mean."

"Don't worry. I won't be going far until I get my

bearings."

"Aye, well. If you're ever lost, ask for the Brig O'Don hotel. It's only ten minutes by bus back to Tilly from there."

We headed inland, passing a service station on the left then eventually more tower blocks.

"St Ninians – that's got a wee bit of a reputation as well but at least it's a step up from Donside Court."

"Where's Donside Court?"

"I'll show you. It's the tower blocks at the side of my place. They're mostly decent people with nowhere else to stay, but a few druggies get their names in the papers. Did you notice the new library? That big glass building on your left? I don't think they'd started building it when you were last up here."

Jigsaw pieces of memory began to fit together. The roundabout. The play park and the Zoology building. Then block after block of uninspiring architecture masquerading as social housing. But up ahead of us a whole rash of new-build apartments had sprouted where there had once been waste ground.

He parked outside the same nondescript terrace of four-storey flats we'd visited seven years ago. And towering over the entire estate, I could see five sets of high-rises - each block nineteen floors high. Brendan's chicken-coop existence was bad enough, but the thought of living inside a set of boxes stacked on top of each other was disheartening. No view to the hills or even the scent of the sea despite their height.

"Home sweet home."

Brendan had told Mum his flat at Tillydrone was only ever meant to be temporary. An investment - close enough to the university to allow him to rent it out to students and buy somewhere closer to the airport when the time suited. But that time never came.

"Let me help you with your cases up these stairs then I'll leave you to settle yourself in while I make us something to eat."

"How long will you be away for?" I asked as he handed me a spare set of keys.

"Two weeks. But I'll be staying over at Jan's a couple of nights, once I'm back. Whenever she's not working we try and get together. But nae worries. I'll give you her number as well as my own mobile - if there's anything you need."

"Did we meet her when we came before?"

"Not Jan," he laughed. "We've only been an item a couple of years. It's still relatively new to me, all this going steady business."

"Where does she stay?" I said.

"She's an apartment out at Midstocket."

"So are you going to sell this place and move in with her?"

"What's this? *20 Questions*?"

I shook my head. "I'm catching up, that's all. Mum never tells me anything about Dad's side of the family."

"That's as much my fault as hers," he said. "I only ever phone Christmas and birthdays. And our telephone conversations are always short rather than sweet."

"I know."

Mum never had much to say when Brendan phoned.

"Your ma doesn't approve of me, if you want to know the truth. We called a truce after Davey left us, but I'm still surprised she let you within a hundred miles of your crazy uncle."

12

WE spent the rest of Thursday night catching up. Give Brendan his due, he didn't ask for all the gory info on how I'd ended up in such a mess. He said he'd caught most of the background from Mum. Reading between the lines, he reckoned I'd been unlucky. But I chose to gloss over the finer details.

After we'd eaten, Brendan asked me if I'd like to see photos of my dad. Mum never spoke much about Dad either, even though I know she'd loved him more than anything else in the world. Maybe the pain was too much - remembering the good times and realising what she was missing.

"Most of them are before he took up with your ma. He was always a hard drinker before he settled down. Could put most men twice his age under the table, and it was me that got blamed for leading him astray."

Someone had stuck the pictures inside an album. Each photograph, complete with thick white border, held in place by four corner mounts. There were holiday snaps taken at the seaside. One or two of people dressed up for some formal occasion - suits with wide lapels and hair styles best forgotten.

"That's you ma's wedding day. She had such a twinkle in her eye."

Mum had the same picture on her dressing table in a

gilt frame.

Most of the others featured Dad or Brendan in full outdoor gear. Brendan was two years older than Dad but you'd never have guessed.

"We'd always fancied ourselves a right pair of teuchters, me and Davey. Country boys who'd been stolen at birth and raised in Tilly by tinks. That's us on Ladhar Bheinn. Out at Knoydart," he said. "We camped the whole week in Barrisdale Bay. July 1988, I mind it was. The summer before he married your ma."

"It's fantastic."

"Aye. It's a right bonnie place. That's Skye you can see in the distance. The Cuillins."

"Mum said you and Dad used to spend most of your spare time in the hills," I said.

"Aye, we did. Every holiday." His eyes seemed to lose focus for a moment. "I wish he was still here, you know."

"Yeah."

"Me and Jan. It's not the same, 'cause she hasn't got the same adventurous streak Davey had. We'd get in some right pickles, I tell you."

"You and Jan go climbing together?"

"Not exactly climbing." His fingers stroked the hair above his right ear. "I'm officially a wuss now, though I still do my fair share of winter walking."

I'd seen the ice axe hanging from one of the coat hooks in the lobby of the flat.

"We spent the Hogmanay before last scouting round Cairn Toul. It was quite something."

There were dozens of pictures taken in the Cairngorms but I also recognised one or two more familiar peaks.

"That's Canisp. Right?" I said. "With Suilven lower down next to the loch."

"Aye," he said. "Your dad and I spent a week at the campsite in Clachtoll. I'd borrowed a mate's motorbike

59

and we went there for an Easter break."

"And Quinag. I've been up there a couple of times."

"It was still single-track out of Ullapool back then," he laughed. "And there were more sheep than cars on the road."

"There's still plenty of sheep," I said.

"We decided to head home along the coast road through Drumbeg and someone at the village shop told us to watch out for anyone carrying a jar of barbecue sauce."

"Cannibals?"

"You've heard it before."

"Dad used to tell us."

"Davey had a wicked sense of humour," Brendan said. He must have caught me studying one or two of the photographs more closely. "Did anyone ever tell you you've got your dad's eyes?"

"D'you think?" I said.

"I always thought so. As soon as I first saw you."

I laughed. "Mum tells Leanne she looks more like our gran, and she goes mad if I say anything."

"Your sister?"

"Yeah."

"But you get on? You and Leanne?"

"Yeah, of course," I said.

"And what is it she does?"

I kept it simple. "She works in an old people's home. And her boyfriend, Steve, works for a builder's merchants in Ullapool."

"Good for her. And what about yourself? What d'you plan on doing when all this blows over?"

Caddy and I had always wanted to go backpacking after school. We'd talked about going to New Zealand.

"I can't decide. I'll probably end up in university if I get round to finishing my Highers. It's all up in the air at the moment."

Brendan nodded as if he knew exactly how difficult it was.

"Me and Caddy planned to take a gap year together," I continued. "But now it depends on what Mum says, I suppose. She didn't want me coming all the way out here on my own, so God knows what she'd say if I told her I was planning on going abroad."

"Speak to Jan," Brendan said. "She did a fair bit of back-packing before settling down. Thailand. Sri Lanka."

Maybe. Maybe not.

"So what does Jan do?"

"She's in her final year at Abertay, studying forensic sciences."

"Her final year?"

"She's been on placement out at the Gartcosh campus in Glasgow since April, so we only get to see each other at the weekends. Most of the time it's lab work, but she's had to attend crime scenes as part of the training. She's hoping to be based there full time once she gets her degree."

"Right."

He obviously caught the look that crossed my face.

"Jan's a mature student, Amy. She's nearer forty than thirty."

"I wasn't thinking about the age difference," I said. But I had been. "I was wondering why she's living in Aberdeen if she's studying in Dundee and working in Glasgow."

"She kept hold of the flat she bought during her previous job. They're like gold dust."

"What was her job?"

"She was an air hostess. What they used to call trolley dollies. Not as glamorous as it sounds. But now she's hoping to qualify as a forensic photographer."

"Different," I said.

61

I didn't press for more details. I'd witnessed enough crime scenes first hand without needing to see Jan's photo collection.

13

NEXT day Brendan took me into town on a shopping expedition. His idea not mine.

"I know what you lassies are like. You'll be wanting to spend time at all the clothes shop in Union Square. Catch up on the latest fashion."

"I'll have to see how I'm fixed for cash first," I said.

"No worries. I told your ma I'd not see you short. And if you plan settling down here, there are plenty of part time jobs. Speak to Jan. She knows most of the bars in town."

"I'm not sure. I don't want to sound ungrateful."

"Ach. Suit yerself."

He mentioned he'd already booked dinner for the three of us at one of the bistros close to the docks for later. Jan was due home sometime between six and six-thirty, depending on the traffic between Glasgow and Aberdeen. But by four in the afternoon I was flagging. I'd had enough window shopping to last me a month. All the time I could sense Brendan was desperate to buy me something fancy to wear, or some girly accessories to disguise the Lochinver look. But all I wanted was an early night.

The thought of sitting down to a meal in some snazzy restaurant with Brendan's lady friend didn't appeal right now. We'd have nothing in common, and I wasn't in the mood for making polite conversation. Things got no better when we'd finished the shopping expedition. He insisted we visit the Maritime Museum. The building was light and airy inside but I couldn't see the appeal. Brendan's boyish enthusiasm soon began to wear me down. It was as if he didn't want me to miss a thing.

Finally, we reached the museum's top floor and he showed me the mock-up of living quarters on board a rig.

The bunk bed resembled a cocoon at best. "You're supposed to sleep in something like that for two weeks at a time?" I said.

"It's only somewhere to get your head down between shifts," he laughed. "Jan says I could sleep on a clothes line."

"Right."

By then I'd figured out what formed the centrepiece of the building and it held a sinister fascination. A scale model of an oil platform rose from the first floor to the third level - a massive twenty-five-foot high skeleton of tubes and girders with a web of cables and piping; stunningly impressive at such close quarters.

I felt sick just looking at it. "Is this the same kind of rig you work on?" I asked.

"Pretty much."

I stared over the glass barrier and felt my stomach lurch.

"We're out on the Norwegian shelf. The Eldfisk. This one's a scale model of another platform that used to work North-East of Shetland. They only have fixed working lives. They're already decommissioning this one."

I blinked away a memory. "Is it close to where Dad used to work?"

He nodded. "Give or take a hundred miles."

I peered over the edge again.

Heights had never been a problem at home. I could happily pick my way along the knife-edge ridges of Quinag or An Teallach without a thought for the sheer drop either side. But unlike mountain tops, ladders and metal platforms have a habit of coming apart without warning.

"So how far down is it?"

"To the sea bed? About eight hundred feet," he said. "The bits at the end of the drills go down much deeper into the bedrock. You're talking thirty thousand feet in some cases."

Eight hundred feet seemed far enough to fall.

"God, lassie. Have you seen yourself?"

Sweat had already broken out on my forehead and I could feel my face growing increasingly hot, as if I was about to pass out.

"I'll be alright," I mumbled. "I need some fresh air, that's all."

I swallowed my nerves as we took the lift back to the ground floor. Then I stumbled outside and Brendan held onto me while I began taking deep breaths.

"Is there anything you want? A glass of water?"

"No. Give me a couple of minutes." I pulled away from him. "It was awful muggy inside."

The pavement seemed to dazzle too brightly. People milled about - chattering, enjoying the afternoon sunlight, oblivious to everything else around them. Their smiling faces and the baking heat put me in mind of summer parties at the White Shore. The buzz and the bustle. There was even a drunk propped up against a wall nearby to complete the scene.

"Is it the medication you're on?"

I shook my head, even though my skull throbbed. "No. I'm probably tired, that's all. I'll be OK. Honest."

He looked lost.

"I haven't been out that much since leaving hospital."

He began to curse his stupidity. Dragging me half way across the city like an excited child, then expecting me to sit in a swanky restaurant with him and Jan until all hours when it was obvious I needed my rest.

"Your ma warned me to look out for you and it's a cat's arse I'm making of things so far."

"No. Honest, Uncle Bren. It's not your fault. I'll be fine."

But we drove back in silence. And as I got changed into my pyjamas and dressing gown, I could hear him on the phone to someone. When I came back through I caught the disappointed look on his face.

"If you've already planned to go out, you should go," I said. "I don't want you ruining your night so you can baby-sit me."

He took me in his arms. "No, doll. I'll never hear the end of it from Jan if I spoil your stay here with us in Aberdeen. I can meet up with her tomorrow or Sunday - give you a little space to yourself the weekend - so there's no need to fret. I've explained the situation to her."

What situation?

After we'd eaten and I helped him stack our dirty dishes in the dishwasher, we sat on the sofa together and he let me rest my feet in his lap. It was kind of nice.

We watched 'Gravity' on Netflix. I'd seen it before but I didn't let on. Sandra Bullock and George Clooney floating in zero gravity while their world falls apart, rivet by rivet, bolt by bolt. All I could think about was the catwalk on Dad's oil rig giving way beneath his boots and that eight hundred foot drop to the sea floor. My father's body plummeting through the air then continuing to sink like a stone through murky seawater - or maybe more slowly. Slowly enough for the brine in his lungs to reduce the amount of water in his blood until his heart failed. I'd often tried to imagine how his body might look, once they recovered it from the water. Bleached white maybe. There's plenty of information on-line about the mechanics of drowning if you know where to go.

14

ANIA had first seen the poster in the local deli more than a month ago.

Czy znasz tą kobietę?

'Do You Know This Woman?'

Paulina's portrait was hardly flattering. More like a child's drawing. The eyes were too far apart and the jaw was not quite right. A little too square. Ania would never have looked twice at the picture if her friend had not gone missing. And since Jonno had warned the girls often enough that running away to begin a new life would never be possible, there had to be another explanation for Paulina's disappearance. Her friend had not simply walked away from her job.

Nie żyje.

This unidentified young woman had been found dead. Her body discovered following an accident. Ania could have asked Jonno if he knew this already, but it seemed most likely he did. Maybe he had been responsible, in which case it was best she say nothing. The other three Polish girls who shared the flat at Rosemount - Ewa, Marcelina and Krystyna - had all given Ania the same advice.

Nikomu nic nie mów.

Tell no one. If Paulina had indeed been killed, then

God would surely bless her soul and let her rest in peace.

But this week, when she called in the local newsagent's for Jonno's cigarette papers, Ania noticed the half page article on the front page of *Głos Szkocki*. The police were no nearer identifying the body of the young woman found in the grounds of an Aberdeen hotel in July. They estimated her age at between twenty and thirty years of age. Red hair. Five foot six inches tall. No external signs of drug abuse but it is likely she had taken cocaine shortly before her death. They had found nothing to identify her by except an embroidered black and white clutch bag, a dark blue evening dress and various items of silk underwear.

The tone of the article suggested the young woman must have been a sex worker. But given her appearance, the chances were she had been working for an unlicensed agency rather than walking the streets. The pastor of the local Catholic church was quoted as saying how, despite the tragedy, such people brought shame on the local Polish community. No mention of how Paulina might have become embroiled in this business in the first place. No mention of Paulina's friends or her respectable family back home in Gdańsk. Her father had worked a fishing trawler before retiring through ill-health. Her younger brother, Jerzy, was training to become an oncologist. Paulina had been so proud of Jerzy.

Ania made a note of the telephone number listed and found a pay phone inside the bus station.

"I am phoning for the young Polish woman. You are searching for her name. She is Paulina Ostrowska."

Ania also gave them Jerzy's name and an address, care of the Copernicus hospital, before hanging up. It was only right Paulina's family should know what had happened.

This city. There were eyes everywhere watching. Secret

Policemen. Immigration officials. Border Agency officers. Jonno had told the girls on more than one occasion they should trust no one but him.

He was the only one who cared about them. He was the only one who knew they even existed. They were his sweethearts - his *kochania*. One mistake, and they would be sent home to Poland, their lives and reputations in shreds. Ania would rather die of shame than have that happen.

15

MONDAY was to be our last night together until Brendan came back onshore on the 27th. I'd felt guilty avoiding his company for the best part of Saturday and Sunday, mooching about the flat or wandering the neighbourhood like an idiot tourist looking for a Starbucks in Beirut. But he shrugged off my moodiness.

"I'll not be wanting to know where you've been from one hour to the next. But maybe we should spend our last night together before I'm back at work. I generally have a few drinks on a Monday before I go offshore, maself and a couple of the lads. But I can make an exception."

"No. No. There's no need," I said. "Please don't stay in just for me." I'd fully recovered from the jet lag or whatever it was.

"In that case, I was wondering," he said. "If you take a drink yerself, we could go off on a jolly. The pair of us. A wee dram here and there while we're stretching our legs."

I could tell from the tone of voice he'd been desperate I agree. A chance to show off his long-lost niece to his cronies, maybe. But life had turned sour the last time I'd had a drink. Brendan would no doubt have received his orders from my mother.

"Say if it's too much too soon."

"No. It's fine."

I didn't need a minder. If I paced myself I'd survive the evening.

We started at the Broadsword. "You've brought your ID with you?"

"I'm never without it."

Challenge 25 such a pain in the ass.

"And you're wanting a spritzer? That's all?"

"Yeah. Just a half glass of white then plenty of ice and soda."

By a quarter past ten we'd visited another half dozen pubs. Most were interchangeable. A standard red Tennents T sign above the door, and small groups of smokers huddled outside each entrance, dropping their stubs in the street like confetti. Many of the pubs had bookies next door and takeaways within staggering distance. One or two even had big-screen TVs inside and I noticed a pool table in the second one we visited. But Brendan was too busy playing tour guide to fit in a game.

Three drinks in, he took great pleasure in showing me the Function Rooms at the back of the Fountain Bar. "It's where I took my wee brother for our first pint together. I mind it's where he met your ma."

Mum rarely spoke about her life in Aberdeen.

"She never said."

"No. She wouldn't have had fond memories of the place. It's a blessing your dad got away from Aberdeen when he did."

"Why?"

"I'll nae go into details. Let's just say he got involved with a wild crowd. Football hooligans who liked to cause a ruckus. Young Davey was never afraid to speak his mind or use his fists whenever the occasion presented itself. He ruffled a few feathers in his time."

"Right."

"But he'd have gone to the ends of the world with your

72

ma. You know that don't you?"

"I know she still misses him."

"Aye, well."

After the first hour all the drinking dens had blended into one. We ended up in Murdos for a nightcap and he suggested I find somewhere closer to the flat, if I ever fancied taking a drink on my own.

"That's unlikely to happen."

"Aye, well. A word to the wise. There's some that need reminding how to behave. Especially when there's an attractive young lassie in the vicinity."

"It's OK. There's plenty of young lads back home who can't hold their drink," I said. "We always used to go round Lochinver on a Friday night - me and my mates. We'd start at the Stag's Head then head for the Caley before chucking-out time."

"Clubbing it after?" he asked.

I shook my head. "That would mean going all the way to Inverness. It's a four hour round trip, unless I'm staying at my sister's. But even then, it's a long drag if you're steaming and bursting for a pee."

"Well, Jan can recommend a few hot spots if you're looking to explore the city. She might even take you on a girls' night out next time she's home. And you're always welcome to have friends come and stay here - take a drink or two, as long as you don't trash the place."

"Don't worry," I said. " I can't see that happening. I'll probably stick with carry-outs while I'm here and try to keep my head down."

"So what about a fish supper on the way home? My treat."

"That would be great."

The thought of making friends in Aberdeen hadn't crossed my mind. Maybe I could invite Matt for the weekend, once I'd got used to my new post code -

separate bedrooms obviously. He'd emailed me almost as soon as I arrived. Hoping I wasn't feeling homesick.

'I've sent you this.'

He'd attached various video clips taken from a drone. Stunning aerial views of the area surrounding Lochinver from as far out as Split Rock to the top of Quinag and across over Loch Assynt to Canisp and Suilven.

I did miss the place, of course I did. There was nowhere else I'd rather be, despite recent events. And I promised myself the day would come when I'd return. I had unfinished business there after all. A few feathers of my own to ruffle.

16

ONCE Brendan left for the airport, the novelty of having his flat all to myself lasted less than three hours.

Flaming phone.

"The papers won't be bothering you," he'd promised as he planted a fatherly kiss on my forehead before leaving. "There's only two people know you're staying here apart from yours truly. Your ma and Jan."

I picked up the receiver, held it to my ear, and waited.

"Amy, it's Mum." Checking up on me already.

Shit.

"Hi."

"I thought you should know. I've had the police here."

"What? Greg Farrell?"

"No," she said. "It was that nice detective that called round the time Caddy was killed."

I remembered him. Hardly nice.

"What the hell did he want?"

"They've got new evidence."

"About who killed Caddy? I know that."

Matt and I had guessed the police would be re-interviewing everyone, once they officially identified the body at White Shore. I'd shaken hands with Rick Tyler's skeleton - his wrists strapped together by the same kind of cable tie they'd used to strangle my friend. That's one reason I'd left Lochinver - but Aberdeen obviously wasn't far enough.

"He asked me to tell you he needs to speak to you again," she said.

"Me? Why do they need to speak to me?"

I could sense the distress in Mum's voice as she explained.

"He said what? They're sending someone from Dingwall to Aberdeen to see me?"

"It's procedure, Amy. He wanted Brendan's address and phone number. He says he'll drive over Thursday morning."

"Shit."

"He wants to go over a few minor details before they close the case. That's all."

"Really?"

"That's what he says."

"Yeah, well. It's a joke if you ask me," I said. "If the police had been on the ball the first time round, they wouldn't need to come hassling innocent people all over again. They sent their top investigators all the way from Dingwall to Lochinver, because they thought our local bobby wasn't up to the job of dealing with a murder, and they made a complete hash of it. Gordon Paver would still be behind bars where he belongs, along with his nut-job of a son, if they hadn't been in such a rush to pin the blame on Rick Tyler."

"Well, they're trying to make sure they're doing everything right this time. The case against Mr Paver is closed. You have to let it go. This is all about establishing who killed Caddy. Let them get on with their jobs then we can all draw a line under the past."

"That's what I've been trying to do," I said. "But I'm supposed to wait for them to turn up here with blaring sirens and flashing blue lights."

"Don't be so dramatic. It'll be nothing like that. DC Galleymore's arranged to interview you at the local police station eleven thirty Thursday morning. Conningham Terrace. It's only a ten minute walk from Brendan's."

17

WHEN the police had questioned me back in December, they'd sent a female officer to the house along with the detective constable, and Mum had been allowed to sit and watch. At least this time I was spared an audience. Two suits and me in an interview room. And as before, a simple witness statement was all they were looking for.

"You've been in the wars since I last saw you, Amy."

"You could say that."

"So, how are you finding life in Aberdeen?" he asked.

"It's all a bit new still."

"But there's a wee bit more action than in Lochinver, aye?"

"I'm not looking for action," I said.

"No."

He introduced his colleague and talked me through the routine. "I appreciate you coming here to talk to us."

"I didn't think I had a choice," I said. Then I sucked in the bitterness that had crept into my voice as I caught the look on the other detective's face. "It's just that I keep getting asked the same questions over and over and I don't see the point."

"Your mum told you why we needed to speak to you again. Right?"

"Yeah. It's about who killed Caddy," I said.

"That's right." I could sense the discomfort they both

shared. The chief suspect in my friend's murder, turning up dead in suspicious circumstances, wasn't helping the situation. "New evidence has come to light, as you're maybe aware."

"You mean the body at White Shore," I said.

"There's that. But we've also spoken to Miss Jepson and she's given us a lot more to go on."

"Kay?" I couldn't hide the surprise from my voice. The last I'd heard, Kay's dad had put her in rehab.

"I'd like to ask you a few more questions about the night you were in Miss Jepson's flat. You and Peter Paver."

"Oh, right."

Kay had been comatose by the time I turned up there, so the chances of her remembering anything of note were less than zero.

"We'd like to go over your statement again. The one you gave the two officers who interviewed you last month."

"OK. But I don't see what any of that's got to do with Caddy's murder," I said.

"Kay mentioned something she overheard. It must have been the morning after the party. You and Peter were talking."

What party?

"You told the two officers you remembered going into Kay's bedroom before leaving."

"That's right."

We'd assumed Kay was still out of it. Paver had pulled back the duvet and kicked her in the backside but she never budged. And when I planted a sweet dreams kiss on her forehead, it was like kissing a corpse.

"She was still asleep so I don't know what she thinks she might have heard. What's she said?"

Whatever it was, Galleymore wouldn't let on. Paver had

been shooting his mouth off. But if any of what he'd said had filtered through to Kay's subconscious, the police expected me to corroborate her statement, assuming they really had spoken to her.

"Maybe you can recall what Peter Paver said about the time he was home on leave last December?"

I stumbled through vague recollections. The party at Strathan, Rick's drugs stash disappearing and something about Peter and the two Ukrainians being on the school bus when Caddy was murdered.

"So Peter mentioned Barto and Damo?"

"Not by name. But I got the impression he was in charge of everything. He's as bad as his fucking father."

The DC gave all the signs of having heard the same story already. Kay's version would tally with mine, up to a point. It left me feeling empty. The thought of Kay being conscious before we left, yet doing nothing to stop Paver and Robbo taking me with them. Maybe it had all been for the best.

He let me continue speaking at my own pace. A fragment here. A snippet there. No prompting. No leading questions. The blank spaces in the recording of the interview surely spoke for themselves.

"You've been very helpful, Amy."

"Thanks."

"As you can appreciate, we're trying to tie everything together. The business with Peter Paver as well as your friend Caddy. It seems he's been involved all along, rather than his father."

It was pointless trying to convince them otherwise.

"I appreciate how difficult it must be having pieces of memory come back like this when you're not expecting them. But I can tell your memory's improving. There's one more thing you can help us clear up before we call it a day."

Sneaky. The doctors had mentioned concussion - a perfect excuse to act dumb. But now my cover was blown. I should have known he'd take advantage because he'd caught me out in a lie before now. I could see the Columbo moment coming a mile off, but there was nothing I could do to stop it. He pulled his briefcase onto his knee, unclasped the two buckles and pulled out a green folder. Then he shuffled through its contents before extracting a glossy black-and-white photograph and passing it across to me.

18

"THIS is Robert Cohen," he began. "Twenty-four years old. He was an ex-squaddie; served in the same regiment as Peter Paver. They were in Afghanistan together and they resigned from the service round about the same time, according to Army records at Newton Aycliffe."

I knew this already. But I'd entertained the idea that Robbo's body might never be recovered, so his involvement would never come to light.

I'd researched on-line about drowning and the way bodies behave after being submerged in sea water for various lengths of time. Gas produced by bacteria forms in the body's tissues during decay and eventually the body floats back to the surface. But if the water is cold enough, it can take several weeks for this to occur. It had taken Dad's body three and a half weeks to reappear less than two hundred metres from the rig. The sea's currents become reduced significantly the deeper one goes. Apparently Robbo's body had been found a week or so ago close to Soyea, less than four kilometres from where Paver's father's boat had sunk. The conclusion was he'd been carried out on the receding tide as soon as his body returned to the surface.

"Do you recognise the face?"

Mug shots rarely look the same as people's faces do in real life. And I'd been in Robbo's company for less than twenty four hours - exactly six weeks earlier. But this was a face I would never forget. Maybe killing someone imprints their features on your memory until the day you die.

"We think he might have been at the flat the night you were there. We're still carrying out checks. DNA and so on. It's also likely he could have been staying on board the 'Meera Rose' while Peter visited you and Kay."

There remained a glimmer of hope. I realised I couldn't keep up the pretence indefinitely. If I confirmed what they thought they knew, they might accept it as truth and leave me in peace.

"Seeing the photo now, yeah. I told the other officers I kept getting fragments of memory. Moments of recognition that didn't connect into a proper picture. I don't remember seeing him at the flat but he might have been on the boat when we got there. There was someone below decks, I'm sure, when me and Peter pulled alongside in the dinghy."

"So you met Cohen on board Gordon Paver's yacht. That's brilliant, Amy."

"Hang on. I didn't say anything about meeting him."

"But you think you recognise his face. So can you remember anything else about him? His clothing perhaps?"

He'd been naked the last time I'd been in his company, but what the hell. I kept it simple. "It might have been an old Army uniform. Combat jacket, you know? And camouflage trousers."

"OK. Did you notice any distinguishing features?"

Tattoos. I'd seen his tattoos when he stripped off.

"No. Nothing," I said. "There are still these gaps, like blanks inside my head. I'm scared that if I suddenly uncover what's been buried deep in my brain, I might discover it's something really bad. Something scary my

83

subconscious wants me to forget. The doctor said I shouldn't force myself to remember. It can make things worse."

"I understand that."

The other officer took back the photograph and slid it inside the folder. Then he took out a sheet of paper and passed it to his colleague.

"We conducted a thorough search of Miss Jepson's flat," Galleymore continued. "There were traces of drugs. Gamma butyrolactone. Cocaine. Three ecstasy tablets and a quantity of marijuana. There were also a number of used condoms on the living room floor."

I said nothing.

"Seven in total."

He referred to the sheet in front of him. "As I say, we're currently waiting for DNA results but we're fairly sure we know what they'll tell us."

He looked me in the eye but again I kept my mouth shut tight.

"A forensic medical examination conducted by the local GP, with Miss Jepson's cooperation and subsequent to an initial interview, confirmed she had not been involved in penetrative sexual activity for some time."

"I don't know why you're telling me all this," I managed to say.

"You had sex the night you visited Kay Jepson's flat. Am I right?"

My head dropped.

"Can you confirm or deny?"

"I don't even want to talk about what might have happened. I was drunk. Peter gave me drugs. I've already told you people everything I remember. Why do you keep pestering me?"

"I thought it was obvious, Amy. This whole story you're giving us is a pack of lies from start to finish.

You're trying to protect your boyfriend, but it's not going to wash."

Boyfriend? What fucking boyfriend?

He checked his wristwatch then turned to his colleague. "Interview terminated at 11:27. We're going to have to begin again, Amy. But this time it's going to be conducted under caution."

19

"**MAYBE** it's best if you begin by telling us about your relationship with Pater Paver. We know you were seeing each other last year. Last August - the weekend before Games Day, to be precise."

I laughed. "Christ. Where did you hear that? It was hardly what I'd call seeing each other."

"But you and Peter were intimate for a time. You had consensual sex."

I could taste the acid at the back of my throat.

"Oh, yeah. But I regretted it as soon as it was finished. There'd been a party at the White Shore. We were pissed and one thing led to another. But I hadn't even spoken to him since then until he turned up at Kay's the night you're talking about."

He closed his eyes and nodded. "That's fine, Amy. We're not here to judge you. But if we later discover you lied by omission, or otherwise wilfully obstructed the investigation, or indeed were attempting to pervert the course of justice in your initial witness statement, you might end up in court having to explain your behaviour."

I felt my cheeks flush red and every tiny scar on my face seemed to sting afresh.

"We're not trying to catch you out. And you're welcome to say nothing else in case you incriminate yourself further. But it won't help your case if you keep quiet until we go to court. Because I promise you, we are going to uncover the truth one way or another."

They gave me time to reel in my thoughts. Dark, murky thoughts that had bubbled beneath the surface of this stupid act I was putting on.

"Can I have a glass of water?"

Galleymore's colleague left and returned with a jug of water and a plastic tumbler.

"OK. I didn't tell the police everything because I was too embarrassed. Mum was in the room the first time they interviewed me." I began to sob. "I didn't want her to hear what happened. She'd hate me, I know she would."

"Take your time," he said. "Talk us through the night you ended up at Kay Jepson's. It's not the first time you've been there, is it?"

Uh?

"Kay's told us everything. We know you were more than friends."

Everything?

That's when I fell apart.

By the time the interview ended it felt like my insides had been scraped raw. The police knew most of what had gone on during my disappearance off the village radar apart from two tiny details. The reason I'd allowed Peter and Robbo to treat me like some piece of trailer trash and the events leading up to their deaths. They even had a reliable witness who was prepared to confirm the identity of the driver and two passengers in Jimmy's truck when we drove away from the Kylesku Bridge.

But it was clear the police still didn't know how Robbo died before his body washed up on Soyea. And not even the threat of a court case and exposure to the media would force me to reveal the truth.

"We'll need to speak to you again, but I shouldn't worry unduly about that for the time being. I've to report back to my superiors at Dingwall. They're going to want to go through the interview question by question, Amy. But it's good that you've finally helped us clear things up."

"So is any of this going to end up in the newspapers?"

The DC looked at his colleague. "I can assure you the Press won't get to hear anything from us. As far as we're concerned, we now know how and why Caddy was killed, and we know who was responsible. Two of the suspects are dead - Peter and one of the Ukrainians. The third has presumably returned overseas. But our search will continue using the services of the local law enforcement agencies. There are still two fatal accident inquiries to be dealt with. Robert Cohen's and Peter Paver's. You'll be called to give evidence at both, I should imagine, sometime during the next few months."

"Oh, shit. No."

"It's normal procedure. The police have a legal requirement to investigate how they both died as well as the circumstances leading up to their deaths."

"But I've already told you all you need to know. Why do I have to go through it all again? They're both scum."

"That's beside the point. It's your legal duty, Amy. And your moral obligation, don't you think?"

He gave me his business card. If I remembered anything else - no matter how trivial - I was to telephone him on his mobile number.

That would never happen. The case was closed. The real guilty party would never be brought to justice.

I walked out of the police station and wept all the way back to the flat, hugging myself until my ribs ached. I'd never felt so alone in all my life.

20

I phoned Mum as soon as I got back to the flat. I needed to hear a friendly voice, and putting off the inevitable wasn't going to make me feel any calmer. I confessed how I'd been given drugs the night before I finished up half-dead on White Shore. Cocaine, GBL as well as a spliff or two. I'd got drunk and ended up having sex with Peter Paver - renewing the fleeting acquaintanceship we'd begun twelve months earlier.

I didn't mention Robbo's role other than to say he'd been there the whole time. Robbo had been the one who drove us around the next day during Paver destructive spree. He'd died along with Paver when the 'Meera Rose' blew up.

"That's awful Amy," she said. "Are you telling me you didn't remember any of it until this morning?"

I hesitated. "Most of it came back to me when I saw the photo," I replied. "The photo of the other guy who was there with Peter Paver. It was like I had a flashback of the whole thing."

"That's difficult to believe."

"For God's sake, Mum. Don't you trust your own daughter? I'd hardly be making up a story that makes me look a complete slag."

I let her absorb that unsavoury fact.

"I'd had concussion, if you remember. The doctor

warned me how certain triggers can bring back unwelcome memories, no matter how deep we try to bury them."

"I suppose you're right."

"And I'm still on temazepan, so God knows what that's been doing to my brain."

"You're right," she said. "I'm sorry."

"It was horrible, going through it all again - all the sordid details. It felt like I was reliving the whole thing."

"Is that what this is all about, Amy? You're ashamed of what you did so you're running away."

"No way."

"Not even subconsciously?"

I let her gather her thoughts and fill in the blanks.

"You can't fool me. Surely you realised the dreadful things you did that night would come out sooner or later. That's why you needed to get away in such a hurry, isn't it?"

If that's what she needed to believe then fine.

"Yeah, Mum. I was ashamed and I didn't want to have to look you in the face when you found out what I'd done. So are you happy now?"

"Oh, Amy, darling. You know me better than that. Come home. We can face this together, you know. You need to be with family. Friends. There are no secrets in this family."

But there was at least one secret that would never come to light. I was as much a cold-blooded killer as Peter Paver.

21

MUM had obviously contacted Leanne as soon as she finished talking to me. My sister couldn't wait to hear my version of events.

"You were shagging Paver again? I can't believe you'd be so stupid."

"So what d'you want me to say?" I asked. "That it didn't happen?"

"That would do for starters. I don't know what to think anymore. You told me yourself you'd had a thing last summer and it was over almost as soon as it started."

"Exactly."

"So what were you doing getting involved again then going off with him on his blowing-up binge? It's mental, Amy."

"It wasn't like that."

I let her ramble on. "You're like one of them silly bitches on the news that flies off to Syria to shack up with a suicide bomber. Or those sad shits who keep on writing love letters to some loser on Death Row while he's waiting for his lethal injection."

Blah-blah-blah.

"What the hell were you thinking?"

"I wasn't. That's the problem."

She must have been able to sense the change in tone of my voice.

"God, Ames. I'm not having a go at you, hon. I'm trying to. . ."

"Help?"

"I was going to say 'understand'. All that crap in the newspapers. I didn't buy a word of it. But if any of this comes out, people are going to start thinking it was true all along. That you and him were in this together."

"They can think whatever they want. I know that's how it looks but it was nothing like that," I said. "I went along with it 'cause I had no choice. They cable-tied my wrists together, for fuck's sake. I thought I was going to end up getting murdered like Caddy."

"OK, hon. I'm sorry," she said. "Mum told me what you said about being drugged as well as drunk. But that stuff about not being able to remember anything. It's all bullshit. Right?"

I wiped the tears from both eyes with the back of my hand.

"I knew from the start you were hiding something."

"Yeah, well."

"Look, Ames. I don't care if you lied to the police or to Mum. But this is me you're talking to. We tell each other everything. Remember?"

Up until recently that might have been the case. But we'd both kept a variety of secrets from each other over the last couple of months.

"I thought you'd hate me. That's all," I said.

"And that's why you're hiding away at the other side of the country."

"Whatever."

I could hear her scratching around for something. A cigarette lighter, maybe. Or a set of keys.

"Listen. I've got to get to work. I'm due in at two. But why don't you come home? You should have your family around you at a time like this - looking after you. It's not right you being all on your own, letting things play on your mind. I know what you're like. Too bloody independent."

I told her I was fine. I didn't need looking after. I didn't need mothering. Then I had a long soak in the bath before changing into my pyjamas, grabbing a duvet and stretching out on the couch. Three o'clock on a glorious summer's afternoon and all I wanted was to be left alone to sleep. I was absolutely fine.

22

THE deeper I sank into the water the quieter it became - as if the silence itself had grown louder, if that's possible. I could feel the bubbles of oxygen imploding in my veins like Rice Crispies, my ear drums popping then collapsing from the increase in pressure. Drowning in slow motion. Then I heard it again. The sound of a telephone in the distance.

There were unfamiliar pictures on the wall. A framed photograph of Ben Alder with its mantle of snow and another of the Lairig Ghru trench between Braeriach and Cairn Gorm. Brendan had bragged how Jan took landscape photographs when she wasn't snapping corpses washed up on the shore.

Bars of sunlight continued to slant through the window blinds but they'd moved from the white rug in front of the plasma TV to the back of the couch - distorted from broad rectangles of brightness to stiletto blades of sharp light.

How many hours had I been under?

There it was again.

"Jesus."

I'd left Brendan's cordless telephone on the breakfast bar in the kitchen. Surely it wasn't my mother again. I wasn't in the mood to speak to her right now. Then I heard a familiar voice come through on the answer machine.

"Hi, Ames. It's only me. Give me a buzz when you get a minute. I want to check you're OK."

I dashed to the next room and clicked the button.

"How did you get this number?"

"I rang your mum."

Shit.

"So how's Aberdeen?"

"Hang on, my mouth's all gummed up."

I cradled the handset under my chin as I opened the fridge door, took out a bottle of Highland Spring and twisted open the cap.

"I still can't believe you went off without saying goodbye properly. I tried ringing your mobile but you never replied. Did you get my email?"

"I keep my phone switched off most of the time. The battery's probably dead anyway."

"Your mum says you're planning on staying away until the autumn."

What else had she told Matt?

"Well, yeah. Nothing definite. We all need a change of scene now and again."

"So how's the Granite City treating you?"

"I've not seen much of it so far, to be honest."

Part of me wanted to cut the conversation short. To come up with an excuse to stop it right there. But another part of me couldn't erase the good times we'd shared, even when the rest of the world had turned bad. Matt Neilson was the last person I needed back in my life - but the one guy I'd never quite given up on despite all his flaws.

"So. . ."

"Have. . ."

"No. You go first," he said.

"It was nothing. What's the news? In Lochinver, I

95

mean?"

"There's none, really. Same old same old."

"OK."

"You watched the videos I sent."

"God, yeah." I said. "Got ourselves a new toy, have we?"

"Dad thought it would give me something useful to do until the elbow's mended," he continued. "I posted them on YouTube as well as Facebook."

I shifted the handset to my other ear. "For saddos like me who don't get out much?"

"It's as bad for me - like I'm back in prison. Steff and Dad still expect me to be there for meal times. And I'm supposed to account for my movements whenever I go out. The usual bullshit."

The usual bullshit whenever Matt was feeling hard done by.

"All part of the deal while you're living under the same roof," I said. "They're only looking out for you after all the crap you've put them through."

"I suppose," he said.

"Maybe it's time you moved out and learned to stand on your own two feet."

"Is that some kind of marriage proposal?"

"In your dreams."

"So why did you bugger off in such a hurry?"

"What's Mum been saying?"

I took another mouthful of designer water while Matt recycled everybody's concerns.

"Tell her I can manage, thanks very much. You've seen that stuff in the papers now they're opening Caddy's case again - my so-called friends spreading new rumours on-line. It's only going to get worse. So why would I want to stick around while everybody's taking cheap shots at me? They've got no idea what happened."

"I know, but give it a couple of weeks and it'll be yesterday's news."

"Yeah. Sure."

"I'm telling you. Most of the idiots who spread that kind of shit lose interest. They'll be back to posting selfies and photos of their fucking cats once the drama has died down."

"Yeah, well. There's stuff you don't know about. More shit that's about to come into contact with the fan."

It wouldn't take much to set the embers alight again. Once I stood in the dock and told the fatal accident inquiries what really happened I'd be vulture-feed again.

"Everybody who knows you realises you're not capable of doing what they're accusing you of. But, Peter. He was worse than his dad, and we both know what a bastard he is."

"Yet he got away with it," I said. "How come nobody ever gave Gordon Paver grief on-line for what he did?"

"I don't know," Matt said. "But you have to forget all that and move on. That's what Dad keeps telling me. We have to accept the fact he's in the clear, even though I feel like taking a swing at him every time I see his ugly fucking mug."

"I don't need anyone fighting my battles for me, thanks very much."

"It's the way he struts about Lochinver like he owns the place," Matt said.

"Why? Are you telling me Gordon Paver's back in the village?"

"Couldn't keep away."

"So where's he staying?"

"Strathbeg House until the sale goes through. Didn't you know?"

"Not really. We haven't kept in touch."

Matt laughed. "I wasn't expecting you to. But you were

the last person to see Peter alive. You'd have thought. . ."

"Thought what? That he'd want me to pass on his precious son's last words before he tried to blow me up, along with the rest of the world?"

"Suppose not."

"Gordon Paver knew what Peter was up to. It wouldn't surprise me if he helped him get hold of the rocket launchers."

"Is that what you think?"

"We'll never know. But it's all worked out rather well, don't you think? Everything Paver Senior was being accused of is now down to his son. He gets away with being the grieving father, his reputation whiter than white."

"I hadn't thought of it that way."

"It doesn't matter anyway. I'm glad I don't have to testify against him."

"There's that," he said. "But what about Caddy's murder? That's still to go to court."

Shit. More grief.

"The cops called round to speak to Dad at the weekend," he continued. "Said they had a couple of leads they need to follow. They're fairly sure they know who killed Caddy and they're expecting to close the case within the next few days. But they still won't let on what they've found out."

"They've been round here as well," I said.

"What? The police?"

Matt obviously hadn't heard I was the prime witness. "They sent someone all the way from Dingwall. Going through my statement again."

"Just doing their jobs, I expect," he said.

"Peter Paver was there."

"What?"

"We got it all wrong. Peter was on the school bus along

with his two Ukrainian pals. They were the looking for Rick's stash and Caddy got in their way."

"And you got this from the police?"

"No. I got it from the horse's mouth. Peter told me everything the night we were at Kay's. He couldn't help himself."

I stuttered my way through the entire story again from the moment I'd seen Jimmy Jump's truck outside Kay's flat to getting hauled into a lifeboat at the White Shore. By the time I finished, I was a snivelling wreck as usual.

"Fucking hell, Ames. I have to come over and see you," he said.

"No way."

"Please."

"And do what? Kiss it all better?"

"I can book myself a hotel room, if it makes you happy. No strings. But I'm telling you, we can't do this over the phone."

23

JAN Malone had style. She'd telephoned in advance and warned me to be ready outside Brendan's flat at seven o'clock on the dot. I heard the horn tooting as soon as she arrived and when I saw her bright yellow sports car I realised I was in for an interesting evening.

She'd phoned the day after my meltdown at the police station, inviting me to her flat for a meal on the Saturday night.

"I don't cook. I leave that to Bren when he comes round. But there are plenty of takeaways close by, and I'll supply the wine."

She sounded brash and so full of herself I wanted to cry off. Develop a tummy bug or a sudden allergy to takeaways. I'd intended leading a life of quiet anonymity in Aberdeen. Home alone with the three Ps. Pringles for sustenance, Prosecco for re-hydration, and Peggy from *Mad Men* as role model. But Jan had other ideas.

"I've had strict orders to keep in touch while Bren's away. And he's told me so much about your dad, I can't wait to meet up. Bring your pyjamas as well because we're going to have a sleepover."

How old did she think I was? Eleven?

"I appreciate you looking out for me. It's sweet of you, but really, there's no need," I said.

"Yes, there is. You're our guest of honour while you're

here so the least I can do is make you feel welcome. I'm not going to start interfering in your life, so don't worry on that score. I've got enough on my plate as it is. And feel free to tell me to piss off whenever you think I'm overstepping the mark. But we're making a night of it on Saturday 'cause there's no way I'm driving back to Toleydrone until next morning."

"Toleydrone?"

"Brendan knows what I think of that sinkhole. It's even worse now they're building an urban village on the old paper-mill site. I mean, how can you have a fecking village that's urban?"

"No idea," I said.

"The sooner the better they get a licence to frack the whole place to Hell."

Jan drove like a maniac. Or at least it felt that way. Being so close to the ground, I felt every pothole, every dip and rise and sweep of road.

"D'you drive, Amy?"

"I'd been having lessons but then other things took over," I said. "Mostly the shit Brendan's probably told you about."

"Well you need to sort it. Get yourself a set of wheels and you're behoven to no one. I'd be lost without my bananamobile."

We stopped outside a row of shops and she told me to choose. "There's a kebab shop, chippy, Pizza Hut or an Indian. Naveed actually does fantastic fish and chips."

I settled for a curry. She came back laden with carrier bags. "I've got four different naans and a variety of dips as well. And they always throw in a free bag of poppadoms."

"But there's loads."

"Ssh. This is my treat and I'm starving. Bren says you need building up, so button it."

Jan's flat was half the size of Brendan's but everything looked gleaming and new. It gave the impression she didn't spend much time at home. The living room was dominated by a huge, white leather corner sofa. But there were also orange and black bean bags strategically placed next to a glass-topped coffee table. A set of bookshelves, filled to overflowing with paperbacks, covered the main wall, and an expensive-looking music system sat where I'd have expected to find a TV.

"How long have you lived here?" I said.

"Since I started doing long-haul flights back in 2000. It's still my favourite bolt hole, but I'm probably going to have to move closer to Glasgow once I get a full-time job. It takes me three hours each way even in my little MG - and the A-bloody-90 on a Friday afternoon does my head in."

I surveyed the sparse furnishings again and the cardboard boxes labelled 'CDs/DVDs' stacked in the corner. It looked like Jan was already packed ready to relocate.

"So what'll happen to you and Brendan?"

"We'll be OK. Or we won't. We like our own space and that will never change. He can always fly down to Glasgow, if he's that keen."

I liked her attitude and I told her. I liked her look as well. Barely any make-up, hair cut short to not need much styling, and she was obviously self-confident enough to wear skin-tight jeans and a skimpy t-shirt that emphasized her generous figure. There was also a framed photograph on one of the shelves featuring her and Brendan in their swimming costumes. Jan looked bronzed and voluptuous, mid-screech, with such an expression on her face that I expected the picture to come with a built-in volume control.

"So what about you, Amy? Is there anybody in your life special enough to travel all the way across Scotland for a bonk?"

A bonk? Christ, is that what her and Brendan called it?

"Not really."

"You don't sound very convincing. And you must have broken a heart or two in your time, a gorgeous young thing like you."

"Not yet, as far as I know."

She topped up our wine glasses and held hers up for a clink. "You can tell me to mind my business if you like. But I reckon the little-girl-lost look is all an act. Make sure you don't settle for second best. You're a stunning young woman, Amy, and I know you deserve better than what life's dealt you so far."

"Brendan been blabbing?"

"He's mentioned one or two things. But you seem to be coping. Or maybe that's an act as well."

I could sense Jan was wanting me to offload. Maybe her forensic training taking over. But I wasn't in the mood to recount the more lurid details of my car crash life.

"He's probably mentioned Matt. Caddy's brother," I volunteered.

Her bottom lip jutted out, on the point of speaking, perhaps. But instead she took another mouthful of wine.

"Caddy's the girl who was murdered," I added.

I knew I'd never get used to saying that line, no matter how many times the topic came up in conversation.

"Me and Matt have got history. He's let me down so many times, I've lost count but I still have these feelings for him."

"That's guys all over," she said. "It's like having a pet dog. Feed it and give it lots of cuddles and you've got a friend for life. But all it takes is for someone to come

103

along and toss a Frisbee and they're off chasing it. All the promises they ever made gone in a flash."

I laughed. "Matt's chased more Frisbees than I've had takeaways."

"So you need to try harder if you want him to stick around. Give his tummy a rub. Dogs like that. But make sure you give his lead a yank now and again as well. Remind him who's boss."

24

MATT turned up, as expected, the Monday evening before Brendan was due home. He'd borrowed Steff's Clio and I'd made sure he got the message. I'd made a determined effort to appear as unattractive as possible - a pair of baggy track-suit bottoms and one of Brendan's check shirts on top of a faded grey t-shirt. I was still a long way from acquiring a new pet despite Jan's expert advice on how to handle a dog.

I'd been desperate to lose the little-girl-lost look since arriving in Aberdeen. All part of my new image. Jan warned me against taking things too far. "Don't go trying to copy any of the lassies round here. They wouldn't know good taste if it sat on their faces and farted. If you go into any of the clubs at the West end of Union Street, you'll notice they're full of office tarts sporting shiny, orange faces and donut hairstyles, or teenyboppers dressed up as Goths."

"What the hell's a teenybopper?"

"Before your time, Amy. When I was your age I thought big hair and the Stevie Nicks look was the height of sophistication. Then I got encouraged to go for the Barbie look favoured by every airline West of Singapore. And now look at me."

She didn't look so bad.

"Is there anywhere I can get a cheap cut and dye job in

a hurry?" I asked.

There was. Within twenty-four hours, the only evidence of my own Barbie look were a few strands of blonde hair still trapped in the plug-hole of Brendan's shower. Welcome to the new me.

"Jesus Christ, what the fuck did you do to your hair?" Considering the fact that Matt had shaved his entire head while in prison, I felt he was over-reacting.

"Nice to see you as well."

"You should have warned me, that's all," he said. "Have you joined some kind of punk girl band? Pussy Riot or whatever they're called?"

"Very funny, not."

He ran his fingers through my stubble.

"So what colour's it supposed to be? Fruits of the Forest?"

"It's fucking garnet, if you must know. Did you bring booze?"

He raised his arm in a salute then handed me a carrier bag containing a box of wine. "It's all for you, *mein Fräulein*. I'm driving, so I'll stick to coffee."

He followed me into the flat and that's when I noticed he'd not brought anything else. No rucksack or holdall.

"So where have you booked?"

He surveyed the kitchen while I folded up the empty plastic bag and put the wine in the fridge. "I'll find somewhere later. There's a Holiday Inn I remember passing about a mile from here. I was in a rush to see you, to be honest. And I've got to head back to Lochinver tomorrow afternoon. I'm due at work again Wednesday."

"You're working? I'm super impressed."

"It's better than I expected. The flat, I mean."

"Not exactly classy but, yeah. It's OK."

"The abandoned cars in the courtyard add a nice touch as well."

"Courtyard? It's more like a bomb site. But people actually drive around in some of those heaps."

"If you say so." He pointed to the large frying pan on the hob. "Is that for us, because you don't have to go to so much trouble. We can eat out."

"It's a tortilla. And there's some garnish drying out in the oven."

"Great."

"We might as well go through to the lounge. The salad is going to be another twenty minutes."

We slouched at opposite ends of the large sofa and I felt the tension that had been building up all weekend slowly fade away as Matt brought me up to speed with events at Lochinver. Who was shagging who and who was the latest to get barred from the Caley.

"Where did you say you were working?" I asked.

"I didn't. Dad's got me a couple of shifts at the harbour office, that's all. It's part-time so far. The money comes in handy but if there's no Spanish boats in there's no work and I don't get paid."

"You don't intend doing that for the rest of your life."

"No way. But it gets me out of the house. I'd go mental otherwise. I'm watching that much children's TV, I think I'm starting to fancy some of those cartoon babes."

"You mean the Powerpuff Girls?"

"Not quite. I've got the hots for that scrawny Viking kid from *How to Tame Your Dragon,* but enough about me." He shook his head. "Did I tell you the police have been round again?"

"No."

"They wanted to speak to Dad and Steff. They said there's going to be some kind of inquest but they're ready to close Caddy's case."

I didn't want to hear about that.

"Let me check on the tea. Put the telly on if you like.

The CBeebies channel should be on there somewhere."

"Good to see you haven't lost your sarcastic streak."

I tore the plastic collar off the wine box and poured myself a glass as the tortilla bubbled under the grill. Then I found some trays and we ate while watching my favourite, mindless quiz show. By the time we'd finished the second course, a frozen cheesecake Jan had made me bring home for our dinner date, I was on to the third glass of wine and ready to confess all.

25

"THE police mentioned another body - Paver's mate, Robbo. He was the one driving the truck. Right?"

I nodded.

"So was he in the flat the whole time?"

"Yeah."

"While you and Paver partied."

I nodded again.

"And was he giving Kay one or was he watching you two get it together?"

"Matt, we don't have to do this." I swirled the wine around my mouth and it tasted like vinegar when I finally swallowed it. "It's hardly going to make any difference now."

He shrugged. "It might do."

"What if I told you he joined in?"

"With you and Paver?" he said.

I mentioned the amount of drink they'd given me and the drugs and I could see Matt's curiosity shrivel up before my eyes.

"It was like it was happening to someone else the whole time," I said.

"You mean you were having sex? The three of you?" Still he seemed to sense there was more I wasn't telling him. "So where was Kay while all this was going on?"

"They'd put her to bed. She was totally zonked out."

"I'm not getting it. You told me that you and Paver weren't even seeing each other before things kicked off so I don't even know what you were doing inside Kay's flat."

"Like I said. Wrong place wrong time."

"But I know what you're like and it's not your style, no matter how much booze they forced down your throat. You'd have put up some kind of fight. Screamed the place down."

"You know me that well?"

"Yeah. I do. What else aren't you telling me?"

I stood and picked up the dirty dishes. Something tugged at my insides. Feelings for the old Matt, maybe. The one who claimed to care. The one who promised to look out for me, always. "I'll be back in a minute."

When I returned with a recharged wine glass, Matt was poised on the edge of the sofa as if he was about to climb to his feet and walk out.

"Tell me again," he said as I sat down. "I want to hear everything."

"You want to hear what exactly? That I let Robbo and Peter take it in turns to shag me?" The words turned to dust and I tried to wash away the taste of betrayal with more wine.

"I don't understand why you'd let them do that to you," he said. "Or how you can be so calm about it."

"Calm? You haven't got a Scooby-Doo, have you?"

"So help me out here. What the hell made you give it up like that?"

"It was Peter," I snapped. "He wanted to screw Kay and I begged him not to."

"What?"

"I told him she still hadn't got over being attacked by those two Ukrainians. She was fragile as fuck. But he wouldn't take no for an answer."

110

He stared down at his shoes. "I didn't realise you cared that much for Kay Jepson."

"You don't know everything, Matt." I wiped my nose with the sleeve of my shirt. "I'd been going round to see her - we'd share a spliff or two and have ourselves a drink."

"Sounds very cosy."

"It was. We had a lot more in common than you'd think."

"Bezzie mates or lezzie mates?"

"Oh, piss off, Matt," I said. "Your trouble is you don't care about anyone else except yourself. Kay had been going through a rough time. We both had, and you were partly to blame."

"Me? How come?"

"Doesn't matter now. But I knew it wouldn't take much for Paver to push her right over the edge."

"So you sacrificed yourself to save your girlfriend? Shit. She must have got to you."

I ignored the jibe. "I didn't know what they had in mind. Not until it was too late."

"What d'you mean?" he said.

"It was two against one. They were already stoned, stripped down to their boxers and high-fiving each other. Peter bullied me to get undressed. Said he'd help out if I didn't get my arse in gear."

"So he forced you."

"Not quite. My brain was like porridge. I thought they wanted a quick grope. A blow-job maybe. I'd have given them one to get it over with."

"What did the police say?"

I sloshed back the remains of the wine. "That's none of their business. I went along with it, so the police won't be interested."

"For Christ's sake, Ames. You know that's not true. If

111

Paver and his oppo threatened you then it's not consensual, even if you signed a fucking contract saying you agreed."

"I mean it. It's over and done with and I don't want to have to rake through it all over again."

The look on Matt's face. I couldn't tell whether it was pity or revulsion. I got up and headed for the kitchen again. "I need another drink. I'll make you a fresh coffee unless you'd like something stronger."

He didn't reply, and when I returned with a bottle of spiced rum and a couple of glasses he still looked broken.

"So? Shall I pour you one?"

"Not if I'm driving."

"And are you driving?"

"That's up to you," he said.

26

I knew something was different. For one thing, I wasn't suffering the slow motion withdrawal of yet another temazepan-fuelled coma. During the recent warm spell I'd taken to sleeping in one of Brendan's t-shirts and nothing else, but I realised I was still wearing my bra and pants. And there was someone lying next to me. I knew instantly it was Matt Neilson.

I rolled onto my back and counted to ten. I felt between my legs. I expected to smell him on me at least, or find traces of something more unsavoury than my own stale sweat enriched with the scent of Morgan's Spiced. There had been recent nights when I might have welcomed Matt's attentions. Something to soothe the irritation. But last night hadn't been one of them.

Shit.

My mouth tasted as if I'd been chewing on a strip of pub-floor carpet. I couldn't even remember brushing my teeth let alone getting undressed for bed.

Matt must have felt the mattress shift as I turned my back on him and curled up into a ball.

"You awake?"

I didn't reply.

"Nothing happened, Ames. OK?"

Still no reply.

"I couldn't leave you. You were in a state and . . ."

"You waited until I passed out then decided to undress me."

"No."

"Christ, Matt. How do you think this makes me feel after everything I told you last night?"

"It wasn't like that. You were still awake when we got into bed."

"And you were hoping I'd let you shag me for old times sake. It must have turned you on, listening to all the gory details."

"Amy, listen."

I clammed up again.

Then I felt his hand graze my hip. "Don't you fucking dare."

"Amy, you were blazing. Totally off your head. I've never seen you as bad."

"That doesn't entitle you to strip me half-naked and jump into bed with me."

"You're making it sound worse than it was. You were raging about Gordon Paver and about the police. What a bunch of useless tossers they are. Then you started going on about me and Kaz Cartwright - how she spiked your drink and some crap about her attacking Kevin Waterson because I asked her to. You kept knocking back the rums like there was no tomorrow."

"So you let me get wasted, then as soon as I'm beyond help you lay me flat on my back. Did you manage to shag me while you were at it, or did you make do with a wank?"

"You'd puked all down your shirt."

That brought me to my senses. "I what?"

"You threw up all down the front of your shirt. It was mostly liquid, but it was minging. We took your top off in the bathroom. I mean I helped you take it off."

"Right."

"I've left your shirt soaking in the bath. It's still there, if you don't believe me. And your t-shirt. That was covered in vomit as well. But I left your bra."

I rolled onto my back again and pulled the duvet up to my neck.

"I cleaned you up as best as I could with a face cloth and I gave you a glass of water to drink. Then I managed to convince you to go to bed, but I realised I couldn't leave you to sleep on your own. You'd have drowned in your own vomit if you'd been sick again in the night. I wanted to make sure you were safe, that's all."

"Sorry. I should probably say thanks."

"I can't believe you think I'd interfere with you because you were too pissed to stop me." He got up and sat on the side of the bed facing away from me. "Anyway, you said you needed a pee first and you told me to wait outside while you went."

"Lovely."

"Then when you came out of the bathroom you'd already got rid of your track suit bottoms and your socks."

"Hmm."

"You crashed out in my arms and I had to help you into the bedroom. And when I laid you down you refused to let go, clinging on to me and saying all kinds of stupid stuff. The drink talking, I expect - but I swear we never did anything. Honest."

"Shit. I obviously didn't know what I was doing."

"Exactly. So you need to watch yourself, Ames."

"What d'you mean?"

"If it had been some other guy in the same situation - let's say somebody walks you home from the pub and you ask them in for a nightcap."

"That's never going to happen," I said. "I'm not in the

115

mood for any male company at the moment. Put that down to the Matt Neilson factor."

I knew if I kept saying it to myself often enough it would make the stupid longing go away.

"OK. I'm just saying, be careful if you're ever out on the town late at night. Aberdeen's nothing like Lochinver. There will always be some creep or other hanging round inside a night club waiting for the opportunity to offer help to any young girl the worse for drink. They're only after the one thing."

"Have you finished? 'Cause you're starting to sound like my mother now."

"Fine. You're obviously in control of everything. But I still think you should have told the police about Peter Paver's attack. There are people you can talk to about what you're going through. Trained professionals."

"What d'you mean 'what I'm going through'? You think I'm losing the plot?"

"No. But I think you need help."

"Thanks, but no thanks. I'm going to have a shower. Make yourself useful and do us each a couple of rounds of toast before you leave. There's sliced bread in the freezer."

27

MATT had been in no rush to leave, and we'd chit-chatted while I nursed a coffee and tried to rearrange my hair. He mentioned Kaz Cartwright briefly, and it seemed there was no need to elaborate on the back-stabbing bitch's exploits.

"I thought you had better taste than that," I said.

"She caught me at a bad time. She told me I was about to be dumped and made it clear she was happy to fill the vacancy. Then, living under the same roof, she'd parade in a skimpy towel or her undies whenever there was nobody else around."

"TMI, Matt."

"I'm telling you what she was like."

"And you couldn't help yourself."

"Kind of."

"So I assume you're no longer seeing each other," I said. More out of sheer bloody mindedness than curiosity. I knew Kaz had left Matt for dead when Paver and his buddy had attacked him.

"Fuck no. She's just a tarted up tink." He went on to talk about trust. Discovering who your real friends are when the chips are down. "I must have been mad."

"So, are you telling me you regretted sleeping with her?" I said. If so, that would be a first, as far as Matt Neilson was concerned.

117

"'Course not. There's things I could have done different, and things I haven't done that I wish I had. But it's all part of life, isn't it?"

"Really?"

He must have read the disgust on my face. He backtracked and gave a garbled speech about the difference between regretting what you've done and regretting not doing something.

"It's different for guys," he said. "We don't fixate on mistakes we might or might not have made the way women do. We look back and look at missed opportunities."

I couldn't help grinning. "Is that something you've read in one of Steff's magazines?"

"Probably. Or *FHM*," he said. "I mean, there's loads of stuff in women's magazines that men don't know about. You'd be surprised. Did you know there are eight different kinds of nipple?"

"I don't even know why they print that kind of stuff."

"It's educational."

"Sure."

I suffered a momentary flashback to Kay Jepson's nipples. They were much darker than mine, and the image came into my head of the tattoos snaking round her breasts like barbed wire. But this didn't seem the most appropriate time to bring up our fiery relationship or the fact I still fancied the bones off Matt despite him being such a prat.

SEPTEMBER

28

BRENDAN must have sensed cabin fever in the air as soon as he arrived home. The neglected puppy act fell short of tail-wagging and face-licking, but I threw him a goofy smile as soon as he walked in.

"My God. Look at that hair. You've dyed it to match the colour of your eyes."

I let him have his fun, dispensing sarcasm and sympathy in equal measure. It was almost like Matt had reappeared in someone else's body.

My daily routine settled into a monotonous pattern. Sleep in late. Open the blinds to check the weather. Put on a dressing gown if it was sunny. Stay in my pyjamas and put on a dressing gown if it was crap. Most of the time it was crap. I had enough to occupy my days without leaving the maisonette. Cooking for us both when Brendan wasn't at Jan's, working my way through his Blu ray collection and box sets, or browsing the free downloads on my Kindle.

Then, the Friday before he was about to leave again, he caught me on the hop. "You're coming out with me and Jan tomorrow, just so you know."

"I'm not sure what I'm doing yet."

"Yes you are. You're coming with us for a wee drive and a picnic so no excuses."

Picnic? Shit. I'd not been on a picnic since Primary 7.

"But you and Jan hardly see each other. You're not going to want me hanging round like a bad smell."

"It's already decided. Jan's idea."

We left at the back of ten, despite the overcast sky that threatened to grow darker as we continued along the ring road South towards the A93. Jan kept reminding him of the speeding tickets he'd accrued during the last six months.

"If you weren't away at sea most of the time, you'd have been banned from driving ages ago."

Brendan muttered his frustration as we encountered one 30 mph restriction after another. "We're not all bloody tourists. I know this road like the back of my hand. I don't need telling what's a safe speed and what isn't."

We stopped for a coffee at the old railway station in Ballater then we headed North into the hills, finally shaking off the convoys of motor-homes, caravans and bikers. The clouds cleared once we reached the Lecht summit. Brendan pulled his car off the road and parked next to a large, timber-fronted building.

"Anybody wanting a pee, now's your chance before we enter Injun country," he announced.

Jan took out her camera and began snapping. The barren hillsides looked rather unappealing with their dismal collection of pylons, abandoned ski lifts and fencing but that made no difference. Then she got me and Brendan to pose together.

"You make a lovely couple," she said.

Brendan planted a kiss on the top of my head. "Did you get that one?"

I tried to pull away, but he placed me in a headlock and kept tousling my unruly hair as we headed back to the car.

"You ever been skiing?" Jan asked when he finally let me go.

"No. Never."

"We can hire the right gear then you can come with us once we get the first hit of snow. Me and Bren managed to come up here almost every weekend last winter."

"I'll see." The thought of fun and games in the snow with this pair was scary.

"I've taken up snow boarding as well. And horse riding, motor biking, even windsurfing," she said.

Brendan draped an arm around each of our shoulders. "Christ, I feel like I'm living inside an advert for sanitary towels."

Jan nudged him in the ribs and he made a grab for her backside. It was embarrassing to watch.

"Next stop, Grannytown," he said, "unless you ladies have a better idea."

"I'm starving hungry but I can wait 'til then. What about you, Amy?"

"Yeah, whatever."

I curled up on the back seat and watched the world go by.

"We should have a day in the hills next time I'm on leave," Brendan said. "Have you brought your walking boots with you, Amy?"

"Yep."

"You'll have to come with us then. We keep saying we should get out more often, blow away the cobwebs. It's funny how other things keep getting in the way."

"Yeah," Jan said. "Like you not being able to drag your lazy lump out of my bed six o'clock on a Saturday morning even when the sun's cracking the flagstones."

We stopped at Grantown-on-Spey. It resembled a ghost town and the picnic turned out to be a pub meal and an

121

ice cream cone afterwards. I wasn't complaining. It was like being on holiday - a concept I had faint recollections of from when Dad had been alive. Jan and Bren wandered around, hand in hand, like they hadn't a care in the world. I should have been wishing myself a million miles away from the pair of lovebirds but I couldn't muster up the energy to be a wet blanket. And all the way back they sang one cheesy song after another. Abba. The Bee Gees. Wet Wet Wet. They got me singing along with them. It would have been rude not to join in.

"You don't mind staying at Jan's tonight, do you?" Brendan asked as we approached the outskirts of Aberdeen. "I like a couple of cannies on a Saturday night."

"What? Me?"

"We can get a takeaway from Naveed's and play board games."

"If Jan doesn't mind. I mean, I don't want to intrude."

"Ach," he said. "Stop being such a misery guts. You're one of the Metcalf clan, so you're going to have to get used to it. There's no way I'm leaving you on your own tonight of all nights."

And I felt my eyes fill up. I should have known he'd remember the date. September 6th. As soon as we got back to Midstocket he took out his iPhone and began checking his messages. I helped Jan gather together dining plates and cutlery, but the next thing I knew he handed me his phone.

"Your ma wants a word," he said as he signalled for Jan to follow him into the next room.

Despite the small talk, it was good to hear her voice. She didn't mentioned the anniversary of Dad's death, but I sensed we were both thinking the same thoughts. I could barely stem the flow of tears by the time our conversation ended, and even though I gave my face a wipe with a tea towel Brendan must have been able to read the signals. He gave me a hug and made me sit on the sofa between him and Jan for the rest of the evening.

We ate Chinese and Jan and I drank cider while Brendan stuck to lager. Then Jan dug out a bottle of mango chilli schnapps and slowly that disappeared. When we got too drunk to continue playing Bucket of Doom, we shared ghost stories and corny jokes and Jan told us about her jet-setting life.

"It was crazy. Milan one day. New York the next. Tokyo. KL. But I spent more time crashed out in airport hotels than here in my own bed. Most of the time I didn't get to see any of the sights. It's not much fun serving plastic food and trying to sell duty-free tat and lottery tickets to people who would rather be allowed to get pissed or fall asleep." I'd never seen Brendan happier.

I woke in the early hours, wrapped in a duvet on Jan's couch and dehydrated. The intermittent drone of passing traffic quickly spiralled into the distant hush of the night. I imagined them both cocooned in the dark, wrapped in each other's arms or spooning. Out of nowhere, I suddenly saw what was missing in Mum's life. Love. Or more accurately, fun. She had no one to laugh with, to cuddle, to tease.

Mum did her best to put on a brave face, but most of her time was spent working to keep a roof over our heads. Whatever she earned went for rent, food and other essentials - including me. We never went anywhere together purely as a treat.

I rolled over and curled into a snug ball. Sometimes life sucks - end of. I realised, despite everything I'd been through, I still needed sexual contact. In fact, I needed sex more than ever - as if my hormones were telling me not to give up on life. I closed my eyes and began to fantasize.

29

SUNDAY lie in. *What else?* I had no intention of bursting into the honeymoon suite, so I lay daydreaming until long past ten o'clock: Matt and Kay morphing into some kind of impossible transgender hottie.

Jan eventually came through into the living room and opened the blinds. "Shit. My mouth tastes like an armadillo's pissed in it. D'you want toast?"

I elected to take a shower first. I couldn't help but smile as I noticed Brendan's shaving tackle laid out above the wash basin next to Jan's deodorant and hair spray. Claiming his territory.

When I came back out of the tiny bathroom, suitably refreshed, Brendan was sitting at the breakfast bar, wearing Jan's dressing gown and leafing through the Sunday papers. Jan stood next to him, weaving her fingers through his greying hair.

"I've got to set off for Glasgow after lunch," she said. "There's some urgent tests we've got to run and I'm on earlies this coming week so I got the call-out. Fun, fun, fun."

"That's OK, hon," Brendan said. "We can find something to keep us entertained. I'll have a look and see what's on at the Vue. What kind of films do you like, Amy?"

I shrugged. "Whatever's on. Something like the

Minions or the new X-Men one."

"As long as it's not rom-coms, 'cause they're not allowed on my watch."

Jan gave him the finger behind his back but he rolled his eyes, giving every indication of knowing exactly how she'd react. Then he picked up the weekend supplement and scanned the listings at the back. That's when I caught sight of the headline on the front page of the local news pull-out.

CRAZED SQUADDIE SLEPT WITH MY EX
BEFORE BLOWING UP THE NEIGHBOURHOOD

30

FUCK, fuck, fuck, fuck, fuck.

It was all there. A two-page spread complete with grainy, washed out colour photographs and three sidebars.

```
MURDERED SISTER
BLIND REVENGE
DRUGS AND SEX AND NO CONTROL
```

Matt's story began with his rescue from the trashed van abandoned at the bottom of the marble quarry. Then he described the time he visited me in hospital, nursing me through my recovery.

```
Some  damage  runs  deeper  than  flesh
wounds.  There  was  so  much  troubling
Amy  that  you  couldn't  see  on  the
surface.
```

Bastard. A mind reader as well as a complete shit.

There was no mention of how exactly I'd ended up being his ex. Just reams of self-indulgent crap. How he'd supported me when Caddy was murdered.

It was like I'd found another sister.
We got close. Maybe too close, given
the state Amy was in.

Yeah. I'd been an emotional wreck, but still good
enough for a one-night stand and another notch on his
bedpost.

He glossed over the business with the Polish girls and
the two Ukrainians. The paper excused the omission by
explaining the matter was due to go to court later this
month. But he managed to squeeze in how he'd rescued
me from the burning minibus following my run in with
Gordon Paver and my subsequent breakdown.

I never realised how obsessed Amy had
become with getting revenge. It's as
if she couldn't move on with her life
until every score was somehow settled.

I imagined the reporter licking her lips as he rambled
on.

I'm sure that's why she ended up
befriending Peter Paver. It was the
only way to get back at his father.

Christ. Did he believe this crap or had he been
misquoted?

Then the story skipped ahead to the night I ended up in
Kay Jepson's flat. Alcohol. Drugs. The orgy that
followed. He made it sound like I'd joined a fucking cult.

This isn't the Amy Metcalf I know.
Peter Paver might have brainwashed her
into having sex with him and his

127

accomplice, but she admits it was never consensual. I feel somehow guilty that I wasn't there for Amy when she needed me. She never reported the attack to the police, and that makes me even more concerned for her emotional well-being.

Shit.

He had the gall to spout this garbage in public, as if I was a helpless, mental wreck in need of salvaging. I felt like he'd stolen part of our life together and decided to share it with the world - a theft of the worst kind.

The only saving grace was they'd used an old photograph of me and Caddy taken during her sixteenth birthday party. That had been the barbecue where we ended up crashed out in her bed, blootered and exhausted.

I'd tied up my long, blonde hair in a French braid for the occasion. I'd also made an effort to look super-hot in a bright orange vest top and tight black hipsters. The fact that everyone could see my bra through the arm-holes had somehow not mattered. Caddy's dad couldn't keep his eyes off me.

There was no curled top lip complete with two-inch scar. No metallic red hair cut to the bone. The chances were my new neighbours in Tillydrone would never connect this teenage seductress with a hot, smoking body, and the sad, sack of shit, new butch bitch on the block. But no doubt my friends and acquaintances back home would devour every juicy titbit. Maybe they'd paid Matt by the word. Give him his due, he'd milked the human interest element for all it was worth. His candour might even earn him a fifteen minute spot on Breakfast TV.

As for me, I was the pathetic victim of my misplaced obsession with bringing Gordon Paver to justice. I actually winced as the knife penetrated the flesh between my shoulder blades.

It seemed Jan's kitchen had become frozen inside a bubble of time. None of us uttered a word as I scanned the article for anything that might paint me in a better light. But there was nothing. I scrunched the newspaper into a ball and Brendan must have seen the look of utter despair that creased my features.

"What is it?"

I couldn't speak. My face caved in and the tears ran unhindered.

He got up and stood behind me, wrapping one arm across my chest and easing the paper from my grasp with the other.

"What is it?" Jan asked.

"Ssh."

I could hear him smoothing the paper back into shape then Jan give a gasp as she presumably saw what I'd been reading.

"Fucking wee cunt," she said. "This is the guy you'd been seeing?"

I felt Brendan's arms tighten and I turned to press my face against his chest. Sobs exploded like well-placed time bombs but he didn't move. I clung on. I needed his warmth. I needed his strength. A solid rock in a sea of hopelessness.

"Put that trash away and get her a glass of water," he said.

As the tide of emotion subsided, I expected Brendan to pull away. To tell me everything was going to be fine. But he stood there, unmoving. I could feel his heart thumping next to me. Breaths long and deep. Fingers stroked the back of my head then a hand pressed against my shoulder. In a way it reminded me of the time Mike Neilson and I had comforted each other following

Caddy's death. That hadn't ended well, but this was different. If my dad had still been here he'd have done exactly the same. I knew it.

"Take your time, lassie. There's no hurry."

God. How had I lost it so spectacularly?

Finally he leant back so he could look into my face and wipe my eyes with the back of one hand. His skin felt coarse as bark yet had the gentlest of touches.

"Take a sip of water." Jan passed me a glass and I felt Brendan's hand wrap around my own, helping me steady it.

"Get her a blanket," he said. "She's shivering like a newborn lamb."

I snivelled and gulped my way to the bottom of the glass then he steered me towards the living room and helped me settle into one corner of the sofa.

Jan followed us in and placed a duvet over my body. "Did you know anything at all about him giving this press interview?" she said.

I shook my head. I couldn't trust myself to speak without blubbing again.

"God, I wish I could get my hands on him right now," Brendan said.

"That's not going to help Amy, is it?"

"Ach, maybe not. But me and him need a friendly chat. Ya ken?"

"There's no point," I said, each intake of breath an effort. "They all know. Everybody knows."

I curled up into a ball and tried to stop myself shaking. My life was an unmade bed, an underpass filled with the stink of piss, an unflushed toilet. It had even earned its own set of sidebars.

LIFE TRASHED
FAMILY IN TATTERS

They left me on my own to rewind but I could hear them muttering in the next room. A door slammed somewhere then I felt the couch sag as Jan sat next to me.

"You OK?"

I sat up and wiped my face the best I could.

"I've made you a coffee."

"Ta."

"Did you bring your phone with you?" she said.

"It's in my bag but it's switched off. The battery'll be flat 'cause I've not used it since leaving Lochinver."

"Only, Brendan would like to take a look."

"Uh?" I sat up straighter and rearranged the duvet over my bare legs.

"He's after Matt's phone number, that's all."

"What for?"

She shrugged. "He says he's going to have a quiet word."

"No way." I passed the mug back to Jan and got to my feet. "I don't need anybody interfering."

"He says he's not. But the lad's gone and kippered you."

I kicked the duvet free of my feet and headed towards the kitchen.

"Amy!" she called out after me. "You need to let Bren do something. Because if he gets it into his head you're trying to protect the wee shite, he's likely to jump in his car and drive all the way across Scotland even though he's due to fly out again Tuesday night."

"There's nothing he can do."

"Maybe not," she said. "But I've never seen him so wound up. We always promised each other we'd never part company with an unresolved argument hanging in the air, or some problem we'd rather not talk about left to fester. It doesn't do to dwell, and I don't want Bren all the

131

way out there in the North Sea with something like this bouncing about inside his empty head. When he's at work, he doesn't need family matters distracting him."

"I suppose not," I said.

"That's why I'm telling you, honey pie. You have to let him help you."

31

THERE it was again. The same photo-fit picture of her friend, Paulina, now filling the front cover of this week's *Głos Szkocki*. Except, when she studied it closer Ania realised it was a different photograph. Her friend looked no more than fifteen years old - the dress she wore most likely her confirmation gown. And beneath the photograph a headline that made Ania's heart swell with pride and fear.

"I take this please also." She passed over a handful of loose change to the shopkeeper and went back outside. She needed somewhere quiet where she wouldn't be disturbed.

Alex had told her he would be back in ten minutes. "One deal and then after I place my bets we're heading home. Get your fucking messages and make sure you're outside the bookies' waiting for me. I'm nae goin' round and round the block like a fucking taxi while you make your mind up what sweeties to buy."

She turned into John Street and stepped inside the Mither Tap. No one looked twice at the skinny, young woman as she took a corner seat away from the bar and unfolded the newspaper.

The article filled two pages.

PAULINA OSTROWSKA (1991-2014)

HISTORIA MOJEJ SIOSTRY
'The story of my sister'

The sidebar said it all - *NIEWIDZIALNI POLACY* - Invisible Poles.

Ania recognised the byline - Witek Tomaszewski. He'd originally helped out at the Polish Centre on Union Street and had written a series of popular articles about the immigration experience in Aberdeen. It seemed Jerzy, Paulina's brother, had been in touch with this reporter, anxious to set the record straight about his sister.

Ania already knew most of Paulina's story since they'd grown up together in the same neighbourhood. As far as Ania knew, Paulina's parents still lived in one of the flats on Abrahama. Her friend's family had been distraught when she announced she was leaving Gdańsk in search of a better life. Their daughter had made it clear she did not plan on working with the other Sweet Peas behind a till at the Groszek supermarket, marrying a neighbour's son and having two babies by the time she was seventeen.

By then Ania was already working weekends at Loopy's World - babysitting hyperactive kindergartners all day long. The opportunity for both girls to escape a life of low-paid drudgery with no hope of anything better seemed too good to miss.

They'd travelled to Amsterdam on student tickets before crossing the Channel and finding part-time work in a series of cheap hotels on the East coast of England, surviving for three years on less than the minimum wage while sharing a tiny bedroom in a workers' hostel. Paulina had written home whenever she could.

Jerzy quoted extracts from his sister's letters. How much she loved living in England. How friendly the people were. Paulina hadn't mentioned the sullen looks

134

from some of the locals. The verbal abuse. The threats. Some words became familiar. Names she could never repeat to her parents. Instead she joked that it was possible to function as a waitress with a five-word vocabulary. 'Tea - coffee - toast - brown - white.' Paulina had also commented on the pace of life - so much faster than in Poland. In this country they spent less time reporting items on the television news than in advertising shampoo during the commercials.

Nie ma czasu na wylegiwanie się - no time to relax.

The pace of life in Northern Ireland had suited them better. Paulina and Ania left together after replying to an advertisement in a Polish employment directory. They'd found work in a seaside guest house and within six months had made friends with three other Polish girls in the same situation. The promise of even better paid work and a large apartment they could share made the previous three and a half years' deprivations worthwhile. Paulina had passed on the good news to her family along with a photograph of her best friend. Then the letters home and infrequent telephone calls ceased.

It was as if Paulina had disappeared off the face of the Earth.

32

ANIA folded up the newspaper and pushed it behind one of the seat cushions before leaving the pub. She felt guilty for not speaking up. For not, somehow, contacting her own family back home in Poland to let them know she was still alive. But Jonno had eyes and ears everywhere.

Alex would be across the road waiting for her, growing more anxious by the minute. She would explain the delay - how she had needed to use the toilet facilities. When she scanned the row of parked vehicles she saw his car in a taxi rank two hundred yards away - its hazard lights flashing and engine ticking over. Alex reached to open the passenger door, Ania climbed in and he drove off with a familiar scowl. Not a word this time.

When growing up in Gdańsk, Ania had considered herself a twenty-first century Rapunzel, trapped inside a castle tower looking out onto three concentric rings of apartment blocks. And despite leaving Poland, she had never really escaped. Identical high-rises shut out the skyline as Alex followed the stream of afternoon traffic out of the city centre towards Rosemount. Back home, the wall of every tower block had been decorated with colourful murals. Splashes of art high above the streets like celebration flags. Even when advertising something as unsexy as construction units, the M-City project had transformed the hell of the Zaspa housing compounds into something worth looking at. Banksy didn't come close. But here the blocks of grey concrete simply added to the gloom of the city. Someone once joked that when you turn on a light in Aberdeen in October it has to stay on until March.

Ania cast her mind back to the summer evening they boarded the 'Meera Rose'. The five girls had dressed for the occasion - a cocktail party on board a rich man's boat while the sun set on a silver sea. But the mood changed once they were locked inside one of the cabins below decks. The Rapunzel story didn't include a pirate ship and two ugly brothers. A pair of heavy-set gangsters in leather jackets and denim trousers forced them back on deck then made them climb into a tiny dingy at the dead of night. Despite the screams and sense of dread, Ania's most vivid memory was the full moon suspended above a strange sea.

Once ashore, the two brothers led the girls along a shingle beach towards a wooden building. The one with the pock-marked skin began cursing at them in Russian. Calling them dreadful names before taking them inside and forcing them to do unspeakable things.

They had taken away Ania's bag - confiscated her mobile phone, passport, key ring and purse. She still had a few Euros folded up inside her shoe but €15 would never be enough for a taxi. And when everything was explained to them, Ania realised her life was now over. They would become prostitutes and earn money for their new masters or they would be taken out to sea and drowned.

After the one with the pock-marked face raped Paulina he did the same to Ania and she wished herself dead. Despite being given alcohol to drink - vodka straight from a bottle - nothing would take away the pain.

Sometime later a younger man joined them and handed out tablets.

"*Leki*," one of the gangsters told her. "Make you strong. Give you energy."

But none of that made the situation any easier. The girls attended a party, little more than a dress rehearsal for life in Aberdeen. All five were instructed to be on their best behaviour. Four men in suits eagerly awaited their company. There was music and dancing, more alcohol and drugs.

At one point Ania managed to stuff one of her folded-up banknotes inside a cushion cover. Her *ostatnia deska ratunku* she told her friends later as they commented on how terrible everything had been - the constant pawing, the loud music, one man with red y-fronts and a particularly hairy back, and the bright, snot-yellow sofa. But any dream of rescue went unanswered.

She'd hidden the remaining €5 note inside the corner of one of the pillow cases after they returned to their living quarters. Another desperate SOS. But no one came.

The months that followed, confined to a single room in an Aberdeen high rise, blurred into a single smear of memory. Despite the same grey expanse of sea visible from her bedroom, Boston and Peterborough seemed a world away from Aberdeen. The outside world no longer existed. She heard the occasional buzz of heavy traffic. But no voices carried up from the city streets. Ground level was a long way down, and even when men came calling, Jonno or Alex would see to it that the bedroom door was always locked.

There came a time when Ania no longer took notice of the days of the week, the months, the seasons. Jonno kept her supplied with drugs. A little cocaine to get into the mood. A little smack to help her chill out and take away the pain. The girls were even allowed the occasional glass of vodka in the kitchen they all shared with their two captors. That was the only time she ever got to speak to her friends - when the drinks were flowing and Alex and Jonno got to party with them.

The police raid in March came to nothing. Someone had telephoned in advance. They all got away in four separate taxis with minutes to spare. But this brief escape from routine merely increased the paranoia. The girls were farmed out to the suburbs and shared out amongst Jonno's most trusted associates. Ania spent three months with a drug dealer named Paul. Most nights they would trawl the cold, wind-swept streets alongside the docks searching for kerb-crawlers, or visit the main truck stop on the airport estate to sell full sex or blow jobs in exchange for free cocaine and a handful of currency.

The worst time came during early summer, sleeping in the back of the car or in stinking motel rooms with cockroaches and stained bed sheets. Getting cleaned up in motorway services and surviving on burgers and Red Bull. More than once, Ania was ready to run but there was nowhere she could run to. Jonno had her passport and other documents.

Eventually the police operation to clear the city of prostitution was relaxed - or so it seemed. Paul was instructed to deliver Ania to the three bedroom flat in Rosemount. Despite the unrelenting pressure to be available for a call-out all hours of day or night, this was an improvement. She felt clean for the first time in weeks.

There were also times, few and far between, when she felt in control, and there were times when escape seemed possible. But there were other nights, her brain blunted by drugs, when Ania realised one job was much like any other. Being paid to serve sexual favours was no worse than being paid to serve breakfast. Tea or coffee? Fuck or

139

suck? After a while the words meant nothing.

But now the thought of her best friend, another discard on the Aberdeen streets without a chance to be mourned or given a decent burial, chilled Ania to the core. Someone in authority would learn of Paulina's history and how she came to be another invisible Pole.

33

BRENDAN offered to telephone his line manager Monday night and beg for compassionate leave - anything to avoid abandoning me for a fortnight. Besides, he had holidays he could take, if necessary. But I assured him everything was fine. I'd had another mini-meltdown when I saw the same article on-line Monday afternoon but that soon passed. Mum had phoned. People back home in Lochinver wished me well. They all knew I was a decent girl at heart and none of it was my fault - as if their opinions made everything better.

I'd lain in bed Sunday night and pinched the inside of my left arm as each sob erupted from my throat. My long fingernails were like claws and I scratched and scraped until it hurt - searching for the tiny scabs that had puckered my skin weeks earlier. I needed something intense to take my mind off this waking hell. Pain would do to start with. The buzz of pins and needles. The sting of a razor cut and a dab of surgical spirit to raise the stakes. If I actually started self-harming maybe that would work. Maybe not.

Mum had tried to convince me returning home would be a better option but I wasn't about to hand over control of my life to someone else. Not even my mum.

"No way. I might bump into Matthew Neilson. The thought of ever meeting him face to face again turns my stomach," I said.

"But they're all going to understand, Amy. No one believes this is your fault."

Maybe. But I didn't need their understanding and besides, there were others out there I'd rather not have to think about. Matt wasn't the only villain of the piece. He wasn't the guy who'd drugged me or the one who raped me. And I didn't need everyone feeling sorry for me, fighting my corner on Facebook. I needed anonymity.

Brendan admitted he'd been unable to contact Matt Sunday afternoon. He'd rung the house and spoken to Matt's dad instead. Venting his anger seemed to have helped.

"He claims he didn't even know about the article until I phoned. If you ask me, the guy doesn't have all his oars in the water."

"So what? I told you to leave it."

None of this was helping. And when Leanne phoned Monday night with another bit of news, the tension increased a notch or two. Mum had gone round after work on Sunday and given Steff a piece of her mind like that was going to make everything better.

"Why can't everybody leave me alone?"

"We're only trying to help."

"I don't need your fucking help."

"Suit yourself."

She told me to ring her back when I was in a better frame of mind. I didn't.

I couldn't sleep Monday night and ended up wandering from room to room, zombified most of the time. Brendan sat up in front of the TV until the early hours, watching over me, saying nothing, brewing coffee, offering a hug when I finally sat next to him and had another weeping session. And when Jan phoned from Glasgow early Tuesday morning I heard him tell her to leave it for the

142

time being.

"She's still asleep, hon."

I wasn't, but the last thing I needed was another shoulder to cry on.

Then sometime after two in the afternoon, my bladder full and my tear ducts bone dry, I got up and went to the loo to freshen up. Brendan was in the kitchen waiting for me when I resurfaced, a little more human, a little less fragile.

"The lad's done you a favour now everything's all out in the open, not that I'm condoning how he's gone about it. But there'll be no more rumours about you and the Paver boy."

I couldn't see it. The thought of what people might be saying behind my back made me cringe.

"He still had no right."

"I know, love. But what's done is done so don't be so hard on yourself, Amy. No bugger round here knows who you are or what happened at Lochinver so go out and treat yourself. Think about making a fresh start."

He picked up his holdall, planted a kiss on my cheek than handed me a wad of cash.

"What's this for? You don't have to."

"I ken. But why not go and enjoy yourself? Treat yourself to something nice. Jan says you know where she is if you need to talk. You're not on your own, mind."

I wiped the drizzle of tears from my face. "I will."

£200 would go some way to easing the pain. But then a handwritten envelope arrived in the post the next day addressed to me and I realised my options had suddenly increased a hundredfold.

34

SHIT. *Was this for real?*

    I kept staring at the figures on the cheque - counting the number of zeros to convince myself I'd got it wrong. But I hadn't, and the enclosed letter explained all.

```
Amy,


So sorry to hear about your recent
troubles. I can't say this has been
Matt's finest moment. Life away from
Lochinver doesn't get any easier, does
it?
Hope this goes some way to making
things more bearable. Sometimes the
past is best left where it belongs -
in the past. I know the court case is
due to start next week as well so you
should consider heading further than
Aberdeen and take that trip of a
lifetime right now.
Remember the night we watched the
Northern Lights together? There's so
much more out there for you to
discover. Whatever you decide, accept
this gift together with my warmest
wishes. Wherever you find yourself I
```

hope things work out for the best.
 Keep well.

 Mike x

Mike Neilson was obviously trying to pay me off and save Matt's skin at the same time. He'd already handed me one cheque for ten thousand pounds less than three months earlier. He'd explained then how that cash had originally been meant for Matt - something to help fund his son's rehabilitation back into society after three months in prison. But following a fall out, Mike felt I was more deserving. I'd stood by Matt from the time of Caddy's murder to the day I visited him at Peterhead and yet he'd treated me like shit.

But this was different. If Mike had been feeling guilty then he'd already paid his dues. I'd shared half the ten thousand with Leanne. The thought of another fat cheque sitting in my RBS current account was scary. The bank would start thinking I was some kind of money launderer.

I stuck the cheque and letter back inside the envelope and put it in my shoe box. The pink cardboard treasure chest that had lain at the bottom of my wardrobe back home was destined to follow me wherever I went. Its contents included my emergency supply of weed, a couple of wraps I'd resisted sampling so far. But what the hell? Maybe I should stop feeling so fucking guilty and start to enjoy myself as Brendan had suggested. I rolled a joint and lit up. Then I pulled out my passport and stared at the ghost of Amy Metcalf. A cute smile under a curtain of blonde hair. Would I even be allowed past Airport Security now my appearance had changed so dramatically?

I'd applied for my passport on a whim the previous summer and never got around to using it. New Zealand had beckoned back then, but my desire to explore the world lost its edge once my best friend died. Even the streets outside Brendan's apartment were a virtual no-go area.

Some days I'd go out early morning when there was less chance of being seen. Circling the neighbourhood like a dog on a long restraining leash. Admiring the sparse patches of greenery along Rattray Place and the well-tended lawns bounded by Coningham Gardens and Formartine Road. Brendan and his neighbours occupied a completely artificial world. I wondered if they knew what they were missing. This corner of Aberdeen was so different from the open spaces of Assynt I'd grown up in. We didn't have much greenery, but we did have the natural tweed of oranges and browns and purples and greys - spattered white with cotton grass in summer and snow patches in winter.

As I regained my confidence the number 19 bus became my lifeline - a secure link with the city centre. I'd wait at the end of Cort Road with the posse of young mothers pushing baby buggies, weighed down by their Lidl shopping bags and a haunted look of abandonment. Occasionally there'd also be a couple of neds hanging around in the red shirts of Aberdeen Football Club, sporting home-made gangsta haircuts and blurry tattoos. And there was always the same old mannie on the corner checking the racing pages as he walked his wee Jack Russell to the local bookies. I made no eye contact. This wasn't the place for a friendly nod or a familiar, have-a-good day smile. This was the big bad city. If anyone had dared give me the look I'd have stared them out.

I usually got off outside Marischal College where Robert the Bruce sat astride his bronze horse, laptop held aloft. Across the road, long-legged cranes swung lazily in the sunshine like overgrown coat hangers. Everywhere the swirl of unfamiliar sounds and colours sucked me in like a whirlpool. I'd reluctantly join the crowds, dodging the showers or drinking in the silvery sunshine and the constant thrum of traffic.

Eventually, I found my way back to the Maritime Museum. I rediscovered it the second time I'd explored Broad Street and beyond. I didn't dare go inside but I lingered at the edge of the harbour and watched the boats. Mostly supply ships for the rigs. There was also the Northlink ferry complete with a Viking warrior emblazoned along its side. I'd become mesmerised watching the boats come and go, and dream about climbing on board and taking off. Exploring the world while everything back home returned to the West coast version of normal. But I intended going a lot further than Lerwick or the nearest oil platform.

Would I be missed if I disappeared? I'd heard of people who booked a flight and holiday literally hours before heading off into the sun. I could simply pack up a suitcase and go. It was unlikely the police had warned Passport Control I might try to leave the country.

Caddy's inquest and the suspicious death hearings - Robbo's and young Paver's - weren't due until the end of the year, and the chances were they could manage without me. There was also the impending trial at Aberdeen Sherriff Court of Stuart Coleman from Rosehall and John Fleming from Torbreck. That was less than a week away. Mum had forewarned me of the local interest it might rekindle long before Matt's bombshell. Maybe it would be better if I was half a world away from all the fresh publicity: the press raking over the ashes, reigniting a community's shame and uprooting so many hurtful memories to sell more newspapers.

Of course, if the police had been doing their job properly Gordon Paver would be joining Coleman and

147

Fleming in the dock facing charges of abduction, actual bodily harm, human trafficking and forced prostitution. But then I'd have had to testify against him, helping the Crown Office to get him locked away for life. Instead he got away with it. No case to answer. And I was spared at least one court appearance. Time for everybody to move on.

I stubbed out the joint and reassessed the situation. Right now I needed a drink. I needed the buzz of alcohol and loud music and company my own age. I needed the smell of hormone-heavy sweat and cheap weed and something else. I needed uncomplicated sex. God, how I missed the sensation of a warm, writhing body - any gender - clamped against mine. It was time I gave in to my urges and started enjoying life. I had a cheque for £20,000 burning a hole in my pocket. Time to think about spending some of it, and fuck the consequences.

35

IF there'd been a morning-after pill for stupidity, I'd be queuing outside the nearest pharmacy right now waiting for them to open. I could smell the guy next to me. A blend of cheap deodorant, testosterone and stale sweat. Maybe the sweat was my own contribution to the state of the bedding - a threadbare duvet, a sheet stained with spillages I'd rather not dwell on too closely and a lumpy, discoloured pillow, hard as a headstone.

I'd spend the dregs of the night perched on my side of the mattress, trying to keep my body as far away from Patryk as possible. I'd only met this dark-haired stranger, tattooed and nicely toned, hours earlier, yet he'd left me feeling confused and loved up and cheap and tantalisingly trashy.

What bits I recalled came rushing back like bullet points. Someone called Vera - the hawk-nosed flatmate he'd claimed to know all his life. Strong, bitter coffee - in china cups not mugs. Polish pastries - sprinkled with icing sugar. Vera called them Polish 'bows' - her mother's speciality. And the abrupt transition from living room to bedroom - my cue to show Patryk what I wanted him to do to me. Gasping for it. Tensed up tightly as my hormones placed my body into anaphylactic shock.

The flat aroma of weed hung in the air even though neither of us had smoked a single joint. And the bedroom smelt of sex as soon as I staggered in. Reassuring, in a way. We undressed in the dark - unfamiliar shapes and shadows all around me as I stumbled onto this strange bed. Its frame creaking under my weight. Trying to decipher the room's geography. Then I found my way under the duvet and began to hyperventilate. I could hear a trickle of sounds from the next room. Music fading in and out and the clink of crockery in a kitchen sink. My eyes adjusted to the dark as he climbed in next to me, then the patch of light at the bottom of the door disappeared followed by the slam of another door.

The only illumination that remained was the streetlight: orange bars filtering through a set of distorted window blinds. They never moved the entire night. There was little to mark the passage of time, after I'd asked him to stop, except the tiny red display on the bedside radio. I watched it counting the hours.

02:40. 03:17. 05:05.

The taste in my mouth made me regret accepting the nightcap.

"Thunder vodka. Is good."

The sickly toffee flavour masked the stab of pure alcohol. Then he'd kissed me and his tongue stole the sweet aftertaste and left me wanting more.

"This is much better."

We'd met inside the only pub I could identify by sight and smell. The Friars - an old-fashioned drinking hole with a full-timbered frontage and the stench of spilt ale on the pavement outside. He'd said his name was Patryk. Spelt it out in case I'd want to write it down and reference it for later. I was guessing East European. Polish or Lithuanian, maybe, judging by the accent. Dark, close-cropped hair and designer stubble. Retro 90s. He swaggered across and, give him his due, he used none of the standard chat-up lines as perfected by every desperate ned from Stranraer to Thurso.

"I don't expect to see you here."

"What?" Had he confused me with someone else?

"Your eyes. They call to me from across the room. They make you look as if someone haunts you."

I make it a rule to ignore any guy who claims he can tell what is going on in my mind when he's never met me before. Charmers who reckon they are reaching out to your soul across a crowded room. In my experience they are no better than the creeps who grab your hand out of nowhere, trace their fingers across your palm and recite your life story.

"Such a pretty face but something in your eyes. A painful memory perhaps."

Shit.

"I'm sorry. I think. . ."

"It's OK," he said. "I don't try to bother you any more or make you feel uncomfortable."

He sat on the bar stool next to me. "I buy you first one drink then leave you alone."

"There's no need, really."

He gestured to the half-empty bar.

"You find someone else who is perhaps better company for you? Five minutes, I promise. Then I go if you ask."

I scanned the darkened room for back-up. It was still early evening so the place wasn't yet wall to wall jerks. What few punters I could see were paired off and dining or part of a large group of office types hovering next to the jukebox. I searched for a friendly face. There were none. Those few lit up by iPad screens barely had the time to gaze in my direction as they continued to vape while checking their Facebook feeds. I probably looked like a seedy skank looking to be picked up or some random Tinder tramp desperate for a fumble.

"Vodka?" he said.

By now the first gin and tonic had long gone. I put a hand over my glass. I wasn't in the mood to be propositioned or seduced. Nowhere near the mood or the zone. I shook my head but before I could stop him he'd taken my glass, raised it to his face and inhaled.

"Ah." He motioned to the barman. "Double Hendrick's please, and a vodka and Coke."

"I wasn't planning to have another," I said.

Then he pointed to the bottle of tonic water, two-thirds full still. "You need a fresh glass?"

I nodded. "OK. Lots of ice, and a slice of lemon please."

He smiled and I noticed his teeth - a little crooked. And his brown eyes. And I cursed under my breath for failing to have an exit strategy in place. My tight, pencil skirt and skimpy vest top hardly functioned as body armour.

We clinked glasses and he leant closer, as if trying to shield me from the rest of the bar. Claiming his own territory maybe. Smiling. Confident but not too cocky. I could smell his aftershave. Something astringent rather than attractive.

"So you are from Aberdeen?" he said.

"No."

"But you are Scottish. I can tell."

"Yeah."

"And what do you do here? A student?"

"Sort of. It's a long story. I'm passing through and I haven't decided what I'm doing next. I'll probably travel first then study."

"Me, I am also a student. Architecture and Technology. RGU."

"What's that?"

He explained briefly. Somewhere South of the city.

"So what are you doing alone in a bar on a Wednesday

night?" he said.

"Just chilling. It's been a shit week so far."

"OK. Is it allowed if we chill together?"

I took a sip from my glass and gave a smirk.

"Or I leave you alone. You don't need a guy like me who talks when you want quiet to think."

"It's OK," I said. "I'll tell you when I want you to go."

"And yes. When you say I go, I go."

Patryk spoke about his family. Russian father. Polish mother. Most of his life spent in a small Polish town close to the border with Ukraine.

"I also have an older sister, Katerina. She is a journalist. There was much corruption in Ukraine with our President. There were protest marches and she reported on them, but it is a dangerous job."

"Sounds the same as here. Politicians are no different, wherever you live."

"You study Politics?"

"I think Media Studies, once I decide. I'd like to specialise in photography or video."

Patryk continued to play things cool. Not making a move. He changed the subject. Cinema. Patryk was a Tarantino fan. He bought me another drink then I got us a third. By now I couldn't help fantasizing how it would feel to press myself against his well-toned body.

He grinned. Maybe he'd figured I was checking him out. "So do you go to the nightclubs afterwards?"

That had been my original intention. I would spend an hour inside the Friars to build up a little Dutch courage then I'd head for Clubland. I'd already researched on-line where I might go in search of company but I couldn't decide whether to choose a gay-friendly bar or simply a place where I could blend in with the young crowd. When it came down to it, I was after more than a hug on a dancefloor.

"We can try *The Tunnels* - or *Liquid* where most of the students go," he said. "Sometimes Vera comes also with me."

Then he must have noticed the smug grin cross my face. "Don't worry. Vera is an old friend from Chelm. Our home town. We live together but we are not sleeping together. And you are also very pretty but I don't know you yet so I don't make assumptions. We are only two people talking. Right?"

He smiled again and I leant in, angling my face so both our mouths were at the same level. Then I let him taste my lips and my tongue. Twenty, thirty seconds.

I pulled away from his awkward embrace and took a longer drink. "Yeah. We're just talking," I said.

Christ! What was I doing?

I scrabbled for my bag that had become entangled in the legs of the bar stool.

"I'm sorry. I don't normally act like this," I said. "Too much drink."

"That's OK. If you don't want to go to a club we maybe go to the *Siberia Wodka Bar*. They do crazy shots there."

I lurched off the stool and slung the strap of my bag over one shoulder. "Better not, but thank you. I'll probably go home instead."

"Then I help you." He followed me to the door. "Where is it you live?"

"Tillydrone. Wingate Place. It's absolutely miles from here. You don't need to change your plans."

"I have no plans." He took my arm. "I help you find a taxi home. Or if you like we can go back to my flat first for coffee. It is on the same way."

"I'm fine. Honest."

But Patryk was insistent. "We find a taxi then we talk about it. I don't have bad intentions for you, Amy."

36

ONLY when I stepped outside the bar did I realise I'd drunk way too many grin and tonics, as Leanne always called them. Patryk held onto my arm and helped me pick my way along the uneven pavement towards the brighter lights of Castle Street. I thought back to Matt Neilson's warning and decided he was being paranoid.

By the time we found a cab I'd almost surrendered to the fact I could well end up getting raped or strangled then dumped in a skip. It didn't seem to matter that much anymore. I heard Patryk ask for my address again but I couldn't bring myself to answer. Instead I grabbed his hand and sank back into the rear seat of the taxi. He squeezed my fingers and, whenever I focussed on our surroundings, I kept seeing flashes of the city like frames from a movie. We headed North along King Street. We passed the floodlit harbour on our right. Darker streets and unfamiliar territory until, up ahead, I could make out the new glass library lit up like an aquarium. A set of familiar high rises came into view and Patryk kissed me but I didn't respond. I needed to pee.

We stepped out into a dimly lit courtyard and Patryk paid the taxi. It had started to rain and he steered me into the lobby of the nearest tower block. That brought me to my senses.

"Shit. I'm sorry," I said. "This isn't such a good idea." I

rummaged in my bag for my mobile and cursed my stupidity once more for not having the sense to charge the fucking thing before coming out. "Can you ask the taxi to wait?"

"If he is still here. This is not a place to wait for fares, so late at night."

I followed him outside and rechecked the contents of my purse. Two twenties and maybe a couple of pounds in loose change. More than enough. But then Paranoia Stage II kicked in and I considered the consequences of a young woman, the worse for drink, getting inside a taxi late at night.

There was no sign of the cab. One potential bullet dodged.

"God. I don't know what I'm going to do," I said.

Patryk moved in closer. "Take it easy. We call another cab and I lend you money to get home if you don't have enough."

"It's not that. I don't even know you. I don't know if I can trust you or what."

I felt pathetic. Stuck in the middle of God knows where with a bladder about to burst. Patryk put his arm around me and shepherded me back inside.

"You are safe here, I promise. Come upstairs to meet Vera. She will talk with you while I make everyone a coffee, then I telephone for another taxi. Ten minutes it comes."

"I'm actually desperate for a wee so I don't need anything else to drink."

We ascended ten floors inside a grubby elevator with flattened cigarette stubs and sweet wrappers on the floor. I counted each floor then it stopped moving. Outside, in the corridor, there was a strong smell of disinfectant, no doubt to mask the stench of urine and beer. He led me along a dim passage away to the left. Three doors along,

156

he took out his keys.

"Vera is probably watching TV. She likes hospital stories, you know? Casualty? Holby City?" He steered me into the cramped living room. I smelt the weed as soon as we walked inside and for a split second I got a flashback. A young woman lay sprawled on a couch. I saw tea lights and heard loud throbbing music. But this wasn't Kay Jepson's flat and the music was the theme tune to some inane reality show. Celebrity Blind Dates or something similar. Vera wore a t-shirt and pyjama bottoms and her spliff had almost burned down to the butt.

"I bring someone home for a coffee, *kochanie*. This is Amy."

Vera rose to her feet, stubbed out her smoke in an overflowing ashtray and gave Patryk the briefest of hugs.

"Can I use your loo?" I said.

Vera opened one of the nearest doors, pointed into the darkness, then wandered barefooted into the next room. I could hear the clink of crockery as I tugged down my tights. When I returned to the living room, Patryk helped me take off my damp coat and removed a stack of newspapers and magazines from one of the armchairs.

"Sit here."

"You know? I should probably go. It's late."

"But Vera makes us coffee. You are our guest so it's OK you stay."

"Does Vera make coffee for all your guests?" I said.

Patryk laughed out loud. "We are like brother and sister. We know each other all our life so when I come to Scotland we share a flat to make it easier to pay the rent and the bills. But there is nothing else. Sometimes I bring a friend home for the night and we sleep together - Vera understands. She can do the same if ever she captures a man."

157

"I'm not going to sleep. . ." I let the sentence die.

"That's not what I mean." Patryk took off his jacket and muted the television. "You are a new friend to us. We make all friends welcome here, that is all."

Vera returned with a tray - cookies and coffee - and Patryk began to talk about his time in Ukraine.

"It is easy to get across the border from Poland," he said. "Fifteen hours from our home to Kiev. I tell my parents I go to visit a friend but instead I join my sister who takes part in the demonstration on Independence Square. The protesters there have tents and we were allowed to stay as long as we wished."

"You were both demonstrating?" I said.

"Of course. You have read about the Euromaidan protests in Ukraine?" Patryk asked.

I shook my head. The British media had enough to occupy themselves with the forthcoming Scottish Referendum.

"Fucking Yanukovych and his cronies. We are attacked while we are asleep," Patryk continued. "That is why we return to Poland."

"The reports from Crimea make us scared for our safety," Vera said.

Patryk pulled out a Polish language newspaper from the pile on the floor. The cover featured a photograph of a young woman and a name and date beneath it.

PAULINA OSTROWSKA (1991-2014)

The rest of the writing meant nothing.

He opened the paper and passed it over. "This is what my sister reports," he said. I saw the by line - *Katerina Balik*. There were photographs of barricades and people holding up placards.

"Does your sister still live in Poland?" I asked.

He shook his head but said no more.

"You should have seen Patryk's face when he saw Katerina's article," Vera said. "He was so proud, he had tears in his eyes."

Patryk closed the magazine and let it drop to the floor.

"So what does your sister's article say?"

"That the Ukrainians are stupid to let Russia steal part of their homeland because of propaganda from Putin and their own corrupt politicians," Patryk said.

"It is dangerous what Kata says. The police attack their own people - using tear gas and hit them with sticks," Vera continued. "And so many *titushky* on the streets every night. Men from outside the city who come there to earn money by attacking protesters."

"It was no longer safe, you understand? That is why we both had to leave," Patryk said. "And now my sister fights for Ukraine by writing about injustice."

He went on to describe the long lines of traffic waiting to cross the border into Poland.

"We take a ride from a musician and his girlfriend. They have a battered Volkswagen campervan and it breaks down five miles after we cross over. They drive all the way from England. That is when I decide to come here to make a new life."

I felt my eyes grow heavy, and once or twice I heard them mutter to each other in a foreign language. Vera finally offered to find blankets and a spare pillow but once we were alone I told Patryk I'd prefer not to sleep on the couch.

"It is not so uncomfortable. But if you want, I call for a taxi," he said.

"That's not what I mean," I said.

We didn't have sex. Not technically. I'd made it clear that wasn't on the agenda. I wanted to keep the entire relationship superficial. But for some weird reason, I wanted to make sure Vera could hear us. Maybe I needed to make her jealous when she realised what we were up to under the bed sheets. I took off my clothes, lay on the dirty sheets, and when Patryk lay next to me I reached between his legs.

"You like this?"

We agreed it was to be no more than a little fun. I'd be gone by morning and we'd probably never see each other again. But there were moments, during the darker hours, when the alcohol began to wear off and I felt I was cheating on myself. The scent and touch of Patryk's body seemed too familiar. It was Matt's lips caressing my bare skin when Patryk's tattooed hands covered every inch of my naked body. I imagined Kay's tongue teasing my nipples and my belly and heard soothing words in a language that made no sense.

I left my mark. A bite on the flesh covering his left collar bone. Sometime later I must have slept. And when I woke for the third time, hungover in a strange bed with the memories of the night still lingering on the air like forbidden perfume, the guilt and anxiety came flooding back. Daylight seeped into the threadbare room, an unwelcome intruder. Patryk lay on his back with his left arm splayed across my belly. I reached for his open hand, traced the slender, reed-like bones forming part of his wrist, threaded my fingers through his and squeezed once. Then I scraped myself off the bed and went in search of my bra and pants.

I made sure no one heard me leave.

37

THERE wasn't a soul outside Donside Court to witness my morning-after face; a face marked for failure. The fifteen minute walk of shame in shoes not made for walking didn't make the experience any more rewarding. The only consolation was that Brendan wasn't home to greet me as I crawled in like a feral cat after a night out on the tiles. I could smell myself on my fingers and on my skin.

First into the kitchen for a glass of cold milk. But that didn't help. I felt as if my stomach was about to implode. I dashed to the bathroom, bent over the toilet bowl and emptied myself until my diaphragm ached from so much heaving. My eyes stung. My mouth tasted rancid. I cursed my stupidity and swore I'd never touch another drop of booze.

Then I stripped off and stood under the shower - needle points of hot water to revive and to cleanse. That's how I ended up hugging myself beneath the downpour, bawling my eyes out. I endured the pain until my bare skin stung, scrubbed red sore until all flesh was worn away down to bare bone and raw sinew. In no mood for toast and coffee, I tossed the outfit I'd worn the previous night into the laundry basket then thought better of it. Everything went into the washing machine along with my bath towel and face flannel.

I put on a pair of woolly bed socks, a clean pair of knickers and my fluffy dressing gown then I scooted under the duvet. It was half past nine in the morning and I had no intentions of climbing out of my bunker for the foreseeable future. The events of the previous few hours replayed in brief flashes of intensity. The sensation of our first kiss. The smoky undertone of his voice. The passion as he spoke about his political conscience. The unfamiliar landscape of his naked body as he moulded it against mine.

Shit. I needed a spliff.

After lighting up, I took out the bundle of postcards I'd kept from way back when. Various greetings from Tenerife, Gran Canaria, and a handful from Lauren and Quinn as they reported back from their travels. Japan. Malaysia. New Zealand.

I could follow in their footsteps. No problem.

I took out my passport again to double check all was in order. The €5 banknote I'd stuck in there earlier this year slipped free and I thought back to Caddy's Facebook post.

'My Only Tip So Far This Month. Thank you Ania and friends'

She'd posted that over twelve months ago along with a photo of the banknote left in one of the Strathbeg bunkhouses. Caddy had come across it while doing one of her weekend changeovers for Gordon Paver. There was handwriting on the back - Polish, maybe. Matt had found it amongst his sister's mementoes shortly after her murder and we'd thought nothing of it until unfolding events suggested there had been something shady going on in the chalet park. A human trafficking operation being conducted right under everyone's noses. Whoever left the message on the back of the banknote had also signed off with a list of girls' names.

Ania, Paulina, Ewa, Marcelina and Krystyna.

We were curious, and Matt and I finally visited Inverness one Friday night in search of someone who might be able to translate what else was written on the banknote. I'd got pissed, but we found a couple of Polish girls at the N-Zone who offered their help in exchange for a free drink. The words hastily added in biro had almost faded to nothing but I could still make them out well enough to read.

And that single word like a punch in the guts - *gwalt*.

I checked the calendar on my smart phone. The court case was due to begin in four days. Maybe I could escape to the other side of the world before the verdict and before everything got stirred up again by the tabloid vultures.

38

WHEN Carl Tyler let slip he had business to attend to back in the UK, Jenny assumed he'd be travelling there alone. She had no desire to leave their Mediterranean love nest, regardless of the British tabloids' latest claim.

LONDON BRACED FOR 30° SCORCHER

Jenny Maclean knew how most of these mini heat waves would be followed days later by a contradictory warning.

ARCTIC BLAST FORECAST FOR HOLIDAY WEEKEND.

While her Facebook friends in Lochinver conducted Ice Bucket challenges, Jenny had been soaking up the Spanish sun; topping up her tan or teaching Jake to swim in their own private pool. They could all go fuck themselves, as far as she was concerned. When the village had swarmed with rumours regarding Rick Tyler's role in Caddy's murder more than eight months earlier, Jenny had been persona non grata. In everyone's eyes she was as bad as the scumbag who shared her bed.

OK, admittedly she'd begun to believe that Rick was indeed the murderer. He'd been screwing Caddy. And much as she'd enjoyed the casual sex, Matt Neilson was little more than a friend with benefits. He'd called her a friend on benefits. How times had changed.

By the start of the local tourist season, Jenny's buttermilk complexion had developed more than a hint of bronze, and she could manage enough phrases in Spanish to get by. Carl Tyler's years on the Costa del Sol, between his short spells in prison, made him look more local than expat - or in Jenny's eyes, more gangster than respectable businessman.

There was something so romantic about the Costa del Crime. It didn't do to look too closely how Carl made his money, but cocaine and booze came free with the ex-pat lifestyle. And all that mattered was that she'd escaped the grind of single motherhood in a one-bedroom flat in the armpit of the universe for a new life in paradise. The Highlands couldn't have been further from her mind when Carl received the email from one of his ex-con buddies in Manchester asking if he'd seen the news. Something about Rick Tyler's remains being discovered on a remote beach on the West coast of Scotland less than a mile from the flat he'd once shared with Jenny.

"Do they say what happened?" Jenny asked.

"Not exactly. But it doesn't look like it was accidental drowning."

"How d'you know?"

Carl tapped the side of his nose before turning his back on her. One of his usual tricks whenever he didn't want Jenny to know something. "It doesn't matter, babes. Let's leave it for now." Then he'd left the room and she heard him make a telephone call. His voice raised. Short, sharp explosions of anger.

Jenny knew better than to pry further.

She thought she might have shed a tear or two on discovering the news. After all Carl's kid brother, Rick, was the father of her little boy. She'd been ridiculously in love with Rick until he disappeared. But that infatuation soon soured, once she discovered he'd wormed his way inside Caddy Neilson's panties while feeding her drugs. The fact that Rick had been dealing was a minor issue. Carl was in the same line of business. But the thought of Rick climbing into her bed with his dick still smeared in Caddy's slime. She'd have cut his balls off if she'd known.

Where Rick had been inept, Carl was the ultimate pro. He crossed every t and dotted every i. Carl had a talent for making money. A talent that allowed them to live in a luxurious villa less than a mile from the exclusive Monte Paraiso Golf Club. If he had business back home, it was likely to be lucrative. Maybe a new distribution contract or a new chain of supply. But then he mentioned a trip to the Highlands. Jenny was to accompany him, and that's when she began to have second thoughts.

"We're going to spend a month in Lochinver? Shit."

"Keep your knickers on. It'll give you time to catch up with your besties. And I've booked us a wee, romantic cottage at the foot of Quinag."

"You're joking. That's the last place I wanna be."

But he'd already planned everything down to the hire car. A sleek black 4x4 so he said. And he'd shown Jenny the booking confirmation for the holiday cottage during their flight to Prestwich.

"Croft House Cottage? Shit."

"You know it?"

"Yeah. It's miles from everywhere."

"That's the idea," he said.

"But for God's sake, what the hell are we supposed to do out there for a whole fucking month?"

Carl tapped his nose.

"That's your answer to everything."

166

"Woah woah woah."

"I don't know why me and Jake couldn't have stopped in Marbella," Jenny continued. "You could have went on your own."

Then she saw his eyes narrow. The telltale signs.

"We're supposed to be a team, you and me. I don't ask a lot of you."

"I'm only saying," she muttered. "I don't want me and the babby to get in the way."

He gave her arm a squeeze. "You won't," he said. "We'll call to see your ma on the way through. I was thinking Jake might like to spend a little time with his nana since we're passing."

"So everything's planned?"

"It is. This business could get a little messy."

"I still don't see why you need me. I can stop there with her as well 'cause I've no mates in Lochinver. Trust me."

"Don't start that again. You're coming, so get used to the idea. It'll be needing a woman's touch."

"If you say so." She wrapped her arms around her son as the plane began its slow descent.

"The papers are suggesting the coppers won't bother looking for Ricky's killer any time soon. So that's down to me. And once I find the fucker responsible, I'm gonna tear off his dick, grind it to a point then shove it up his arse."

Jenny felt the blood grow chill in her veins. "So what am I supposed to do while you're playing hard man?"

"You'll get your chance to help out. I'm gonna need to do some catching up with a couple of Rick's known associates."

"Like who?"

"We'll start with lover boy."

39

"IS that you, Matt?"

He didn't recognise the voice.

"Who's asking?"

"It's Jenny. Jenny Maclean."

For a second or two Matt considered ending the call. Jenny Maclean had been part of his not so glorious past. Rick Tyler's girlfriend, make that ex-girlfriend, was someone he'd comfort fucked after his dad threw him out. But she'd disappeared shortly after Matt's run in with Slippy and his two Rottweilers, and he'd not given her a thought since.

"Christ. I thought you and Carl had buggered off to Spain."

"We stayed in Bearsden for a couple of months. My ma's. Then Carl said me and the wean could go off with him. We're back for a few weeks and I want Jake to meet his granny again. Carl's got a business deal he needs to handle in person."

"OK. So why call me out of the blue?"

"I wanted to see you, that's all. Catch-up, you know."

"You're joking."

"I'm not," she said. And her voice began to break. "I saw all the latest stuff in the papers about Caddy and you and Amy."

"So?"

"I felt bad. I'd been thinking Rick was a killer all along like the police reckoned he was."

"Well, we all got that bit wrong. But Rick still had it coming."

"What d'you mean?"

"I mean, he wasn't exactly selective in the company he was keeping. And he didn't have the sense to get out while he could."

"That's not fair," she said.

"Christ, Jen. I warned him to get rid of the drugs the weekend before Caddy was killed. Didn't I come round to the flat on the Tuesday morning to tell him the cops were sniffing round?"

"Suppose so."

"Anyway, it was obvious you found a better option, the way you went off with your new boyfriend after Slippy's goons gave me a pasting. It's a long hike from Bearsden to Lochinver for a quickie - if that's what you're after."

"Fuck you, Matt. Me and Carl are back in Lochinver if you must know. The Hanley place."

"Out by Loch Assynt?"

"Aye. He's booked the cottage for the next few weeks. That's why I'm calling. He says he's got a proposition to make you."

Now it made sense. Carl Tyler, the wannabe gangster who'd stood idly by while Matt had seven shades of shit beaten out of him then made off with Jenny, the baby and Steff's car.

"Tell him from me, he can fuck off. I've got better things to do than listen to his shite."

"He knows how you must feel about him. The way things turned out. But he's only asking you to hear him out. He owes you big time, and there's a drink in it for you, so he says."

40

IT had been so empowering to discover I still had what it took to snare a guy. The right mix of pheromones and sexual charisma, and maybe the look. Not much consolation in the grand scheme of things, but it proved the scars were beginning to fade. Physically and emotionally. Recovery and reconstruction had been painfully slow, and I wasn't kidding myself that it would all be party time and rampant sex from now on. Complete rebirth was a long way off. But I felt comfortable inside my own skin. The first time I could admit that in ages.

That sudden sense of self-belief made my plans that much easier. I rang my sister to break the good news.

"Are you serious?"

"It's what I need right now," I replied, cradling the telephone handset under my chin as I tapped ash off the end of the second joint of the day. "I'm getting cabin fever here, and I'd rather be away from Aberdeen now this court case is about to start. It'll be in all the papers."

"But why go abroad? Mum'll have a dickie fit."

"That's why I'm phoning you, not her."

"But, shit. You're going to have to tell her sooner or later."

"Yeah. I'll do it as soon as I get to Amsterdam. It's not a rush decision, Lea."

The line went quiet for a few seconds.

"You sure?"

"Yeah. I've booked my flight for a fortnight from now. October the third. There's a few bits I need to sort out before I leave. But don't you even dare suggest coming all the way out here to try to get me to change my mind. It's not happening."

"I wasn't going to. But, Christ, Amy. How you will you manage? You're going to need somewhere to stay. That won't be cheap. And have you even looked at finding work out there?"

That's when I told her about Mike Neilson's cheque.

"How much this time?"

"Same again. Ten grand." A little white lie.

"Christ, I don't get it. Why does he keep sending you cash?"

"I already told you. He feels responsible for the way things turned out. Caddy dying the way she did and all the crap I've gone through. Matt's betrayal was the final straw. He's on a guilt trip."

"So what? I think it's totally bogus. Are you sure there's nothing been going on between you two I don't know about?" she said. "I mean, Mike Neilson's only an accountant in the Harbour Office, so I don't see how he can afford to finance your extravagant lifestyle."

"Very funny. But that's not the point. How he spends his money is none of my business."

"How convenient."

"Yeah, well."

"Personally I'd have torn the cheque up. And heading off to Amsterdam is the most stupid idea I've ever heard."

"Why stupid?"

"It's another one of you knee-jerk reactions, Ames. You can't keep running away from life."

"I'm not," I said.

"What about Brendan?" she asked. "Hasn't he tried to

171

talk you out of it?"

"He doesn't know yet. I'll probably have a heart to heart with him when Jan's not around."

"So you're happy talking to him, but can't be bothered to tell your own mother. It's a bit mean, don't you think?"

"I know, but I can't handle telling her to her face. If I say anything before leaving, she'll be on the next train to Aberdeen. It's hard, Lea."

"Only 'cause you're making it hard. No one's making you leave. And you're going to have to have a better story ready when you explain to Mum how you're paying for all this or she'll be round Mike's house shouting the odds. Does Steff know what her husband's up to?"

"I doubt it, so don't say anything. Not even to Steve."

"I wasn't going to. Not after the last business. But promise me you won't go planning any long distant flights to the other side of the world without phoning me again."

"I won't."

But already the possibilities had become increasingly intoxicating, once the travel bug dug its teeth into me and the bite marks began to itch. I'd mapped out several itineraries in my head. Amsterdam for a week or two then a flight to Abu Dhabi or KL or Singapore or Bangkok. New Zealand was doable. Lauren always said the best stories were those written inside the pages of a passport. My passport was still a blank sheet but I was desperate to scribble the first word, even if I was only on line one, page one, chapter one.

I'd rediscovered another itch as well. That itch.

Patryk had known how to scratch it until I purred and curled up like a contented cat. He'd let me steer his fingers towards the sweet spot and it seemed the louder I moaned the harder he got. Days later, I was still on heat. When I wasn't trawling the internet in search of cheap flights, I was wandering the neighbourhood, desperate to catch sight of him yet hoping I wouldn't. I felt torn in two - the thought that I'd met someone who I fancied a month before leaving for a new life on the other side of the world.

Once or twice I spotted the woman out in the street. Vera. Not my new best friend forever. If she saw me out of the corner of her eye, she didn't let on. The first time she'd been carrying a large blue plastic bag. She'd gone inside the local laundrette then minutes later wandered into the newsagent's next door for a pack of cigarettes and a magazine. The second time, she'd been on a supermarket shopping trip. Vegetables and fruit, two plastic containers of milk and a bottle of wine. I was conscious I was stalking her. But there had been no sign of her flatmate.

The chances were, I was the last thing on his mind. But I didn't give up. I took to roaming his neighbourhood all hours. Early morning, when dawn was still a pinch of bruised sky out across the grey expanse of sea. Late night, when the street lights took on a sickly shade of orange, and the only sounds of life were the clink of bottles kicked by a drunk on his way home or the snarl of a taxicab heading back towards the city centre.

I even started visiting the newsagent's next door to the laundrette each morning on the off-chance I'd bump into Vera and begin a casual conversation.

"Hi. It's Vera, isn't it? So How's Patryk? Tell him I'm asking after him. Maybe we could meet up for a drink. The three of us. Only, I'm planning on leaving Aberdeen in a couple of weeks. Don't know whether or not I'll bother coming back, ever. It would be nice to say goodbye properly."

But the opportunity didn't arise. Patryk was still a no-show and I'd not seen Vera in the last four days either. I

173

bought packets of liquorice allsorts. A travel magazine - its front page spread providing a touch of Twilight Zone serendipity. Backpacking Special. And down amongst the bottom shelf local small press publications, I spotted a familiar magazine.

Głos Szkocki

I recognised the face in the photograph. And beneath the two meaningless words, one short headline.

PAULINA I ANIA - PRAWDA

I bought myself a copy, even though I couldn't understand a word. 70p guilt money maybe. Then I headed back to Brendan's flat, love and wanderlust curdling like sour wine in my gut as the shame of having so much unfinished business kicked in.

41

THE Caley Hotel bar on a dismally grey Thursday afternoon possessed all the ambience of a funeral parlour. Two tourists shared one of the window seats, poring over a map, and a guy in yellow wellingtons propped up the bar while the young barmaid slowly worked her way around the room, table to table, duster in one hand and a can of polish in the other.

"What'll you have?"

Carl had changed since the last time Matt had seen him. Tan a little deeper, suit a little sharper, demeanour a little sleazier. He also looked strung out on something - something more than sheer delight in his return visit to the Caley. Matt ordered a pint of 80/- and Carl asked for a bottle of Budweiser. Then they found a cosy corner far enough away from the rest of the clientele and the jukebox to discuss business without being overheard.

Carl clinked the bottle against Matt's glass. "Cheers."

"I shouldn't even be drinking with you after the last episode."

"Shit happens. You've gotta move on."

"Yeah. It's probably easier when you're in a villa in Spain than in a hospital bed in Inverness. It was you who got me involved in that shit in the first place. I don't remember you weighing when Slippy's boys started roughing me up," Matt said.

"Not my place. But it's why I'm back here now. To put things right."

"Forget it," Matt said. "It's too late for that, so if you're here to make more trouble, I want no part of it. I'll finish my pint, to be sociable, then I'm off."

"Woah woah woah. Let's rewind. There's a lot been happening since the last time we met."

"I've got better things to do than reminisce about the good old days. I'm not in the mood so, like I say, you're wasting your time."

"You were inside, last I heard," Carl said as he ran a thumb along the top of his bottle. "Can't have been easy."

"It was pure shit, 24/7. But you'll know that yourself," Matt said. "It's not something I talk about with anyone."

"But you got through it," Carl continued.

"Yeah." Matt raised the bottle to his lips and drank deep. "And like I say, it's done with. So thanks for the drink but I've got things to do. People to see."

"So you're not curious about why I'm back in the neighbourhood?"

"Not really. Jenny said something about a business deal. A proposition. But I'm not interested."

"It's about Rickie." Carl lowered his voice forcing Matt to lean in closer.

"Rick?"

"The police don't seem interested in finding out who killed him, let alone clearing his name."

"Yeah, well. He'd been a bad lad, hadn't he?" Matt said. "The police have got better things to do."

"That's not the point," Carl said. "They must realise he didn't kill your sister. If the stupid fucker had come to me when he fell behind on the payments, none of this would have happened. But he's still my kid brother, so it's my job to set the record straight."

"And how are you going to do that?"

"Oh. I'm going to get the bastards who killed him."

"Good luck with that," Matt said. "You're six months behind schedule."

"What d'you mean?"

"Two of the guys are already dead and the third one's well gone. He disappeared off the radar as soon as the shit hit the fan at Paver's chalet park. That's why the police have closed the case."

Carl raised the bottle to his lips and took a slug of beer. "I'm not interested in what the police are doing, Matthew. They couldn't be arsed getting their facts straight the first time round. They had my brother in the frame for your sister 'cause it suited them to show everyone how quick they'd been to solve her murder. They probably earned an extra gold star for improving their crime statistics. It's a fucking joke."

"Even so, it's finished with. You can't exactly get back at someone if they're already dead."

"Is that what your sister would want you to do?" Carl asked.

Matt met the man's gaze and could barely hide the sneer from his voice. "What d'you mean?"

"You're giving up?"

"Shit, I've been through this hundreds of times. The bastards who killed Caddy are dead, so leave it." Matt drained his glass, got up from his seat and made his way to the Gents. Then as he rinsed his hands under the cold tap he thought back to Amy and her crusade against Gordon Paver. It was like they were both fated to relive everything over and over. Carl Tyler was a loose cannon at best. A hard man who talked the talk but had nothing up is sleeve when the chips were down.

"I thought you'd walked out on me," Carl said as Matt returned to their table.

"I needed a slash."

"So have I touched a nerve?"

"I told you, whatever you've got in mind you can count me out," Matt replied. "I've got better things to do. You know what it's like. Life goes on. So give my love to Jen and enjoy the rest of your holiday. I hope the weather stays fine for you."

"You've not listened to a fucking word I've said."

"There's no point, is there? Unless you've got some brilliant plan to contact the dead and tell Peter Paver to his face what a cunt he's been." Matt grabbed his empty glass and headed for the bar.

"What about his old man?" Carl called out. That stopped Matt in his tracks.

"Gordon Paver? He comes complete with non-stick coating. The cops couldn't pin anything on him so I don't know what you're hoping to achieve."

"But he was involved in Rick's death. Right?" Carl continued.

"The two Ukrainians were doing his dirty work by the look of it. Gordon's too fucking clever to get caught even if he put them up to it."

"It doesn't mean he's innocent," Carl said.

"As far as the police are concerned he's squeaky clean. He even grassed on his own son when they reopened Caddy's case. Swore blind he didn't see Peter's meltdown coming."

Carl gazed around the room. "Who's dealing round here now?"

Matt shook his head. "No idea. If you're looking to score, you're asking the wrong man."

"So what about our wee pal with the fishing boat? I assume he's still around?"

"You mean Slippy?" Matt leant closer until his face was level with Carl's. "If you're after doing business with that psycho, count me out. I've already been inside once and that was one time too many. I don't deal drugs anymore. Got that?"

Matt headed towards the bar.

"On your way, then," Carl called after him. "But I could do with some local help. And there's a wad of cash if you know anyone who might be interested. It's a driving job, that's all. No need to get their hands dirty."

Matt could have walked away, but there was something in the tone of Carl's voice that hooked him and drew him back once he'd planted his empty glass on the bar. "I don't want anything to do with whatever you've got planned, so forget about Slippy and go back to working on your fucking tan."

Carl laughed. "He's got a reputation as a hard man in these parts. Big deal. He wouldn't last five minutes where I grew up. Fucking plastic gangster."

"I'm telling you. Keep out of his way. Nobody messes with Slippy. Not even the cops, if you know what I mean."

"That's what I'm banking on, so sit the fuck down and let me tell you what I've got in mind."

"Nah," Matt said.

"Listen. The guy's got a short fuse and all I'm going to do is light the blue touch paper and stand back."

"I already told you. I'm not interested."

But still Matt waited and they left the bar together. He watched Carl click the key fob to unlock his hire car then climb behind the wheel.

"Can I give you a lift anywhere?" he asked.

"No thanks."

"Fine. As long as there's no hard feelings." Then before closing the car door Carl said, "I thought you'd like to be around when Gordon Paver gets what's coming to him, that's all."

"What's that got to do with anything?" Matt said.

179

"Well, I'm going to have a wee chat with our mutual pal and ask him to tell me what he knows about Paver's shady dealings."

Matt laughed out loud. "You think Slippy's going to grass on Paver?"

A broad grin crossed Carl's face as he closed his eyes and began clicking his joints. "Oh, yeah. I'm going to make it clear that it's in his best interests to cooperate. 'Cause if I remember right, your man has a soft spot for his daughter. It would be a shame if something were to happen to her. Right?"

42

THERE had been a time when Matt might have forgiven the Cartwrights anything. Kaz and her older brother Baxter - or Barcode as his mates called him. Barcode had buddied up with Matt in Peterhead. Kept Matt sane when he thought the whole world was conspiring against him. Offered him hope when his girlfriend dumped him after her one and only prison visit. Shown him how life could return to normal on the outside. Given Matt a sofa to surf on when he walked out of his happy home.

He'd even got Matt into Slippy's good books by putting in a word for him. Driving round in a white van filled with dodgy gear hadn't been Matt's first career choice after leaving Peterhead, but it kept him busy and the hours were regular.

Kaz had been the one who broke the news to Matt how Amy planned on dumping him as soon as he turned up in Lochinver. Admittedly, she'd also made it clear she was available should he be looking for a replacement. It proved he still had what it takes despite being locked up for three months with only his left hand as company. Most females of the species couldn't resist his charms.

Unfortunately, Kaz Cartwright wasn't in the same league as Amy Metcalf. Amy left him craving more than bodily comforts. She was a beautiful, delicate soul he felt obliged to protect. She was hot. She was sexy. She was vulnerable and complex. Kaz was simply a snotty-nosed prick teaser with an attitude, looking for attention rather than affection. Worth a fumble but little more. She took great delight at parading about in her scanties, sticking her hand down the front of his boxers when she thought no one was looking. Yet many a time, when they were alone, she'd cover herself up and put on the modest virgin act. Matt wasn't allowed even a kiss in case he spoilt her make-up.

More to the point, she didn't have feelings for him despite the dripping panties act. She'd been ruthless enough to abandon him at the marble quarry when Robbo and Peter Paver left him for dead. She couldn't be bothered to make an anonymous telephone call to the emergency services. She'd even changed her Facebook status to 'Single' as soon as Matt was found and the police became involved.

But now Matt needed her help. Hers and Barcode's.

"Fucking hell, bro. How's it hangin'? I didn't expect to see you round here again."

"Nice to see you too," Matt said. "Aren't you going to invite me in?"

Before Barcode had a chance to respond, Matt ducked under the arm holding the door open and headed towards the kitchen. "I'll put the kettle on. We need to talk."

"Why? What's happened now?"

"Nothing yet," Matt said. "But I need a word with you and your skanky sister."

"You what?"

"You heard me. Is she here?"

"Hold on," Barcode said. "I think you'd better leave. I don't want any trouble, but you're either stoned or looking to get smacked."

"Erm, actually no. I'm looking for some help and you're the first two people I thought of."

"Mattie, listen. . ."

"No. You listen," Matt said as he reached for the kettle. "We'll grab a coffee and I'll tell you all about it. Where did you say your sister was, by the way?"

"Kaz is taking a shower, but you'd better be gone before she comes out. She won't want to see you in this kind of mood. And her ma's told her to have nothing more to do with my mates - and that includes you."

"Well that's a shame 'cause I want to see her. And she'd better play nice. 'Cause if anyone finds out you've been shipping drugs for our mutual friend, you'll be back inside. Am I right?"

"That's crazy fucking talk," Barcode said. "You're on licence same as me. We'll both end up getting recalled if you grass me up."

"If I'm honest, I don't give a shit. I'm already starting to miss Peterhead," Matt said. "Pass me the mugs."

"Suit yourself, bro. But cross me or Slippy, and you won't see daylight again. You'll be carried out of Peterhead in a body bag."

Matt turned and gave Barcode's left shoulder a squeeze. "You're so hot when you get angry. Did you know that?"

"Fuck you."

"Whatever. Just so we're clear, I don't intend doing anything stupid unless I have to. That's not why I'm here."

"So what's with all the bullshit threats?" Barcode said.

"I'm laying down the ground rules. If you know what's good for you, you'll listen. Listen hard. And I hope your precious sister feels the same way. Instant do you?"

Matt spooned coffee into the two mugs then went to the fridge for some milk.

"The dealing has got nothing to do with Kaz," Barcode said as he poured boiling water into each mug. "Keep her out of it."

183

"Wish I could but she's already up to her eyes in it. I'm wondering how she'd cope with all the other young offenders. 'Cause I can't see her fitting in myself. Too high-maintenance."

"You're talking shite. Kaz hasn't done anything wrong."

"We'll have to see what she says when I bring up Kevin Waterson's little accident. Sugar?"

43

MATT had never seen Kaz so angry, her face blazed with fury as he accused her.

"I never did anything."

"Oh, but I think you did," Matt said. "In fact, I know you did, because I put the idea inside your stupid little head when I spoke to you from prison."

Kaz swiped a strand of wet hair from her face and stared at him even harder. "You know that's not true."

"Shit. You're the one who brought up Kevin's name in the first place. Called him a freak. Stalker material. Said he needed teaching a lesson."

"Those were Amy's words," she said. "And it was all talk anyway."

"After you spiked her drinks you mean?"

A flush of guilt crossed her face. "Amy got pissed without my help. And she was stone cold sober when she started slagging you off. She mentioned the creepy messages she'd been getting. How they were freaking her out."

"Only I never sent them," he said.

"Duh. I know that. We'd worked out it must have been Kevin Waterson. He still gives me the creeps even now."

"Enough to scald him and leave him scarred for life?"

"That's rubbish," she said. But Matt could detect a misstep in her voice. A flicker of uncertainty in her accusing gaze.

"You can't kid me, Kaz. That was the whole point of the phone call - to soften me up. You knew Amy was going to dump me so you got in first. You dropped that bombshell then pretended you cared. All part of a sick act."

"You're off your head," Barcode said.

"Maybe. But hear me out," Matt said. "'Cause your sister's twisted little plan worked. She began rubbing it in, how I couldn't look out for Amy like I'd promised to. There was a nut-job out there giving her grief and this stupid bitch decided to help out so she could get inside my pants."

"You should be so fucking lucky," Kaz said, but Matt ignored her.

"This conniving little cunt started playing with my head like a pro. Asking what I'd have done to Kevin Waterson if he was locked up inside with me."

"That's complete crap."

"So you don't remember asking if I'd knife him?"

"I was curious," she said. "'Barcode told me about the bother you'd had."

"Yeah. Curious. Asking if anybody'd ever had his balls cut off in there. And I said no, because you'd get found out. But there were other, sneakier ways. Bleach in the milk. Dissolved sugar in a pan of boiling water. Then four days later, Kevin gets napalmed on the landing outside these flats and you expect me to believe it was a fucking coincidence."

"So what?" Barcode said. "There's no proof she even spoke to you about any of that."

Matt drained his mug then ran it under the cold tap. "I'm disappointed in you, bro. I thought you knew better."

"What d'you mean?"

"I mean the small print. Don't you remember what it

186

says on the form when you apply for a telephone card inside? All calls may be monitored."

"That's bullshit," Barcode said.

"Ah, well. We'll have to see. Let's hope they didn't keep a recording of that particular conversation. 3rd of June wasn't it?"

Kaz took a pack of cigarettes from her bag. "I don't even know why you've come round here making trouble after all that time. It's ancient history."

"Yeah. No wonder you can hardly remember doing it."

"Look, if this is about me going off and leaving you in the van, well I'm sorry. But the police would have been wanting to know what you were doing up at the quarry, and why I was there with you. I didn't want to get involved."

"The coppers weren't that fussed, to be honest. They assumed it was somebody trying to send a message to Slippy. None of their business."

"I know," Barcode said. "He's still spitting blood."

"Yeah, well. I've got my own message to deliver to him now, so I need you two to help me."

"No fucking way." Barcode looked across to his sister whose face had already begun to drain of colour. "Whatever gripe you've got with Slippy, leave us out of it. He's got himself a Heisenberg hat - did you know? The kind Walter White wears. It makes him look even more of a head case."

"Nice touch, but I'm not that interested in his latest fashion statement," Matt replied. "He might think he's a big fish in a little pond but there are fucking sharks out there, and they can smell blood. Slippy's blood. So if you know what's best for you both, you'll do as you're fucking told. And you'll not breathe a word to anybody else."

"You're trying to blackmail us," Kaz said.

"Call it what you like."

"You're off your fucking head if you think I'm going to help you mess with Slippy," she continued.

"Oh," Matt said. "Don't worry, Kaz. All I need you to do is arrange a wee get-together. Tomorrow night, if you can. Call it a post-referendum party. Invite all your pals. And here's a couple of hundred quid for booze."

"I don't get it."

"Make sure Cindy O'Connor's on the guest list."

"Why would I do that? No one round here can stand the snotty-nosed bitch."

"Tell her there's been a truce. Tell her anything, But make sure she turns up."

"And then what?" Baxter asked.

"Then when she gets muntered, you and me offer her a free taxi ride home. By the time Slippy gets the news his daughter's gone missing, he'll have more than enough to keep him occupied without chasing after you two."

"What do you mean 'gone missing'?" Kaz said.

"It's best you don't know," Matt replied. "Start phoning your mates. And tell young Cindy she needs to be there or be square. It'll be a night to remember."

44

THE build up to the Referendum with a capital R had passed me by like a slice of history I was destined not to be part of. The euphoria of the past few weeks began to swell like a tsunami of hope. All my pals back home suddenly discovered they had a political conscience. Mum phoned and told me about the music night planned for the Stag's Head that Thursday - a music night to end all music nights. But then came the hangover - the morning-after despair. I'd caught wind of the changing mood as I scanned the internet in the early hours. But I had other matters to concern me.

By half past eight the next morning I was trawling the streets surrounding Brendan's flat. One last shot. I'd gone on-line long before the first results came in, searching for RGU. The Robert Gordon University. I even took the virtual tour. Then I racked my brain for his sister's name. The journalist. Katerina Balik. Presumably she wasn't married - or if she was, she might have kept her maiden name for professional reasons. Maybe that would be enough for me to find him.

I took the first available bus into the city. Everyone muttering. A curse here and there. Some faces turned in upon themselves as they got to grips with a missed opportunity. Others with their smiles cut free like party balloons. Life would continue the way it always had.

The university building itself was dazzling. But the staff at the front desk refused to confirm whether or not a Patryk Balik was one of their students. They were also unwilling, or unable, to confirm what classes he took, even if he did study there. So I hung around the Architecture department like a stray dog looking to be adopted before I spotted him walking across the forecourt with three other student-types. The same eyes. The same confident tilt of the chin and unfeigned smile as he recognised me.

"Amy? What are you doing here? I don't understand?"

He leant forwards to give me a peck on the cheek but I pulled away. "Don't get any ideas. I needed to see you about something, that's all."

Christ. That opening line would be enough to send most guys heading for the emergency exit.

"Right." He straightened the strap of his shoulder bag. "Only I have an 11:30 lecture."

"That's fine. I can wait for you."

His face clouded over. "There is trouble between us? You have something personal to tell me?"

"God, no. It's nothing like that."

"OK."

"There's nothing to worry about, but I need your help and I didn't know how to get hold of you. I tried waiting outside the flats a couple of times but I didn't see you there."

His gaze slid away somewhere else. Some other place where Amy Metcalf was nothing more than a one-nighter, maybe. "I have been at a friend's. But, look. I'm already running late. We can meet after my class if you wait for me here."

"Yeah. What time do you finish?"

"I'm free after one. There's a Costa coffee bar inside the main food hall. Grab yourself a drink and wait for me

190

there."

"See you later."

I let him give my arm a squeeze. No kiss. No smile. I'm not sure what I was expecting, to be honest, but I sent out a silent prayer for him not to let me down or do a disappearing act.

I grabbed a can of Diet Coke and chose a table as far away from the main entrance as possible. Shitty brown plastic chairs, huge glass windows, sunshine slanting across the table bright enough to make me wince. I sat people-watching while my imagination flew back and forth between Lochinver, Aberdeen and Amsterdam. Things were happening too quickly.

I checked the time on my mobile phone for the hundredth time. 13:12. He obviously wasn't coming. I'd have been better off concentrating on packing my suitcase instead of following this wild goose chase. Then he walked in and I saw the look of irritation in his eyes.

45

"YOU must be thinking I had forgotten," he said.

"No. I assumed you'd had second thoughts."

"Second thoughts? Not really, but I don't know what you are expecting from me. We can still be friends."

"Don't worry about the other night. We had sex without strings. It was good but I'm not into you."

"Fine," he said. "No strings - so let me get you another drink." Relief shone from his face like a beam of sunlight.

He returned with two coffees and by then I'd already opened out the newspaper on the table. A two page spread. One photograph. One headline. And a block of poorly printed, unintelligible copy.

"This is Polish, yeah?" I asked.

He flipped back to the front page. "Yes. *Głos Szkocki.* Scottish Voice. It's a local newspaper for Polish speakers who live in Aberdeen. My sister sometimes publishes articles inside it."

"I know. You showed me a copy of the same paper in your flat. Have you read this week's issue?"

He scanned the front page again. "No. But Vera is sure to have one lying around the flat somewhere. She keeps up with the local news."

"Fine." I didn't pursue the matter. Instead, I took the paper from him and smoothed the double page spread across the table. "You can read what that says, right?"

"Of course."

"So can you translate it into English for me?"

He mumbled to himself as he began to read. "Two girls. Paulina and Ania. The headline says 'truth'. It's the usual stuff. Young girls come here to look for work and sometimes things don't work out. It's their story, that's all."

"What else does it say about them?"

He shrugged as he scanned the pages. "Their childhood. They grow up together in the same town. Gdańsk - a big port on the Baltic. Then they come to the UK. Waitressing. They learn the language. They fit in. Then it is not so good here any more."

His gaze skipped ahead to the next column and he was silent for a while.

"What?" I said.

"There is a story about a boat. Somebody brings them here to Scotland and tells them they will now be sex workers. It's not so good."

I felt the blood grow cold in my veins. "Go on."

He shook his head. "They are brought to Aberdeen to work." He closed the paper and stared me in the face. "But I think you know this already."

"Some of it, yeah."

"What do these girls have to do with you?"

I swallowed the lump in my throat. "Is there more?"

"Oh, yeah," he said. "Not such a happy ending, if you want to hear about it."

"What d'you mean?"

He pointed to the photograph on the front page. "This girl - Paulina. She was an escort. She was paid for sex. She took drugs and now she is dead."

Somehow I already knew this.

"A tragic accident it says here. She fell from the

balcony of a hotel. That was almost three months ago. But for a long time the police did not know her name because she carried no identification documents."

"She died here, in this city?"

"Out by the airport. The police put posters up and some time later someone telephones them with her name. This other girl, Ania, maybe."

"And you're sure Paulina's death was an accident?" I said.

"They're saying she was with a client when she died. She carried no documents and very little money. That is how the police worked out what she is involved with."

"What do you mean?"

"It means she works for someone instead of for herself. A pimp. Someone who keeps her passport safe and takes whatever she earns for himself. They are saying she is a nobody - her and this Ania. One of the *niewidzialni Polacy* - the invisible Poles. Not such nice girls anymore because they give our people a bad name. Especially for those in our home country. We are not all junkies and whores and criminals."

"And what does it say about Ania?" I stabbed my finger at the second name in the headline. "What has she got to do with all this?"

"She tells this journalist, Witek, some sad story. How she wants her friend's family to know the truth. They did not choose to live like this. They are given drugs and raped when they are brought here against their wishes. But, Christ. They must have been fucking stupid, that's all I can say."

"And this Ania also lives in Aberdeen?"

"It doesn't say. Witek writes very little about her. Only her first name. No address. She wanted Paulina's family to know the truth, that is all. She probably does the same work. *Kurwa* we call a girl like this."

I took the €5 bill out of my purse and placed it face down between us on top of the newspaper.

"What is that for?"

"Read what's written on it. Both sides."

His gaze flitted from the banknote to my face, and his expression grew grimmer as he presumably absorbed what he was reading, word by word.

"Turn it over. Look at the other side."

His fingers fumbled with the money but I saw his grip tighten once he'd finished reading the five names.

"I don't understand where you get this," he said.

"It's the same girls. Can't you see? Ania. Paulina. Another three. Ania left this behind for someone to find."

"And you found this?"

"No. It was Caddy, my friend. She found it." I gave him a brief version of the story.

He shook his head as if the thought was trapped inside his skull and he wanted to dislodge it. "But you don't know for sure these are the same girls. Your friend found this such a long time ago, Amy."

"The same time the girls were brought here in the boat. Think about it. It's obviously the same girls." I took another newspaper out of my bag. " Do you know about this? It's all over the papers this week. Men trafficking Polish girls from Northern Ireland to Aberdeen. Two of the guys are up in court right now. But these five girls - I bet the police don't know anything about them."

"So what do you plan to do? It's lucky for them the police don't know, yeah?" he said.

"Maybe, but it's still not right. The guy who brought them over in his boat has never been charged. He got away with it."

"And this man, you know who he is?"

I nodded. "His name's Paver."

"So it is a sad story, and sometimes bad people do bad

195

things and don't get caught. But I think it is safe not to become involved with people like this man."

"Safe? Is that why you and your sister couldn't wait to leave the Ukraine, because your friends were being attacked? Because sometimes life sucks and it's best to pretend bad stuff never happens?"

He got to his feet and slung his bag over his shoulder. "That is not fair. Katerina was my priority. I had to make sure she was safe."

"And I'll never be safe while Mr Paver is able to walk away free from everything that he has done."

"That sounds like paranoia to me, Amy. But it's your life so you get to choose how to live it. I have to be somewhere else in half an hour so I say goodbye and wish you good luck."

"I'm not finished," I said.

"There's nothing more you can do, Amy. You should leave things be."

"But there is something I can do, if you'll help me."

"Help you? I want to be no part of this mess, you understand? I am an immigrant. I come to this country on a student visa, so it is easy for the authorities to send me back to Poland if I cause trouble."

"It'll be nothing like that. I want to meet with this girl, Ania, that's all. I need someone I can trust to be there with me when I talk to her. Someone who can speak Polish."

46

THE Rotterdam Effect had a lot to answer for. Most imports into the UK from the rest of Europe as well as Africa, the Middle East and Asia passed through the port. And before his Peterhead vacation Barcode had taken regular trips between Newcastle and the Netherlands. He'd been one of Slippy's trusted mules. Not the kind who swallowed condoms of coke or stuffed a couple of baggies up their rectum before boarding a KLM flight from Schiphol to Inverness. But the kind who travelled to and from Amsterdam in a battered campervan and knew when to keep his mouth shut.

Slippy had made a small fortune smuggling in amphetamines, pep pills and ecstasy from the continent. But that had never been enough. Five years ago he'd expanded. First blues and cocaine, then the wonderfully expanding world of illegal highs. Jiffy bags of bath salts, plant food and incense added to his wide-ranging stock but also increased the risk of discovery. In the end he subcontracted the entire operation.

Slippy continued to take a cut of the profits, but the risk of tarnishing his respectable reputation as a local fishing boat owner and successful entrepreneur was no longer an issue now that everything had been farmed out. It seemed ironic that Mr Big's darling daughter was about to fall foul of her own father's dodgy dealings.

"How long is she going to be out for?" Kaz asked.

Barcode shushed his sister. "Let me and Matt worry about that. Get her bag and her jacket then go back inside. Enjoy the party and pretend nothing's happened."

"But what do I say if her mum and dad phone and ask where she is and when she's coming home?"

"Tell them what you like - she was a no-show or she felt sick and had to leave early. But you need to turn the fucking noise down, or you'll have the coppers round."

"So what are you going to do with her?"

"Does it matter? Make sure there's none of her stuff left inside the flat. Keys. Mobile phone. Whatever. And rinse out that fucking glass as well."

The sound of the party carried down into the street and Matt heard the volume of the music suddenly increase as someone opened the door to the landing. "We need to go, guys."

"Got it," Barcode replied. "You take her arms and I'll grab her feet. And Kaz, don't let anyone come down the stairs until we're gone."

They bundled the girl's body onto the back seat of Steff's car then, once Kaz returned with Cindy's bag, Matt fired up the engine and headed towards Lochinver.

"You sure you know what you're doing?" Barcode asked as he wiped his hands on his trouser legs. "If Slippy finds out we're involved in this, we'll be fish bait."

"Yeah, well. I won't say anything if you don't."

"And what if there are coppers about?"

"Stop your fannying. I'll keep to the speed limit. And if we do get pulled, I'll ask them to keep their voices down because it's my wee sister asleep in the back. We're both stone cold sober - right? And it's my mum's car so everything's legit. Why would the coppers think we're up to anything?"

"'Cause as soon as they try to wake her or shine a torch

198

in her eyes they're gonna know she's taken something."

"Exactly. So we're doing the responsible thing. Taking her home."

"Mhmm."

Matt had already checked on-line. According to the wisdom of Wikipedia the Rohypnol effect would last between four and six hours. Long enough for them to deliver Cindy O'Connor into the hands of Carl Tyler before she showed signs of waking up.

The choice of Blue Curaçao for the welcome cocktails had been genius. Barcode supplied the blue capsule from his private collection - souvenirs of his chequered past. Kaz dropped it into Cindy's vodka concoction as soon as she walked in and the young girl presumably registered nothing unusual about her drink. Fifteen minutes later, Cindy complained of feeling dizzy. Kaz accused her of being a lightweight before escorting her off the premises. No one offered to help. No one took any notice.

"What's the plan when we get to the cottage?" Barcode asked.

"We drop off the fare then head back to Ullapool. It's up to Carl what he does with her then. We'll be well gone before she even wakes up."

"You sure?"

"Of course I'm fucking sure. I'm only doing this for Caddy. I owe her one more good deed, then we're quits."

47

CARL came out to meet the car as soon as they turned in through the gate. He signalled for Matt to park the vehicle at the rear of the cottage then held his fingers to his lips as Matt and Barcode got out.

"Kill the lights."

Matt reached in to switch off the headlights and turn off the engine while Carl peered inside the back of the car.

"Any problems?"

"No. Everything went sweet as a nut," Matt replied. "Most of the ones at the party were so pissed they won't even remember she'd been there."

"So let's get her inside, yeah?" Carl said. "We're in the middle of fucking nowhere. Sound carries for miles."

Barcode and Matt each placed one of Cindy's arms across their shoulders.

"I know it's pitch black out here, but anybody could be watching. The old dear across the road doesn't miss a trick."

A single light shone behind the cluster of trees a short distance away, otherwise the entire area was swathed in darkness. Even the stars were hidden above the canopy of low cloud.

"I assume this is the tradesmen's entrance," Barcode said under his breath while Carl guided them through the back door into the tiny kitchen. "How are we supposed to keep the noise down if we can't see a fucking thing?"

"It works both ways so shut the fuck up. You don't know who's driving past this time of night."

A faint light shone beyond the doorway into the living room.

"Jenny's blocked out the window in the upstairs bedroom but you'll still need to watch your step. These fucking stairs. . ."

The girl groaned as they propped her against the wall then began to haul her up the staircase one step at a time; Matt at her head and Barcode at her feet.

"Let me pass, and I'll give you a hand."

The staircase had a tight turn half way up and Carl began to curse as the girl's shoulders slipped from his grasp. "OK. Sit her on one of the steps then me and Matt can each take an arm."

For such a frail specimen, it took their combined efforts to manoeuvre Cindy O'Connor to the top of the staircase and through the low doorway into the tiny bedroom.

"Fucking hell, it's like a bloody shoe box in here," Barcode said.

"Big enough for what we want. She's not going to be here long enough to care how big it is."

The room itself was too cramped to contain much more than a sofa bed, a chair and a blanket chest. A combed ceiling swept down below head height to the door at one end, and a tiny window at the other covered by a heavy blanket suspended from a flimsy rail.

"Lay her on the bed." Barcode and Matt stood either side while Carl straightened out the girl's body on top of the quilted eiderdown patterned with dark green Christmas trees. "How much did you say you gave her?"

"Just the one bluey," Barcode replied. "So can we go now?"

"Stay here while I go and fetch Jenny," Carl said. "I

might need a hand here."

He gave them the thumbs up and left the room.

"Who the fuck's Jenny?" Barcode said.

Matt explained.

"So you really will shag anything with a pulse?"

"It was nothing like that," Matt said. "We were both going through a rough time. Looking out for each other."

"Sweet. And now she's cutting you in on the deal for old times' sake. That's class, even if I say so myself."

"What deal?"

Barcode pointed at the body on the bed. "This deal. I mean, I hope you're getting a decent cut. How much are they asking?"

"What you on about?" Matt asked.

"The ransom. 'Cause you'd better count me and Kaz in as well, considering the risk we're taking, or I might be telling somebody what we've been up to tonight."

"How are you going to do that after I take this to your tongue?" Carl stood at the bedroom door with a pair of wire cutters in one hand and a length of sash cord in the other.

"I was kidding," Barcode replied.

"There is no ransom, just so we're clear. You'll get paid for your trouble once this is over with, but if either of you breathe a fucking word about what you've seen here tonight I'll be using these later. Comprende?"

Barcode nodded, then watched in silence as Jenny appeared behind Carl, wrapped in a long woollen sweater. "Bloody Highland weather. I forgot how cold it gets."

"Hi, Jen," Matt said.

She managed to flash him a smile.

"Nice tan."

"I know. I should be working on it right now instead of freezing my nipples off in this fucking dump."

"OK, boys and girls," Carl said. "Enough of the cosy chit chat. Jenny, I think it's best if you strip her."

48

CARL tugged off the young girl's boots and removed her wind-proof jacket before standing aside to allow Jenny to unzip her dress and slide it off. Then she unbuttoned Cindy's blouse, pulled it free, rolled the girl onto her back and unclasped her bra. No one spoke a word as she rearranged the half-naked body on the bed and removed her tights. The tiny room seemed to hum with an uneasy silence and the scent of the young girl's body spray hung in the air like a forbidden rumour, teasing their senses and testing their nerve.

Carl finally broke the silence. "Leave her knickers for now." Then he began to cut the cord into equal lengths. "I'm going to tie her wrists to the headboard in case."

"In case what?" Barcode said.

"In case she wakes up. What d'you think?"

"Right. Stupid question."

"So does that mean we can we go now?" Matt asked.

"Not until I say. Did you check if she's got her mobile with her? It might make things a little more tasty."

"There's no phone signal out here," Matt said.

"I need to take a few photos, that's all. Let Daddy know what his little princess is up to."

Jenny searched through the pockets of the young girl's jacket. "I don't see it here."

"Kaz could have put it in her bag," Matt said. Barcode

gave him an accusing look. "It's still in the back of the car."

"So what are you waiting for?" Carl said.

Matt studied the young girl's body while Barcode went back downstairs. The first time he'd seen Cindy O'Connor, she'd been sporting a football shirt and pyjama bottoms. A sixteen-year-old with an attitude from Hell. But now she looked little more than a kid - a kid testing out a woman's body for size. The same age as his sister, Cindy had the same big hair, the same threaded eyebrows and a voluptuous pout to her mouth that could switch from scowl to smile in seconds. But Cindy's breasts looked barely formed - pale, pink nipples surrounded by darker, puffy flesh revealing she was no longer a child. And her hips were relatively narrow, her bone-white legs more skinny than slender.

Matt couldn't help but stare at the triangle of fabric that covered the young girl's crotch. He tried not to fantasize about what might be revealed if Jenny was asked to remove the rest of the young girl's underwear.

"Keep your mucky thoughts to yourself," Carl said.

"Fuck off."

"It's a friendly warning, that's all. You and that scally pal of yours. No one touches this kid unless I say so."

"I never intended to. What the hell d'you think I am?"

Carl's smile made that only too clear.

"I'm not a fucking cradle-snatcher like your brother," Matt continued.

"That's enough," Jenny said. "I think she's waking up."

Matt stared in anguish as Cindy's head began to rock from side to side. "Don't let her see me, for God's sake."

"She's still zonked out, so cool it." Carl began to stroke the young girl's hair. "It's OK, doll. No one's going to hurt you." Then he turned to Jenny.

"Get me a wrap."

Jenny reached in the deep pocket of her cardigan and pulled out a small plastic bag. Carl peeled it open with a fingernail and placed a small mound of white powder on the tip of a finger.

"Once she's taken a snort of this, it won't matter what the fuck she sees or what she remembers."

Barcode came back into the bedroom carrying a small, red leather clutch bag then passed it to Jenny. Then he gave Matt a nod. "I think you and me should hit the road."

"Woah woah woah," Carl said. "Find out if there's a fucking phone in her bag, Jen. And you two, grab her feet."

"You what?" Matt said.

"Her feet. And spread those legs."

Jenny fished out a small chrome-effect smartphone. Then she stood at the foot of the bed between the young girl's legs and held the phone to her face.

"OK, boys. No need to say cheese. But keep hold of them ankles and spread her as wide as you can. I want Slippy to see exactly what we're doing. Make him think his daughter's about to get gang-banged. That's assuming she hasn't been shagged stupid already."

Matt counted ten flashes. Before each one Carl rearranged the girl's body. Squeezing her bare breasts hard enough to leave finger marks. Pressing his hands against her throat. Pulling down the waistband of her pants to reveal her pubes. Feeding the fingers of his right hand into the hidden crease between Cindy O'Connor's open legs. Then the final humiliation. The young girl's underwear pulled all the way down to expose her vulva.

"Did you get it all?"

"Take a look." Jenny handed Carl the phone and he began to check the photographs. And all the while Cindy lay dead to the world. By the time it was all over Matt couldn't look Jenny in the face. She smirked at his obvious discomfort. "Feeling horny yet?"

"Fuck you, Jen. There's no need for this kind of twisted shit. She's still a kid."

"I remember the crap me and Jake had to put up with when Rick was dealing. That's down to Slippy, so this spoilt little bitch deserves all she gets."

"OK people. Let's cut to the chase." Carl used the fingers of one hand to smear more cocaine inside the girl's nostrils and along her bottom lip. Then he held the phone in front of her face and took one more photo.

"Give Daddy a happy, smiley face for the family album."

49

TWELVE hours. Twenty-four. Thirty-six. Forty-eight, and still not a peep from Slippy. Matt had telephoned Barcode more than a dozen times since midday Saturday.

"Still no news, bro and I'm saying 'Thank fuck' because if he came knocking on my door I'd be shitting myself."

"And you've heard nothing?"

"Someone said he's away to Stornoway for the weekend. He went over on the ferry Friday night so he probably doesn't even know about Cindy."

"Of course he fucking knows," Matt said. "If Carl's even bothered getting in touch."

"Maybe you should phone Jenny and see what's happening her end."

"There's no point. You know what it's like trying to get a phone signal out there. What about Tommy and Ken? Have they been sniffing around?"

"I saw them working on the boat yesterday afternoon," Barcode said. "Then they went into the Seaforth for a couple of pints as usual. I'd been watching the pier most of the day and they were both acting like nothing's happened."

"So what the fuck's Carl been up to?" Matt said.

"Search me. He's your pal not mine."

"Whatever."

"Maybe Slippy's got the message and he's been in touch

with Paver," he said.

"And maybe he's managed to work out where his daughter is and his boys are on the way round there now with a fucking baseball bat or an axe. You've seen what they're like when he lets them off the leash."

"I doubt it. This is personal. Slippy's going to want to handle it himself."

"Fuck," Matt said. "I'm thinking about finding somewhere to lie low until this all blows over."

"That's what Kaz said. She's already gone to her nan's in Inverness."

"To stay?"

"I've to phone her when it's all over. But, shit. I hate all this waiting, not knowing what's going on. It's like sitting on a time bomb."

"Yeah," Matt said.

"Slippy's going to be raging. And if he's on the warpath, you and me should both get the fuck out of town."

"Any bright ideas?"

"Amsterdam? I've got contacts."

50

INSIDE the flat the clock continued ticking. Brendan was due home in twenty-four hours and my flight was booked for eleven days from now. October the 3rd. Less than forty-eight hours had passed since I'd last met up with Patryk: an entire weekend spent fielding telephone calls from Mum, Leanne and Jan. All after a piece of Amy.

I managed to convince Mum that everything was fine, despite not being in touch recently. I was busy settling in and I'd made new friends. A Polish couple who lived close by. No reason to worry. I'd got over Matthewgate and was looking forward to a weekend away, sometime soon.

"Are you planning on coming back here to Lochinver?" she asked.

"No. I was thinking somewhere like Amsterdam. Brendan's girlfriend says it's a great place for a city break."

"As long as you're looking after yourself."

Jan had also been on a fishing expedition.

"You sound different. Like a girl on a mission. Has anything happened?"

Where do I start?

"Not really. What d'you know about Amsterdam?"

"I absolutely love it. And if you're planning on a

210

weekend away, I can get in touch with one or two mates from uni. We could all chav out together. I know the best bars. Places to eat. And we'll have to go down the *Rossebuurt* where the ladies of the night strut their stuff in their window parlours."

"The what?"

"Prozzies, Amy."

Christ.

The last thing I felt like doing right now was joining a hen party trawling Amsterdam's red light district.

"I'll let you know."

I remained barricaded inside the flat, and give Leanne her due, when she phoned she convinced me it was nothing more sinister than to check I was OK. No attempt to make me reconsider my plans. Beside, plans have a habit of changing.

13:32 Monday I received a text.

`Can we meet this afternoon? Patryk`

I rang his mobile from Brendan's landline. He suggested we rendezvous in Seaton Park near the fountain. All very Jason Bourne, considering he was the one who'd accused me of being paranoid.

There had been floods here the previous Spring. Swathes of bright greenery still bore muddy, brown patches like mould where the underlying ground remained waterlogged. But the flower borders were full of colour and most of the punters stretched out on the benches were there to sample the sunshine. No druggies during daylight hours. No dossers or muggers.

Patryk had company, but even from a distance I realised it wasn't Ania. The guy carried a battered brown brief case and wore a green Gore-Tex coat. Hardly summer wear, even in the Granite City. His dark hair, feathering to grey at the temples, was cut short and his wire-framed glasses added to the sense of professionalism.

"Amy. This is Mr Tomaszewski."

He extended a hand.

"Amy. Amy Metcalf."

"Witek."

"Have you spoken to Ania?" I asked.

Witek smiled then shook his head.

"It is not so easy as that," Patryk said. He'd contacted Witek through the offices of *Głos Szkocki*, throwing in his sister's name as guarantor. One fellow journalist to another.

Witek took over the conversation. "She asked me to be discreet. This young woman is under constant scrutiny by the men who hold her and her friends against their will. Men who make a great deal of money from this business. The authorities do not listen with sympathy to girls like Ania unless she gives the names and addresses of these men. Can you not understand why she speaks to no one?"

"But she has spoken to you."

"No, Amy." He opened his briefcase and took out a buff folder. Inside were two flimsy sheets of blue writing paper covered in a childish scrawl. I couldn't read a word of it but the message was crystal clear.

"Ania wrote this?"

"It was inside a plain envelope pushed under the door. No return address or contact details."

"So there's no way to get in touch with her," I said.

"No."

Fuck!

I dug my nails into the palm of each hand deep enough to leave their mark. "But if she's so frightened why did she bother writing to you in the first place?"

212

Witek folded up the letter and placed it back inside the folder. "I had published an article two or three weeks ago telling Paulina's story. Paulina was her friend. Some people from the local Polish community say girls like this bring shame on their families and their country. Then once the police identified the body at the airport, Paulina's brother asked me to publish a few words."

"And?"

"Ania must have read both articles. She wanted to tell the world what was the truth. Her friend was a sex worker but she was not an evil or uncaring person."

"She was a victim," I said.

"Precisely."

"So, I'm wasting my time." I kicked at the stone wall surrounding the fountain.

"Not necessarily," Witek said. "There is maybe one way to get Ania to contact me again."

"How?"

"Patryk has told me about your banknote. Maybe we can use that. Offer a reward for information."

51

"WHAT'S new?"

"You shouldn't be here, Matt."

"Well, how else am I supposed to get in touch with you? There's no mobile phone signal out here in mamba country."

"But still."

"Don't worry. I'm parked down by the loch, and I've already seen Carl's 4 x 4 outside the Deli."

"I'm just saying. Carl's getting more and more wound up. If he finds out you've been back."

Matt leant against the wall of the porch and shielded his eyes from the glare of the afternoon sun. "How d'you mean 'wound up'?"

"Never mind. You'd better come inside. He's gone for a pint, and he's bringing back some pies for our teas."

"Very nice. So has he been in touch with Slippy yet?"

I heard her click her tongue. "It's weird. It's like her old man doesn't care."

"Is that what Carl's told you?"

"No. He replied straight away. I saw the text. Said he'd kill Carl if he harmed a hair on his daughter's head. The usual. Then he said he'd be in touch, but we haven't heard from him since."

"When was that?"

"Saturday night."

"Three days ago," Matt said. "He'll be planning something, playing for time."

"That's what Carl says. But I'm on edge here, on my own so much. Every time a car passes or I hear the wind in the rafters."

"How often does he leave you on your own?"

"It's like I'm the one who's locked up here. I've had a belly-full. And Cindy's in a state. Carl's got her tied to the bed most of the time. We've only got a slop bucket, and I'm the one who has to empty it. It's rank."

"I bet."

"A couple of times she managed to kick me in the face when I tried to help her do her business."

"So let her rot."

"That's what Carl says. But she's starting to smell, Matt. As soon as you open the bedroom door. She won't even let me wipe her clean down there. She curses me and lashes out."

"So what's Carl's master plan?"

"Don't ask me. When he's home, he's stoned most of the time - coke or weed. And he spends most afternoons at the Caley or the Stag's Head. Says it's the only place he can get a signal. It's the holiday from Hell, out here in the middle of nowhere with no one to talk to."

"So talk to me."

"That's what I'm doing. I'm worried, Matt. Carl's on about sending Slippy another message, if he doesn't hear anything by the weekend."

"What kind of message? You mean more porn shots? Christ."

"Not photos," Jenny said.

"So what?"

"Carl's asked me to varnish her nails - his idea of a sick joke. He's threatening to use those wire cutters and put one of her fingers in the post."

52

I'D not intended telephoning Matt Neilson ever again in this lifetime. The thought of hearing his voice, let alone making polite conversation, was enough to make me heave. But the clock continued to tick. The front page article would not appear in the Polish magazine until Friday afternoon. I had time to kill, and I needed something more than scribbles on a banknote to convince Ania I was on her side. I believed her story and I was desperate to help.

"Is that you, Amy?"

"It's not a social call. And if I wasn't desperate, you're the last person I'd be telephoning."

"OK. But you know why I did what I did. Right?"

"Cash? Attention-seeking? Seeing your name in print?"

"Nothing like that, Ames."

"Or maybe you wanted to humiliate me in public," I said. "But spare me your feeble excuses. I need a favour, and it makes me sick to the stomach even asking. But you owe me big time."

Christ. Why was it so hard?

"So I was wondering. . ."

"Wondering what?"

"Remember those photos? The ones Vanessa took at Caddy's funeral?"

I guessed he'd not been expecting that.

"Uh, you mean at Stoer cemetery."

"Yeah. I was wondering if you still had them. On your laptop, or whatever."

Matt had asked his mother to email them to him because we suspected they included photographs of Jimmy Jump's Klondykers. The two Ukrainians who had been acting as Gordon Paver's gofers. Balto and Damo.

"They're on a memory stick. I'll see if I can dig it out. But what the hell d'you want with them?"

"Something new I'm working on. Like a scrapbook of Lochinver. I'm thinking of going away for a few months, so it would be nice to have a few mementoes to take along. You know?"

"God. Funeral photos?"

"It's an important memory, Matt. Remember how much better you felt after we dragged you out to the kirk? You'd never have forgiven yourself if you'd missed your own sister's funeral service."

"S'pose. Which photos do you want me to send?"

"Send them all and I'll sort through the ones I'd like to keep."

"Can do. So where are you thinking of heading?"

"I think I'm going to work my way through the alphabet. I'll probably start with Amsterdam and see what happens."

53

THEY turned up late at night. Steff was in bed and Mike upstairs in his study, working through his accounts or watching on-line porn with his headphones stuck to his ears. Matt didn't care what his dad was up to, as long as he wasn't in the same room, breathing the same air, searching for something new to argue about.

"For God's sake, I'll answer the door, why don't I?" No one heard Matt. He left the empty Corona bottle on the coffee table, muted the volume on the television and turned on the lights.

There it came again. The incessant rattling of the door knocker.

"OK. OK. Where's the fire?"

As soon as he opened the front door, Matt recognised the three visitors even though their dark clothing and headgear masked most of their features.

"Christ, you scared the shit out of me. What are you doing here this time of night?"

Slippy fumbled with the zipper at his collar before pulling it down enough to uncover the bottom half of his face. "Get your fucking coat. You're coming for a wee ride."

Matt felt his stomach twist tight. "It's late. I mean, what's this supposed to be about?"

"In the Jeep and we'll tell you. But don't be thinking

about doing anything stupid. Ken, you go inside with him."

"My dad's still up. If he hears us, he's gonna want to know what's happening."

"Then you'd better get your dancing shoes on, pretty boy, and get a move on. I haven't got all fucking night."

Matt slipped on his trainers and grabbed a jacket off the back of one of the kitchen chairs while Ken surveyed the interior like one of the cardboard estate agents from 'Homes Under the Hammer'.

"See anything you like?"

Ken's sense of humour bypass seemed complete. "Are we done here?"

Matt sat in the front, next to Slippy. "So, where are we going? 'Cause I'm supposed to be working tomorrow morning. There's a Spanish boat due in at 07:00."

"This won't take long."

They took a left, past the Boathouse and the Caley. Slippy continued driving out as far as the breakwater. Then he swung the vehicle round in a semi-circle and parked it next to the slipway.

"You seen your wee pal, Baxter, recently?" Slippy asked.

The question caught Matt unprepared. "Not since the weekend. I mean, I called round Thursday morning for a coffee. That's all."

"So you didn't get an invite to the party?"

"What party?"

"Fuck, if you're messing me about now I'm going to have to get Tommy or Ken here to carry out a little more dental work. And it won't be their boots they're using this time."

"God's honest truth - I wasn't at any party, and I've not seen Barcode. I phoned him Sunday afternoon, that's all. I was after some weed but he said he was all out."

219

Slippy began tapping the wheel of the Jeep. "So he didn't say anything about where he might be heading."

"No way. As far as I know he's at home."

Slippy laughed. Not a pleasant laugh. "Trust me, Mattie boy. Your wee pal isn't home. In fact there's nobody home at number 7. Right, boys?"

"Yeah, boss," Tommy said.

"He's gone, and so is that wee cunt of a sister of his. And I'm curious what made them suddenly decide to leave town. I mean, it's not like they're away on honeymoon even though they're meant to be shagging each other."

"Right," Matt said. "But he said nothing. I swear."

"So what about that fucker Tyler? The twat in a suit that came to see me on the boat that time? You remember him, right?"

"Rick's brother? What about him?" Matt said.

"You've been in touch."

"No way. As far as I know he's in Spain."

"Aye, well. He's back here, I'm told. And I want him found."

"OK. But I don't know why you're asking me." Matt watched the windscreen mist over.

"I'm asking you because I know you're a bright lad. You know when to keep your gob shut, and when to keep your neb out of folks' business that doesn't concern you. I'll no forget what happened up at the quarry."

"Right."

"So consider this a friendly warning. You and Tyler were seen together at the Caley a week ago Tuesday. Am I right?"

"It was nothing."

"Am I right?"

Matt nodded. There were two men in the back seat of the vehicles itching to put their baseball bats to good use.

220

"And that fucking toe rag has taken my daughter. Or at least, he knows where she's being kept. And he's doing things to her. And when I find him he's going to wish he'd stayed the fuck away. Am I making myself clear?"

"Yeah. I'll ask around, if that's what you want."

"Oh, I want more than that," Slippy replied. "I want you to deliver your pal a message. I want my wee daughter back unharmed within the next forty eight hours. Forty eight hours, not an hour more. And if I don't, he's going to find himself in a world of grief. Him and that Weegie slag he's shacked up with. Now get the fuck out of my sight before I lose my temper."

54

£1000 NAGRODY KIM SĄ TE DZIEWCZYNY?

"We keep the banner and picture below the fold," Witek explained. "That way it doesn't draw so much attention in case there are others who recognise the names. Others who would do the girls harm if their identities became known to the authorities."

"But that means Ania might not see it either."

"It is a chance we will have to take."

Amy had given a scanned copy of Caddy's banknote to Witek for inclusion on the front page of the next issue. He'd only printed the side containing the names for obvious reasons. Would Ania see this? Would she have the courage to respond? Would a cash reward be enough motivation for her to come forward?

Three days later I got my answer.

"How are you, Amy?"

"Fine. Have you heard anything?"

"Someone's left another note at the newspaper offices," Patryk said.

"Ania?"

"It doesn't say, but it looks like it. They've included the picture torn from the paper, the name of a pub and a time. Two-fifteen tomorrow afternoon in the town centre. Have you got the cash?"

I had the cash. I also had the photographs. I'd begged Brendan to let me borrow Jan's laser printer, even though she was out of town. He didn't press for an explanation and I didn't give him one. I took the opportunity to mention how I'd be leaving Aberdeen as we crossed town, en route to Midstocket. Catching him unawares; unprepared to give a negative response. It felt easier when he was driving because I'd not need to look him in the eye. Instead, I watched the traffic as he grunted a number of reasons why it wasn't such a good idea.

"But you're the one who said I should go off and enjoy myself."

"Yeah. But when Jan said she'd spoken to you about Amsterdam, we both thought you were after a weekend away not a complete change of lifestyle."

"I'll keep in touch."

"That's not the point, Amy. Are you meeting somebody out there? Some guy you haven't bothered telling us about? And what about these photographs?"

"It's private," I said. "I was hoping you and Jan would respect me enough to trust me when I say I know what I'm doing."

The point was, of course, I didn't. I wasn't even clear myself why I was prepared to throw away a thousand pounds on nothing more than a gut feeling.

55

THE Mither Tap was busy. Most of the lunchtime crowd didn't seem in a rush to return to their desks. But no one appeared to be paying particular interest to the young woman sitting next to the pool table where a game was currently in progress. She nursed a glass of fruit juice but had no intentions of finishing it anytime soon. She seemed too preoccupied, studying the clientele and watching each new customer as they entered the bar.

Alex had dropped off Ania in John Street ten minutes earlier. She'd waited until his car passed through the box junction at the end of the road before approaching the bar. Then she ordered her drink and searched for a safe place to sit. Somewhere where she could observe anybody entering or leaving.

Ania had specified a time in her note. She would speak with the journalist for fifteen minutes - not a minute longer. The toilets and fire door were close by. The door had a simple crash bar to keep it shut. If this was a trap, she'd cause a distraction by throwing her glass of juice over the pool table then head for the fire exit. She'd find her own way back to Rosemount if necessary.

For once Alex had been in a relaxed mood during their journey across the city. "Jonno said to give you half an hour. I've a man to see about a dog and a couple of bets to place. But don't keep me waiting or you'll feel the back of ma hand. Outside the bookies no later than twenty to three."

14:12 a couple came in, took off their coats and shook off the drops of rain. The guy's gaze met Ania's - a glint of interest in his eye - but then he turned to his partner and spoke to her while she studied the jukebox.

Another pair came in. Two young lovebirds. The guy was in his twenties, unshaven but with a neat appearance. The girl was younger. She'd made little effort to groom herself and the spiky red hair made her stand out from the crowd for all the wrong reasons. A feminist by the look of it. Not someone Ania had a lot of time for.

They kissed briefly and the young girl came to stand next to the pool table while the guy went to the toilets. Then the girl came closer and reached out a hand. "Ania?"

How could she tell? Ania nodded, her body suddenly coiled tight like a spring on the point of being released.

"I'm Amy. This is Patryk."

The guy had appeared from nowhere. He gave a brief smile of recognition before introducing himself. He was Polish, but not the journalist she was expecting. Patryk had read Ania's story and wanted to help. He spoke of his own family in Chelm, his studies. He seemed a straightforward kind of guy. Ania told a little of her time in Britain before making it clear she hadn't come to chat.

Then he introduced the girl with the red hair. Somehow Amy had discovered the banknote left inside the pillow case. She took it out of her jacket pocket along with an envelope. Ania held the €5 note between her fingers for a moment or two, trying to figure out whether or not it was the same one. The ink had barely faded over time. What had she been thinking? So much had happened.

She explained that she would have to leave at two thirty. The driver would come looking for her if she didn't show up. She didn't want their money. She didn't want their help. She wanted them to allow her to get on with her life.

The red-haired girl remained silent as Patryk explained why she was offering so much money in exchange for information. Amy had also suffered at the hands of these men. Not perhaps the ones who now held Ania and her friends, but there was a connection. The man who ran the operation had also employed the two Ukrainians who kept Ania and Paulina imprisoned at the chalet park.

"Amy doesn't speak Polish," he continued. "But she knows the people involved. This nightmare can end right now if you trust us enough to answer a few questions."

Except there was no nightmare, and Ania knew better than to trust anyone except Jonno and Alex. The girls were safe while they stayed together. Alone in this harsh, cold world, Ania realised, she could never survive.

Then Patryk passed her a slip of paper. An address where they could talk in private. Somewhere safe to stay while they decided what to tell the police.

"*Nie jestem zainteresowany. . .*" Ania apologised for wasting their time and got to her feet. The fire exit was less than five steps away.

"What's she doing?" Amy said.

"Wait. *Żadnej policji.*" Patryk shook his head from side to side."We only want to help you."

"*Alex. Alex mnie zabije.*"

"*Gdzie jest Alex?*"

"*Zapomnij.*" Ania began to move towards the door but Patryk took hold of her arm and steered her back towards their table.

"*Nie!*" She wanted to push him away. To escape into the street and find Alex. But she couldn't risk there being a scene.

He motioned to the girl and she took out a handful of

black and white photographs then placed them gently on the table.

Ania felt her legs grow heavy before slumping back into her seat. She stared at the pictures and the blur of faces became familiar. She saw the two Ukrainians. Her body shuddered as her hands grazed their features. She saw the other three men who had come to the party at the house. The house with the snot-yellow sofa. She pointed at each one and gave details of how she knew them. Maybe this would end once she answered their questions.

The girl with the red hair shuffled the pictures and asked Ania to look once more, as if she didn't believe her story.

"*Jeden. Dwa. Trzy. Cztery. Pięć.*"

"Ask her is she a hundred percent sure," she heard Amy ask. Then a group of men in boiler suits came in through the outside door and Alex appeared from nowhere like a runaway train.

"What the fuck's this?" he said.

His hands reached over to snatch the photographs before making a grab for Ania. But already she had left her seat, smacked her palm against the fire door's crash bar and escaped into the street. She ran off into the rain while Patryk and Alex exchanged words.

"Leave her alone," Patryk said.

The knife came from nowhere and he was forced to back off while Alex shoved the photos inside his jerkin then followed Ania out into the rain.

56

ANIA wasn't what I'd expected. This slim, almost sophisticated, young woman with long dark hair, a figure-hugging trouser suit and a hard edge to her smile that made her seem older. I could tell she was nervous. She wore a black rubber band around her left wrist and plucked at it like a child tugging at a comfort blanket. Her gaze flitted left to right, lurching to a man feeding coins into the jukebox before latching onto Patryk.

Even before I slid onto the bench seat next to her, I saw her flinch as the door to the toilets nearby slammed shut. She reminded me of a wounded fox rather than a frightened rabbit. One wrong move and she'd attack rather than run.

Patryk sat next to me and introduced himself before beginning to speak calmly in Polish. The young woman's features seemed to relax but her voice grated with tension. Their heads bent closer to each other and I was no longer there.

I took out the €5 banknote, unfolded it and let her hold it between her fingers for a moment or two. Then she closed her eyes and the words tumbled out like an avalanche.

"What's she saying?"

"Wait, let her finish," Patryk said.

I watched as her fingers traced the names scribbled in

pen. She shook her head then handed it back to me.

"She'd forgotten about this," Patryk continued. "She had given up hope long ago."

"That's to be expected," I whispered.

"There's another note as well. She remembers being driven to a house with big windows and a wooden floor. There was a yellow, leather sofa and she left a note inside one of the cushion covers but no one came."

"Christ. Tell her that's why we're here," I said. "Does it matter which note we found?"

Ania's eyes fixed on mine as if she understood every word.

"She says she has a new life in Aberdeen. She wants to forget about the past. She says she doesn't need anyone's help any more."

"What about the money?" I'd already pulled out the envelope from the inside pocket of my waterproof jacket.

Patryk laid his hand on top of mine. "She doesn't want the money either."

"Shit." I slid the envelope back inside my jacket and felt the bundle of photographs crinkle against my side. "So why did she bother contacting the paper?"

"She wants to put an end to it all. This business with Paulina has gone on long enough."

Patryk continued speaking to her in Polish but already I could sense the mood shift. Ania looked at her wristwatch, placed both hands on the table and eased herself to her feet.

"What's she doing?"

Patryk reached out for her and forced her back to her seat. "Wait."

They began to argue in Polish and I tried to intervene but Patryk turned on me. "In five minutes time someone will come looking for her. If you want to show her the fucking photographs, now might be a good time."

I laid them on the table. Six print-offs on glossy white paper. 21 centimetres by 30. A view of Stoer cemetery with about a dozen people in shot. Me, Matt, some other kids from the neighbourhood and Caddy's mum and dad. A close up of Mike and Steff with Gordon Paver standing to one side. Gordon and the two Ukrainians. Two shots of Gordon and his co-conspirators from the local Business Group. And one of me and Matt on our own.

Ania seemed to freeze for a moment then her fingers stabbed at the picture of Barto and Damo. She didn't need to speak. Her frightened expression made it clear she recognised them both. Then she shuffled through the other photographs. Three more men in suits. She didn't seem certain and I caught hesitation in her body language.

"Ask her to look again."

It couldn't be right.

Then she spoke to confirm my fears. "*Jeden. Dwa. Trzy. Cztery. Pięć.*" One. Two. Three. Four. Five.

"Is she sure?" I asked.

She nodded. "*To ten.*" This one.

Before I could respond again I felt a hand grip my shoulder from behind. Someone scooped up the photographs and roared in anger as Ania sprang to her feet and smashed her way through the fire exit.

Chaos everywhere. Cursing. Raised voices. The ear-splitting clamour of the fire alarm. The jukebox twice as loud. But I was somewhere else. Not a good place.

Ania had identified the two Ukrainians as expected. No surprises there. She'd also pointed out John Fleming and Stuart Coleman. But she made no sign of recognising Gordon Paver. Instead she'd pulled out the second picture in the pile and looked me in the eye as twice her finger rested on another familiar face.

57

WE sat at the back of the bus. I didn't catch the number. We'd taken the first one that came along. I was desperate to get away. Anywhere.

The bus was a crawler and as it picked its way through the city traffic, from one red stop light to the next, Patryk told me how he'd lost Ania in all the confusion despite following her into the street. We'd both seen her race out of the bar and he was close enough to watch her climb into a car parked across the road from the pub.

"She sits like a zombie in the passenger seat. Then the guy - the one who snatched your pictures - he gets into the car and drives off as if nothing had happened."

I barely heard what he said.

"What do you think it was about?"

I couldn't answer. I couldn't think straight. My mind was mush. It took twenty minutes cruising the city streets before my heart calmed down. I'd seen the look the driver gave me. I was scared he might come back. Scared of what I'd got myself into.

"She's not thinking straight," I said. "Two strangers walk into a bar. It's like the opening to a bad joke. Why should she trust us?"

"I did my best to explain why we were there. You saw how she reacted when the driver turned up."

"Yeah. She's been fucking brainwashed. That's why she

got into the car even though she had a chance to run."

"You think so?" he said.

"She doesn't trust anyone except him, even though she knows exactly what he will do if she tries to escape."

"Even though he keeps her prisoner," Patryk said.

"Better the devil you know."

"So you are wasting your time."

"Maybe," I said. "Sometimes it's better to put up with shit than to start a new life where everything is different. People don't like change. Familiar shit is safe shit."

"And if she tries to get away, it could get worse. There are immigration people everywhere."

"Is that what she said?" I asked.

"She said a lot of things."

"So she feels safer where she is," I said.

"Yes, even though I mentioned you have a spare room in your uncle's flat."

My situation wasn't a great deal different from Ania's. Did I really think I could escape the circus my life had become by flying out to Amsterdam? Leanne told me once that you can't run away from life no matter how you try. But God, my whole world had been turned upside down, and all because I thought I was being smart. Thought I was some kind of superhero out to rescue the universe. Those girls - they didn't want saving. They weren't looking for justice or revenge. And Paver had got away again. I'd shown Ania his photograph and she'd not even flinched. She hadn't picked him from the line-up of usual suspects.

"Do you know where we're supposed to be going?" Patryk asked finally as the bus slowed down at the next stop.

"Let's wait. I need to think." I didn't know who to trust anymore.

I kept a close eye on the on-board electronic timetable.

232

Gerrard Street. Fraser Street. Millbank Place. Kittybrewster - Ashgrove Road. Kittybrewster - Lilybank Place. Woodside. Then I saw the Fountain Bar on our right.

"We should probably get off here," I said.

Patryk looked out of the window. "You recognise this place? I'm not sure."

"It's OK. I know where we are." I remembered seeing the Coral bookmakers when Brendan took me out drinking one time. The Embassy was upstairs and the Function Rooms were at the back. As we turned the corner into Don Street, I pointed to the four high rise blocks towering above the rooftops ahead of us.

"OK. But how far is it to walk? We're going to get soaked."

"We'll be fine," I said as I pulled up my collar. "It's only about twenty minutes from here. What else did Ania tell you?"

"She didn't say very much about herself," he said. "It was mostly about Paulina and what the newspapers were saying."

"Did she mention the time they spent at the chalet park?"

"You mean when she came over on the boat?"

"Yeah."

"Not really. She spoke about a party in a house with shiny floors. The journey in the minibus. Five hours with her wrists cable-tied to her seat. But most of it was about her home in Poland. That is nothing to concern you."

"Suit yourself."

We continued in silence the rest of the way. The streets were quiet - most people at work or on the school run. I'd be home in time for tea. The rain stopped and most of the pavements were quick to dry in the sun. We picked our way through a neat little housing estate. White bungalows with dormer windows and neat little gardens at the front. It all looked so normal.

When we reached Dill Place I said I'd ring him once I'd made a few other calls. "I go right here. I'll be fine."

"You sure?"

"Yeah. I'm sure. And thanks for today. I'll ring you later in the week."

And thanks for bringing my world crashing down on my head. I had to telephone someone else first. I needed to speak to Matt Neilson - probably after I'd had some time to work out how to break the news to him.

58

"YOU'RE still not making sense so tell me again. Who the fuck were those two you were getting cosy with?"

Ania clenched her body, waiting for Jonno to twist her hand again but instead Alex grabbed a handful of hair from behind and tugged it back. The pain sending sharp needles into her skull.

She bit back a sob and tried to calm her breathing. "I didn't see them before in my life."

"No, no, no," Jonno said. "I'm still no getting through, am I?"

Alex continued yanking her hair, forcing her head against the back of the dining chair. But then she felt his grip loosen.

"Open your eyes, Ania, and look at me." Jonno, in his combat jacket and faded denims, stood a couple of feet away, leaning down so his face was at eye level. "I haven't got all fucking day."

"Shall I get the bag?" Alex asked.

The bright fluorescent lights had made her eyes tear up. She saw blurry shapes. The kitchen cupboards. The cooker and the refrigerator. Then she felt Alex's arm wrap around her throat and something was pulled down over her head, covering her eyes, her nose, her mouth.

"How long, boss?"

"We'll see. Keep her still."

The plastic refuse bag was wrenched tight against her face as its loose ends were tugged into a knot beneath her jaw. All her concentration suddenly became focussed on her breathing, even though the smell and taste of polythene made her want to gag. She needed to stay calm, but the instinct to survive quickly took over. Within seconds she was panting for air. Her pulse raced, her drumming heartbeat throbbing inside her skull. Each sound became amplified. The crinkling of the bag against her skin. The scraping of the chair against the floor. Muffled voices, and somewhere the urge to cry out.

Then daylight again. The bag torn from her head and Alex grabbing her shoulders and shaking.

"Have we got your attention now?" Jonno said.

Ania managed to shrug away Alex's hands as she drank in the air. Then she leant forward, resting her own hands on her thighs. Fingers clenched. Knuckles white as she balled both hands into fists.

"I didn't run when I had the chance to get away, did I? They offered me money but I didn't run. I got back in the fucking car like I always do."

"So what d'you want? A fucking medal?"

Ania shook her head, her throat still burning.

"I want their names, Ania," Jonno continued. "And I want to know how they found you, and what the fuck you said to them."

"It was Amy. The girl. And some guy from Chelm called Patryk. He speaks Polish and I pretend not to speak English."

"So you'd arranged to meet them?"

"Of course not. I never saw them before in my life."

The slap came from nowhere. A crack across the left cheek that made her teeth clack together.

"Bullshit. It's all bullshit."

"I told you, they looked like a pair of fucking social

236

workers," Alex said. "Poking their noses where they're not wanted."

"Let her answer," Jonno snarled.

Ania spat something out. Blood salty on her tongue.

"What about these?" He waved the sheaf of photographs in front of her face. "Do you think I'm fucking stupid?"

"No," she managed to say.

"Who are they - this Amy and Patryk? Are they in these pictures? Someone sniffing around?"

"Yes, I mean no," she said.

"Make your fucking mind up 'cause I'm starting to lose my patience again."

"The girl. She is there but her hair is different now. Shorter. Darker. And she has a scar above her mouth. But the boy she is with, I don't recognise."

"So why you? I mean, fuck. They turn up with a bunch of photographs and offer you money, yet you act as if you know nothing."

Ania shrugged, her lips drawn into a grimace as she gathered her thoughts. "It was a newspaper article. The front page of *Głos Szkocki*."

"Speak fucking English.

"Sorry," she stifled a sob. "I saw a photograph of Paulina in the newspaper asking if anyone recognised her. But they write lies about her."

"So?"

"And so I telephone the number. Two weeks ago."

"Fuck me." Alex muttering behind her back.

"I tell them nothing about here. Just about coming to Scotland from Amsterdam. The hard work we do to survive. Something good to make her family proud - to remember she was not such a bad person no matter what other people say."

"Pass me a fucking tissue," Alex said.

"The girl called Amy knows everything about Paulina - how she was brought to Scotland on the boat. She's the one who had the pictures. She says she knows the man who has the boat. She knows where we stay before coming here to Aberdeen."

"How the hell can she?"

"It doesn't matter for now how she knows our story or how she found me. But when she showed me the photographs I recognised the faces. She already knew their names and she wanted me to help her when she goes to the police with her story."

"Shit."

"But I fix everything. I told lies for you and the other girls to protect our life here. I'm not so stupid to give them information they can take to the authorities."

"You did what exactly?" Jonno said.

"I agreed to meet with them and when I saw the pictures I don't tell the truth." She reached out for the photographs and laid them on her knees. "This one - they are the two Ukrainians. But this girl, Amy. She knows that already. I can tell."

"Right."

"And I see the news this week on the television. Three of the men who have sex with us the night they have a party. I recognise them all."

Ania's fingers jabbed at the next picture. "*Jeden. Dwa. Trzy.*"

"So you didn't lie."

Then Ania raised her face as if pleading for understanding. A friendly gesture such as an arm across the shoulder or a hand on the back of her neck.

"I only point to three men. This other one, I say nothing about." Her finger rested on another face. "He is the one with the big boat. He still comes here sometimes, yes? And to the back room of the club?"

"Paver," Alex whispered.

"I don't tell them anything about him. The girl I think knows I tell a lie because she asks again and I tell Patryk I am sure. I say again then Alex comes and I run away from them. Don't you see? I come back to warn you. This Amy, she already knows everything about what happens last year. She says she wants to take me away from here. She gives me an address where she stays. Somewhere safe."

"You remember it?" Jonno said.

Ania reached into both pockets of her coat and began to grow frantic.

"It was on a piece of paper," she said.

"Shit."

"So what do we do?"

"What d'you think we do?" Jonno continued. "We speak to Paver."

"He'll go fucking radge."

"He doesn't need to know the whole story. We'll give him a heads up about his little friend, Amy. He's bound to know where she's staying. Then we'll let him decide what he wants to do about the situation."

OCTOBER

59

"HOW'S things?"

Matt sounded tired. "You know - the usual shit. It's been pissing down with rain all night and there's supposed to be another storm on the way. A follow up to Hurricane Bertha, so they reckon."

"I didn't mean the weather, Matt, but thanks for sending the photos."

"No sweat."

I could sense there was a question on the tip of his tongue.

"I don't buy that scrapbook crap, by the way."

"I knew you wouldn't."

"So what's going on?"

"That's why I need to speak to you," I replied. "I showed them someone."

"Showed them? Showed them who?"

"Remember those Polish girls? The ones who left the note Caddy found?"

"Oh, for fuck's sake."

"I found Ania."

"Whatever."

"Seriously," I said. "And I showed her the photos."

"Why would you do that?"

"I was hoping she would point out Gordon Paver's ugly mug. Some kind of confirmation he'd been involved all along. There'd been a party before they were shipped out to Aberdeen."

"God, Amy. We've already been through this so many times. I wish you'd give it a rest."

"Well. I can't. And anyway, Paver wasn't there. He's squeaky clean as usual."

"There you go," Matt said.

"But she remembered the Ukrainians and two of Paver's buddies. The two up in court this week."

"So why are you phoning me? Let the police do their job and move on."

I began to hyperventilate. There was no easy way to say this. "I can't move on. She pointed out one more face from the party. Someone the police haven't even interviewed, as far as I know."

"And this guy was at Caddy's funeral?"

"Oh, yeah."

"So, are you going to tell me who this mystery man is?"

I could sense the scorn in his voice and that made me feel even worse. "It's your dad, Matt. She said your dad was there."

I expected the silence at the other end to last longer, but Matt had always favoured the spontaneous approach when handling most problems in his life.

"That's bullshit. She made the whole thing up."

"But why would she lie?"

"No idea. But you don't even know it's the same girl who left the note in the first place. There must be hundreds of Polish girls called Ania."

"Maybe. But this one remembered being brought in by boat. She described the bunkhouse where they were locked up. Paver's chalet park. She recognised the other four faces in the photographs, and we already know they were caught up in this business. She even described the inside of the house - the furniture, everything."

"Big deal."

"Matt, I'm only phoning you because I don't know what the hell to do for the best. If this comes out, can you imagine what'll happen?"

"To my dad you mean?"

"To everybody. You and Steff. I wish I'd never bothered getting involved."

"So let it lie."

"But I can't," I said. "This is mega. It's not something I can conveniently forget about, just like that."

"So you're going to soothe your fragile conscience by exposing my dad and wrecking our family on the word of some Polish tart," he said. "Seriously, Ames. Can you see my dad risking everything just to have a freebie in some all-night orgy out at the chalet park? It's a joke."

"Yeah. But six months ago, you were ready to believe me and your precious dad had been shagging each other."

I heard him give a snort. "I never actually believed you'd let him screw you."

"Thanks for that. But trust me, your dad's no saint. He fancied his chances, even though I was his daughter's best friend. I'd barely turned sixteen, yet he still came on to me."

"That's 'cause you probably gave him the green light - some kind of teenage crush."

I felt the flush of embarrassment swell inside my breast. "It doesn't mean he had to take advantage. He was up for it alright. I even had to fight him off the day after Caddy was found murdered."

"So what do you suggest I do now?"

"It's up to you. But all this could come out in court if they put the screws on Fleming or Coleman. They'll say

243

anything to save their skins."

"I doubt it. It'll be hearsay at best. And you've got no proof that will stand up in court other than the word of some Polish junky cunt. I bet she's an illegal immigrant, running all sorts of scams to pay for her drug habit. I suppose you offered her money for this so-called story."

"No."

"And she didn't even ask?"

"No."

"Well, that's something. 'Cause when there's cash involved, people will tell you whatever they think you want to hear."

"Or promise to keep silent for a price," I said.

"What?"

"Twenty grand. That's a lot of cash if you wanted this story sweeping under the carpet."

"Fuck me. So that's what this is all about," he said. "You're trying to blackmail my dad."

My throat filled with bile. "God, Matt. Is that what you think of me?"

"You're the one who mentioned twenty grand."

"You really are a fuckwit," I said.

"So why else would you ring me asking for money?"

"I'm not," I replied. "The money's already in my bank account."

"It's what?"

I told him about the two cheques I'd received from Mike as well as the money he'd given Kay Jepson. I heard Matt mutter a curse before hanging up the phone.

The empty silence that followed was worse than any falling out.

60

MATT needed time to get his head around recent events. Steff had been twittering away about what to make for tea, but he couldn't think straight. He'd told her he wasn't hungry. He was going out. Mind reeling with the implications of what his so-called friend had told him, he was haunted by a single fact.

Amy had been right.

He wiped the sleeve of his jacket across his eyes. Tears blurred the lights of the harbour and their reflections on the loch. A stiff breeze had sprung up out to sea, causing some of the mooring cables to snap at the sides of the boats. This wasn't the storm that had been forecast, but it created enough swell to keep the small fishing fleet tied to the jetty overnight.

11:15 came - evacuation time at the Caley - and he tagged on to a pair of stragglers. They'd spent most of the night propping up the bar, discussing the state of the local fishing industry and the fallout following the failed referendum.

"The world's gone to fecking shite."

"Yeah." A mumble.

"Stuck-up nobs at Westminster don't give a monkey's for anybody outside London."

"No." Another mumble.

"Though I suppose there'll be one or two round here

who'll be pleased."

"Probably." Matt drained the dregs of his glass and zipped up his jacket. He'd long lost interest in the argument. There had been talk of going back to someone's house for an after-party but his heart wasn't in it.

"What about your dad?"

"How d'you mean?" Matt asked, his radar now on high alert.

"Well, his job's gonna be safe now. Right? 'Cause the French and Spanish boats will keep bringing their catch here if we're not going independent."

"Right."

"The threats were no more than scaremongering South of the border."

"If you say so," Matt muttered. "But, look. I'm gonna pass on the party. I've got stuff I need to do." He pulled up the hood of his jacket and headed off into the rain. He'd given up trying to excuse his dad's involvement with Paver. The so-called orgy might well have been a one-off as his dad confessed. A drunken episode best forgotten. He'd been dragged out to Brackloch on a jolly and had no intention joining in the night's sexual activities. But that didn't mean he wasn't a two-faced, hypocritical bastard.

Matt had already worked out only two choices remained, now he'd confronted his dad. Tell him about Carl Tyler's plans to force Slippy's hand and see how he reacted. Or keep his mouth shut and wait for things to develop. In the end he'd said nothing more. The problem was, something might come from the court case in Aberdeen, as Amy had pointed out. If Paver went down, then so would Mike. Much as Matt relished the thought of seeing his dad hauled off to prison and humiliated in public, there was Steff to consider. And Caddy's memory.

His sister's name would be forever tarnished if their

father was discovered to be in cahoots with the guy who raised a monster like Peter Paver. Peter, the nut job responsible for Caddy's death. There was only one sensible solution. Matt had to think of the greater good and consort with the enemy.

He sought shelter in the lee of the creel store then he pulled out his mobile phone. Three rings.

"Hello."

61

"**I** don't know who else to talk to. Christ, it's a mess."

Shit.

"Is that you, Matt?"

He sounded pissed.

"I'm sorry - and please don't hate me, Ames. But you know what it's like. It's my family, and family always comes first."

I slid my body up the bed until I was propped against the pillows. "D'you know what time it is?" Two o'fucking clock in the morning. What was Matt playing at?

"You know me and my old man never got on that much. I've always been a waste of space, as far as he was concerned. None of us could ever reach his high standards. No wonder Vanessa left."

"None of us are perfect," I said.

"I know. But I'm a hundred times better than he is. A thousand times better. I still remember the way he kept eyeing up Caddy's mates, whenever she had them round our house for sleepovers. I thought he was trying to act the Cool Dad, but I realise now he had other reasons."

"For God's sake, your dad isn't the only lech in Lochinver," I said. "We used to mess with their heads whenever we caught them checking us out. Opening the top button of a blouse or pulling down the trouser waist-band to show a little more flesh."

Me defending Mike Neilson after all I'd said about him the previous day.

Matt gave a sniffle. "That doesn't mean he's allowed to make a fucking move on you when his own daughter's body's still in the mortuary."

"It wasn't like that, Matt."

"And what about the way he reacted when they told him Rick and Caddy had been seeing each other? All the shite he started spouting?"

"He was in shock, Matt. We all were."

"I know, but it was all an act 'cause he must have known exactly what had been going on between her and Tyler. Him and Paver kept that bit quiet to save their own skins."

"Does that mean you've had it out with your dad?"

"Yeah," he said. "It's knocked me for six, his dirty little secret. And we've both agreed to keep a lid on it. This'll kill Steff if she ever finds out."

I pulled the duvet up to my chest.

"He denied everything at first. Then when I mentioned the cheques, he spun some yarn about helping with Paver's accounts - conveyancing and stuff."

"What does that mean?"

"For starters, he's been feeding money through the Harbour books - money laundering I suppose you'd call it. Paver's bought property out at Brackloch under a different name. Some offshore company. And Dad's registered a load of cheques down as mooring fees, even though Paver's fucking boat's lying at the bottom of the sea."

"Cheques?" My heart hit the panic button.

"Yeah."

"So are you saying the money he sent wasn't from your dad?" I felt sick to the stomach.

"Not directly. No."

249

Fuck.

"You know what Paver's like - a pillar of the local community and all that jazz. Catholic guilt and so on."

"What about the party with the Polish girls?"

"Dad said he was pissed. Everybody was pissed or stoned. He reckoned it was nothing to do with human trafficking. They were all up for it. But when I said you'd spoken to one of the girls who was there, he went to fucking pieces. Said his whole fucking life would be over if this ever got out."

I know that feeling.

"He could have saved his skin if he'd spoken out when they took Paver in for questioning," I said.

"He didn't dare say a word to the police. Paver warned him to keep his mouth shut long before the coppers took an interest."

"I don't get it," I said.

"There's video-tapes. Paver had cameras hidden inside the house. He filmed the whole lot."

"Shit."

"He told Dad that Steff would get to watch everything if he ever breathed a word."

"God. What a bastard."

"The coppers must have pulled Strathbeg House apart but they found no evidence. No cameras. No video-tapes. But Dad still doesn't trust Paver. I'm scared he'll do something stupid."

"What about the money he gave me?" I said. "If the police find out about the cheques, they're going to come after me."

"Only if they find out. And they won't get anything from me."

"OK. But promise me you won't do anything stupid until we talk about this properly. I'm half asleep and you sound like you're on another planet."

"I won't. But that's not why I'm phoning."

"So what are you after, Matt?" I asked.

"Carl Tyler's back on the scene."

"Rick's brother?" I said.

"Yeah. Jenny's with him. They're staying out near Loch Assynt."

"And what's that got to do with anything?"

He gave a drunken belch then proceeded to tell me about Tyler's crazy idea to get even with Gordon Paver.

"I don't understand how you even know any of this," I said.

"Jenny phoned me as soon as they got here. Carl told her to get in touch."

Jesus. It got worse.

"Please don't tell me you're involved with that pair again."

"It's not as bad as it sounds. And anyway, Slippy knows where they're holding his daughter so everything's going to be OK."

"You've rung Slippy?"

"Sort of. I spoke to his wife earlier."

"Christ, Matt. You know what Slippy's like. The man's a psycho. Him and his boat crew will tear Tyler apart if they've done anything to his daughter. Did you say Jenny was at the cottage as well?"

"Yeah. She baby-sits Cindy while Carl goes on the razzle every night."

"Fucking hell. When did you ring Slippy's wife?"

"I don't know. A couple of hours ago, I suppose. That's why I'm phoning you."

"And what d'you expect me to do?"

"Don't know."

"I hope you've warned Tyler they're on the way."

"I tried ringing Jenny's mobile but there's no signal."

If I didn't know better, I'd swear I heard him sobbing at

251

the other end of the line.

"I assume you shopped Tyler and Jenny to avoid the truth coming out about Paver and your dad."

"Not really," he said.

"That's what this is all about, isn't it? You're saving Paver's skin, even though you know what he did to me. What his psycho son did to me."

"Ames."

"I can't believe you'd take sides with Paver against me and your own sister," I continued.

The line clicked then went dead.

"You still there?" I felt my skin grow clammy, fearing the worst. Slippy wouldn't hang around. He'd snatch his daughter back and be home in his own bed long before the emergency services turned up to repair the damage.

62

"DANILENKO, you dirty dog? How are things behind the Iron Curtain?"

The line crackled at the other end and Gordon Paver could barely make out the individual words. "Who is this calling?"

"It's Paver."

More clicking and hissing.

"Can you hear me? It's Gordon Paver."

"Mr Paver. Long time no speak. I was sorry to hear about your son."

"Yes, well. . . not such a shock if you knew Peter. He was born with a death wish."

"*Niech spoczywa w pokoju.*"

"You're breaking up. So, anyway. How are things in Ukraine?"

"I don't expect to hear from you so soon. I thought for our good health we agreed not to contact each other again, unless there is trouble, yah?"

Gordon brushed a couple of hairs from the lapel of his suit jacket. He could hear the sound of raised voices in the background. "You're still breaking up. Can you find somewhere else to talk?"

"Wait. I go into another room."

Muffled sounds and the slamming of doors.

"You there?" Gordon asked.

"We are having a drink to celebrate the weekend. Much vodka and many pretty girls, but yah, I listen now."

"So there's a little clean-up operation I need doing over here and I thought of you."

"Ah. I'm not so sure. There are too many bad memories of Scotland."

"I know. But we had some good times here, did we not?" Paver said. "You made a small fortune, if I remember rightly. And you know I always look after my friends."

"The safe house was good times. But you are making a bad joke I think. I am having too many good times here also."

"So you're still in Kiev smashing in skulls with the *titushky*."

Gordon heard the Ukrainian laugh at the other end of the telephone. "No. I am in Belarus now. I have my own table at the Laguna nightclub in Minsk. Champagne, vodka and beautiful girls who want to take their clothes off for me. You should come and join me here. I have no reason to return to Scotland."

"We go back a long way, Damo."

"Yah. But I have new business ventures to take care of now. There are many opportunities to make money here without having to break any more skulls. Desperate people with very much cash who want to reach England."

"But you always enjoyed breaking skulls, as I remember. And I have one or two lucrative business ventures of my own. We could discuss ways to combine our expertise."

"Maybe. But I understand the police put a stop to the Polish market," the Ukrainian said.

"Not exactly. One or two girls are still on the books, if that's what you mean. The police don't know everything. But something else has cropped up."

"Something else?"

"A minor problem. That's why I need you back here."

"For when?"

"Can you get to Warsaw before tomorrow night."

"Warsaw?"

"Chopin airport."

"Impossible. I take six or seven hours to drive," Damo replied. "The roads are not so good, and there has been snow for many days."

"Whatever it takes, be there. I'll text you the flight details. One change at Amsterdam. You can be in Aberdeen in five or six hours at the most."

"I fly to Aberdeen? Why the fuck would I fly to Aberdeen?"

"I'll have two of my men meet you at the airport," Paver said. "You still have the necessary paperwork, yeah? Fake passports and so on?"

"I am legal, yah. I can come and go. But I don't understand what it is you expect me to do."

"I'll tell you more, once you get here," Paver said.

"So maybe I don't agree. I have a good life in Belarus. You find someone else to do your dirty work, maybe."

"I thought you'd want to be here to see to things."

"Why me?"

"Because this is personal."

"How do you mean?" Damo said.

"Remember the boy you caught hanging around the chalet park? The one who drove you off the road, the night Barto died?"

"The pretty one. Yah, I remember him. We tried to drown him one time but he has more lives."

"Well, he's been sniffing around again. He's a loose end that needs tying off for good this time."

"But you should maybe deal with him yourself."

"I could do, but his father is a friend of mine and some

255

information has come my way that has to be handled delicately."

"So? Do you forget I don't have such a delicate touch?" Damo said.

"No. But you've never let me down. I want Matt Neilson gone. Make sure you do a proper job this time. I'm relying on your discretion. And there's another problem. He's not the only one stirring things."

"So who else do you talk about?" Damo asked.

"There's the little blonde piece who turned up at the house the night we shipped the girls out. Remember Amy? The one we left inside the sleeping bag? You said you wanted to keep her until later, but Matt went and spoilt your plans."

"Ah, the little girl with the tight little ass. Yah."

Paver could sense the Ukrainian's mood changing. "She's in Aberdeen, far enough away I thought. I even made arrangements for her to take a long holiday, but it seems she's not interested. She's been in touch with one of the Polish girls."

"So you want Amy gone also."

"That's why I'm phoning you."

"But I get to fuck her first - yah? The same way I fuck the girl with the piercings?"

"I'll leave the finer details to you. But she has to be stopped one way or another. And I don't think the friendly warning you gave that bitch junkie is going to be enough to stop young Amy."

63

THE idea of Croft House Cottage as a crime scene was absurd. It hardly qualified as a suitable setting for kidnap, blackmail and violent murder.

Over the years, the two downstairs rooms and the tiny bedroom hidden in the roof space had served as home for a local shepherd and his family. Crouched close to the foot of Quinag, it gained shelter from the bitterest winter winds. The remains of a sheep fank lay perched on a broad shelf of scrubby ground close to one of the burns cascading down the mountain's slopes. Derelict now, it harboured ranks of bracken already turning red as the summer receded. Closer at hand, another collapsed stone enclosure held rolls of rusted wire netting and a twisted, galvanised metal gate. Both ruins the only evidence of its past life.

Now the whitewashed cottage, complete with satellite dish, wheelie bin and Upvc windows, catered almost exclusively for the high-end holiday trade. The idyllic setting with Loch Assynt a stone's throw away attracted those seeking a tranquil retreat from the rat race. Or those with high-velocity rifles, and a thirst for blood and a hunger for a trophy stag. The sounds of gunfire often went unnoticed up here, regardless of the season.

But this morning all was silent. Carl's 4 x 4 wasn't parked outside the front as it should have been. Indeed, there were no immediate signs of anyone ever having been there apart from the damage to the double doors separating the porch from the foot of the stairs. One had been torn off its hinges.

Matt had already checked the downstairs bedroom. A red flight-case lay open next to a dressing table - most of the clothes inside still neatly folded. Colourful blouses and dresses. Lacy underwear and rolled up, woollen tights. One pillow had slipped onto the floor and the duvet was pulled back to reveal a pale green bed sheet. Both were covered in fresh bloodstains, tacky where the discharge was heaviest.

But there were no bodies.

He made his way to the bathroom, fearing the worst. A hair brush and a bottle of body lotion sat on the glass shelf above the wash basin. Shaving foam. A disposable razor. Two travel toothbrushes and tube of Colgate. Three cotton buds, a hair grip and a roll-on deodorant. Two bath towels, still damp. A white, fluffy bathrobe left where it fell inside the shower cubicle.

No blood. No bodies.

The living room smelt of weed. An ash tray on one of the coffee tables held four stubbed-out cigarette ends. Two empty lager cans and a wine glass the only other signs of a party. Jenny had left her heels in the doorway to the kitchen. Matt took in the evidence, expecting to find fresh signs of the attack around every blind corner. The kettle was cold. A collection of plates and cutlery filled the sink - the washing up water scummed with a greasy mixture of cooking oil and coffee dregs, also cold. He could smell fried bacon. The bread bin had been left open - inside an empty plastic Warburton's wrapper and two breakfast rolls. Both stale. Matt's stomach gave a lurch.

No bodies.

He returned to the cramped passageway next to the porch and looked to the top of the tiny staircase. Two weeks ago they had hauled Cindy O'Connor's limp body up these stairs. He'd helped Carl and Barcode lay her on the sofa bed and watched as Jenny undressed her. Then he'd left the young girl there; two weeks a prisoner, fearing for her own life as Carl and Slippy played out their macho games.

The bedroom was empty now, the mattress bare. The only remaining trace of Cindy O'Connor was the lingering stink of human faeces, made worse by the early morning sunlight blazing through the tiny window. The curtain rail had been wrenched free of the wall and the thick blanket used to block out the light now lay on the floor. Matt sat on the edge of the bed and pressed both palms against his forehead. Maybe Carl and Jenny had managed to get away, despite the blood in the bedroom. Anything could have accounted for that.

OK. They'd not had time to pack, but given the dramatic arrival of Slippy and his henchmen that wouldn't be such a surprise.

Christ, the stench up there. Matt closed the bedroom door and made his way downstairs. The air here was as stale. Damp. Musty. He needed to clear his head. If Slippy and his boys had called, they'd left in a hurry. Time for him to hit the road as well. He walked over to Steff's car and noticed scuff marks on the ground. Two deep ruts veered past the porch entrance and around towards the rear of the cottage. The dew-covered grass had been churned up sometime recently, and fresh tyre tracks led across the small patch of lawn to the back of the property.

Matt could hear the steady trickle of the burn that drained off the steep hillside to the North into a wide pool at the rear of the cottage. The last midges of the season

259

danced before his eyes. A sunny autumn morning and the presence of stagnant water nearby enough incentive to draw them closer, despite a hint of frost on the skyline. The ripe scent of decaying flesh inside a confined space no doubt enough of an attraction to keep them out of their beds.

The Vauxhall lay on its side in the burn, tilted at an angle so the water level came more than half way up the windscreen on the passenger side. Apart from a swipe of mud smearing one of its rear wings, the vehicle looked as if it had gently rolled off the lawned area into the water. Its tinted windows were closed up tight but Matt could make out the shape of someone slumped against the steering wheel.

A garden spade lay on the grass. The edge of its blade glistened with something wet. Fresh dew maybe. Or fresh blood along with clumps of matted hair and human tissue.

Matt retched and turned away. Deep breaths. He clenched his fists. There was nothing he could do here. Just him and a dead body inside a car. No doubt there would be police involved. Statements to take. A case to investigate. Matt couldn't afford to be seen here - to be found at the scene of a bloody crime.

He peered again through the windscreen. Matt recognised Tyler's features, despite the signs of carnage. But there was no trace of Jenny, unless she was tucked in the passenger foot well or laid out on the back seat, already drowned.

He turned on his heels. As far as anybody knew he'd never been at the cottage. Ever. Then his mind flashed back to the time he'd been abandoned in the flooded quarry, trapped inside a van with the filthy, cold water almost reaching up to his collar. He recalled the desperate need to remain still as the sound of groaning metal echoed his every movement. Precious seconds slipping away. The sense of helplessness that threatened to overwhelm him. Drowning on fear.

He picked up the spade and braced himself for the sudden shock of cold.

64

HE was out in the street waiting for me. A scrawny guy in a white hatch-back. I'd noticed the car as it sat in front of a red light next to some road works. He seemed in no rush to drive away, even though the motor was running. Then once I'd walked past, the engine went silent and someone called my name.

"Amy?"

I turned to face him. A stranger for a split second, then my heart missed a beat. This was the guy who'd barged into the Mither Tap before making off after the Polish girl. He had the same weasel features. The same ferret face. I picked up the pace as I crossed the grassed area. Brendan's flat was less than a hundred yards away. The driver called out again. Somehow he knew my name, but I wasn't in the mood to stop and exchange telephone numbers.

I dodged round the back of the maisonettes and slipped in through the unlatched fire door. The rear staircase was dark: a minefield, littered with kiddies' bikes of all shapes and sizes, and a shopping trolley with a wonky wheel. As I reached the first floor, I heard him on the stairs behind me. I turned and kicked out at anything within reach. A baby buggy clattered as it tumbled down the staircase. I made a grab for the handrail, continuing up the second flight, orientating myself towards the correct exit. A silent prayer of thanks when I saw the inside door had also been left unlocked.

One floor below, I heard another door slam open followed by a curse. Brendan's flat was within reach now. I had the keys in my left hand. I let the bundle of Sunday papers and supplements drop as I fumbled with the lock. The separate deadlock inside often proved difficult to open. Brendan had told me I could use that whenever he was away, if it made me feel safer. I'd never taken him up on the offer, but once I got inside the two would surely hold while I telephoned for help.

Then out of nowhere, another figure materialise right in front of me. He'd been waiting in the corridor all along. Close up, his heavy-set features looked familiar. This was someone else I'd seen recently. A face in one of the photographs taken at Caddy's burial. One of Jimmy Jump's so-called Klondykers - the one who survived.

I'd been shown mug shots of the Ukrainian brothers by the police following the incident with the minibus back in March. Damo and Barto Danilenko. Like a pair of evil bookends. Damo had escaped and fled the country. Surely this couldn't be the same, pock-marked monster who had attacked my friend and left her for dead. The psycho with a taste for head-butting had fled the country long ago, according to the police.

"Remember me, Amy?"

He knew my name.

I turned my back on him and slid the key into the lock. I felt it resist before clicking open. Weight on the door now, desperate to get inside. It held fast. Panic. Then my fingers twisted the door handle and I felt his hand on my shoulder as the door opened. Pressing down hard.

"I break your neck, simple as this. But if you have good sense you make no sound. We go inside, yah?"

65

I couldn't let this kind of shit happen to me again. I refused to allow the latest in a long line of fanatical nutcases to treat me like a perpetual victim; there to be used, abused, then spat out into the gutter like a piece of trash.

"Let me go," I shrieked as he pushed me into Brendan's cloak room.

He tightened his grip, bearing down with his entire weight, fingers grinding against the bones of my shoulder. Then he placed a forearm across my throat and yanked my head back.

"I say no noise."

There was no way he was coming inside the flat with me. I writhed and twisted, desperate to break his stranglehold. But he was strong. It felt like I was trying to fight my way through the entire wall of the building.

"Damo!" a voice called out.

The pressure slackened as my attacker gestured towards his partner to hurry. "Come hold the door."

I didn't think of the consequences. I lunged forward and reached for Brendan's weatherproof jacket. One minute the loop of his ice axe was in my hand. The next I swung it in a downward arc with all my force so the serrated blade of the pick struck the Ukrainian on the shin.

He yelled and instantly let go.

I turned to swing again. This time the blunt, flattened blade caught him on the side of the head. He spun away from me, one hand already reaching for the wound to stem the flow of blood. I shoved him into the corridor and slammed the door shut. Breath on hold, I fumbled both deadbolts in place, then sat with my back against the door. My heart was racing. Black dots like midges dancing before my eyes. Temples throbbing. Hands shaking.

Finally, I carried the ice axe into the living room and searched for the telephone. Brendan was still at Jan's. I'd not heard a word from him since the weekend. He wasn't due back here until next morning - the day he was scheduled to fly offshore again.

Speed-dial.

Three rings. Four. Five.

Christ. Pick up, for God's sake.

I heard fists pounding at the door.

Six. Seven.

I held the cordless handset against my ear and went back into the lobby, the axe raised above my head. If they somehow managed to get in, I'd not make it easy for them.

Eight. Nine. The big guy could probably tear the walls down if need be.

```
'The mobile phone you have called is
not available. Please hang up.'
```

Shit. Where the hell was Brendan?

My next option. The operator answered after two rings. Which service?

"Police."

I wanted to be put through to my local police station - the one round the corner that could send a squad car

265

within seconds and chase away the big, bad men.

No such luck.

"I'm being attacked in my uncle's flat."

Name - address - who is attacking you - are they in the flat with you.

"They're outside the door." It was hopeless. I swear I could hear the wood splintering as they continued to pound on the door. "Can you please send someone here now?" I said.

Maybe if I started screaming for help, they'd get off the phone and come round here instead of making polite conversation. But the girl on the other end of the telephone seemed in no particular rush.

She said five minutes. She said to get into a room as far away from the front door as possible and barricade myself inside. And, as an afterthought, she told me to remain calm.

I was way beyond calm.

I took my trusty ice axe with me and locked myself in the loo. I'd needed a pee as soon as I left the shops, but somehow that wasn't a priority anymore. Besides, there was no way I was going to be dropping my knickers right now with those two desperados on my tail.

Then the pounding stopped. The silence seemed to stretch - five minutes more like five hours. I heard movement close by. The thud of something falling, followed by heavy footsteps on the laminate floor of the kitchen. More than one guy, by the sound of it.

I clamped my fingers around the shaft of the axe and closed my eyes.

They were inside the flat.

"Amy!"

A familiar voice. Or was my brain playing tricks with me?

"Amy? Are you here?"

66

NO matter how much Matt tugged at the handle of the driver's door, it refused to budge. In the end he rammed the working end of the spade into the narrow gap between the hinges and the front panel and used all his weight to prise the door free of its frame. He pushed and pulled, forcing the spade further into the gap. There was resistance to begin with, then he heard the metal groan in protest. Water began to pour out of the vehicle through the space at the side of the door frame. He shoved his entire weight onto the spade's handle one more time and the door opened.

Most of Carl Tyler's face was a mass of bloody flesh and a haze of hungry insects hovered around his head. Somehow they had already found their way inside. Matt straddled Carl's body as he clambered across to the passenger seat. His hands touched something slumped low down in the passenger foot well. He felt a handful of hair in the water, tantalisingly out of reach. He slid his hands lower. Jenny's face seemed to be resting on her knees. He reached across and placed both hands under her arms then tried to pull her upright. But it was hopeless. The girl was a dead weight.

The more he tried to pull her upright, the more the vehicle shifted as its bulk settled deeper into the peat bed of the burn. Matt was conscious of time draining away.

He tried to reach further inside the foot well, grabbing for Jenny's water-sodden body like a drunkard requesting a dance. Her hands were shackled together. Cable-ties looped around her ankles as well.

"Hang on. I've nearly got you," he gasped.

Then Carl's body slid free of its moorings and Matt's head went under.

"Shit!"

Fighting hard to regain his breath. Vision blurring. Dread already a sour taste at the back of his throat as he felt how cold the girl's body was. Adrenalin turning his blood from liquid to fire, but all too late. This wasn't clammy cold from being immersed in water but deathly cold. He hauled himself out of the vehicle. There had been a knife. A kitchen knife buried under the clutter of dirty dishes.

Matt's head filled with images of Jenny's drowned body. The girl had been wearing a dressing gown. He'd felt the coarse towelling covering her shoulders as he reached for her arms. The flimsy nightshirt she wore underneath had clung against her breasts like a second skin. He'd felt her nipples like tiny pearls sewn into the fabric. Searching for something. A heartbeat. Lungs fighting for one last breath.

He emerged from the cottage once more; spade in one hand, knife in the other. The woman, dressed in long boots, white slacks and quilted body-warmer, barely seemed to acknowledge his agitated state. Instead she trained the rifle on him and he could detect the steel in her voice.

"What the hell are you doing on my property?"

67

AS we approached Ledmore Junction, Brendan pointed out an arrowhead of geese flying north over Canisp. Heading in the same direction as our car, maybe. A sign of an end to summer - nature following its own familiar course. There were times when returning home made sense, regardless of the hazards that might lie ahead.

I hadn't taken much persuading, even though the immediate crisis appeared to be over. Brendan was sure I'd over-reacted. The police could find no signs of forced entry other than fresh splatters of blood on the wall of the corridor. The two policemen had asked Brendan to produce some ID when he turned up, asking why they were knocking on his door. Then once inside, they checked with me that Brendan was indeed my uncle and not, in any shape or form, the person I'd reported as my alleged attacker fifteen minutes earlier.

"We'll keep a squad car scouting the neighbourhood for the next hour. And if you have any more concerns. . ."

I didn't.

"They obviously heard the sirens," Brendan said. "Thieving numpties. They've got a fucking nerve, trying to knock off my gear in broad daylight."

"They weren't trying to break in here to steal your stuff."

"The chances are that's exactly what they were up to."

"But they knew my name. They were waiting for me."

I mentioned the car at the lights - the scrawny guy from the Mither Tap behind the wheel - being followed up the fire escape stairwell - and one of Paver's Ukrainian associates already waiting for me outside the flat.

"You disturbed a pair of no-marks, that's all. They were only after one thing."

"Yeah. Me."

He stood and rested his hands on my shoulders. "For God's sake, Amy. Why would they be after you? You've had a nasty shock, that's all."

"It's Gordon Paver, all over again. He sent them after me."

"Don't be a nelly," Brendan said. "It'll be a couple of local druggies. And with the police on their trail, they'll no come back here in a hurry."

"But I recognised them. The guy in the car is involved with the Polish girls. You've seen the court case. And the one waiting for me out in the corridor worked at Strathbeg chalet park. He's one of the Ukrainians."

"You're no making much sense, lovey. What do you know about Polish girls?"

I followed him into the kitchen and told him about Ania and my feeble attempt to rescue her. I knew I'd brought this on myself, and the last thing I wanted to do was involve Uncle Brendan in all this crap. But I was losing the plot.

"Listen, Amy. I mind when my mother died. I'd keep seeing her face. In the back window of a bus. On the television news whenever there was a crowd. I even saw her behind the counter at Superdrug one time, but it was my mind playing tricks. There'll no be any Ukrainian gangsters in Aberdeen, I promise."

But I feared different. I could feel my entire body shaking with tension.

"I'd rather not stay here," I said.

"There's nothing stopping you moving into Jan's flat while I'm away. Let me make a phone call."

That would hardly make me feel safer. If Paver's men could find me at Brendan's, there was nothing to stop them finding me again. As far as I was concerned, Aberdeen had become another war zone.

"I don't know."

Maybe I could reschedule my flight to Amsterdam. But when Brendan came back into the kitchen, I could tell something had happened.

"I've been on the phone to your ma."

My blood turned to ice as I feared the worst.

"It's all over the village. There's been an accident at one of the holiday cottages. Two tourists drowned."

"Drowned?"

"Somewhere near Loch Assynt. There's police everywhere."

Shit.

"Why did you phone my mum?"

"I thought it best. We agreed I should get you home for the next week or two."

"You're sending me home," I said, deflated at having to give in so easily.

"I told her you were feeling a bit homesick and I thought it best you get away from Aberdeen. Let things quieten down here. Eh? What with the court case. It'll be in all the papers again."

"OK."

"I didn't mention anything to her about this morning," he continued. "But your ma agrees, a break away from here might do you good. Then once this business is over with, you're welcome back here again. You know that."

That would work. I'd done everything I could to help those poor Polish girls and it got me nowhere. If anything

I'd ended up stirring a hornet's nest or whatever that Swedish girl in the film had done.

"I'd better check what time the trains to Inverness leave in the morning."

"There's no need. I'm not back offshore until my next stint's due. There's holidays they owe me, and I've already spoken to Jan," he said.

"What about?"

"We can pack our bags tonight and I'll drive you to Lochinver first thing in the morning. I've booked a B and B for four nights but I can always stay longer. It'll be good to see the old place again."

I knew what he meant.

The highest tops of the Fannichs and Beinn Dearg held a grey scatter of wet snow or frost, but the sky above An Teallach blazed golden in the late afternoon sun.

"God. That's a wonderful sight."

"Yeah." I shielded my eyes as I gazed West.

"I might even do a little hill-walking if the weather stays like this."

We stopped at Ullapool for a bowl of soup at the Ceilidh Place then I plugged in my MP3 player and closed my eyes, zoning out with Adele until we reached Ledmore Junction. That was when Brendan pointed out the geese.

"They're the first ones I've seen this winter."

It wasn't strictly winter. Not yet. Everywhere about us, the heather and bracken had turned russet, and the air was so still it seemed the landscape was frozen in time. Waiting. I stared at the loch as we came closer to the ruins of Ardvreck Castle. So placid this afternoon. The water barely rippled against the shoreline.

"There's no signs left of what happened."

"You mean the landslide?" he said.

"It was here." I pointed to the freshly exposed rocks on the right side of the road.

"That's the way it goes. Bad things get forgotten and life returns to the way it should be. Will you try to see some of your old pals while you're home?" he asked.

I shook my head. "There's only Matt."

"Aye, well. You're better staying away from that wee shite."

"I know."

"That's where it must have happened," he said. Up ahead, two police cars were parked outside the gated entrance to Aubricia's Hanley's house. "And there's another two across the road." He pointed to a police Landrover and a van. Both sat on the gravel at the front of Croft House Cottage; Steff's little red Clio next to them.

"That's Mrs Hanley's holiday cottage." I said. "She usually has hunters staying there this time of year for the deer stalking."

"It must be where the two were drowned."

"Yeah."

If the drownings were a result of Matt's telephone call, the police were sure to figure things out sooner or later. Matt knew everything. He knew about the cheques. Once that came out, the police would be wanting to interview me all over again.

Christ.

I couldn't stomach the guilt of saying nothing with Paver's money sitting in my bank account. The right thing to do would be to give it back. But part of me felt I deserved it for what they'd put me through; Gordon Paver and his cronies.

68

MUM came out to the car to greet us. She looked tired. Drained of energy somehow.

"God, I've missed you so much," she said as she gave my shoulder a hug. "How's she been behaving?"

"Mum!"

"Ach, she's a wee treasure," Brendan said. "I didn't even know she was there, most of the time."

"Well, let's get you both inside. I've made us a bite to eat."

"You're not working?" I asked.

"Not tonight. No."

We ate at the dining table. And apart from a sarcastic comment about my new hairstyle, I got off lightly. Through most of the meal, Mum and Brendan talked about the old times. Holidays at Achmelvich camp site. Nights out at Aberdeen when Dad wasn't working. It was difficult to accept that Mum had had such a full life long before Leanne and I turned up.

Finally, Brendan made his excuses and left. "I'm only staying up the road, so I'll call round tomorrow afternoon."

"Fine. And I'm sorry we can't offer you more than a sofa to sleep on but you're welcome to come for your breakfast."

That wasn't strictly true. Mum and I had often doubled

up in my bed when Leanne and Steve came to stay, but I let it pass.

"It's already paid for. I'll be starting the day with a full Scottish. But we can go out for a meal one night, if you're both free."

I helped Mum clear away the dishes before retreating to my bedroom. Time to unpack and unwind. But less than fifteen minutes later I heard a tap on the door.

"Fancy a coffee?"

"Can do."

I wasn't in the mood for a catch-up, but I felt guilty staying away for so long. Mum deserved a little of my precious time.

"I've been speaking to Leanne," she said.

"Oh."

"She tells me you're planning on going away."

"I was, but that's on hold. I'd have talked with you about it anyway," I said. "It's something I'd been thinking about for ages."

"I'm only asking."

I sipped my coffee. Too hot as usual. "Did she tell you anything else?"

"About the money?"

Shit.

"I didn't know what you'd think - didn't want you finding out, 'cause I know how things would look."

"You mean between you and Mike Neilson."

"There's nothing going on. Never has been."

Another sip. I was praying Leanne hadn't mentioned the other cheque Mike had given me months earlier.

Our shared money. Our shared secret.

"So this is all above board?" she asked.

"I thought it was when I read his letter. He said it was a gift in return for standing by Matt. Visiting him when he had his breakdown and going all the way to Peterhead."

"Right."

"He knows what Matt's like, the way he uses people."

"I understand, Amy. I'm not having a go."

"But I should have realised there was more to it."

"How much was it for?" Mum asked.

"Enough for me to jump on a plane and fly anywhere in the world. He even told me I should make a fresh start."

"I don't understand."

"I didn't either. I thought he was trying to make up for all the shit that happened recently. But I'm thinking there's more to it, and maybe I should pay it back."

She nodded, as if she knew there was only bad news to follow.

"Go on."

"Mike was paying for me to keep my mouth shut. I think he passed on the money from someone else. Someone who wants me as far from here as possible."

"What are you talking about?"

"It was Paver. According to Matt, Mike Neilson's been handling Paver's accounts. Making sure the police can't trace any dodgy dealings back to him."

"And Matt's known this all along?" she said.

"God, no. It was me who found out the connection between Mike Neilson and Gordon Paver. I'd been doing some digging. There'd been sex parties at Strathbeg House, and Mike was there one night. One of the Polish girls identified him from a photograph."

"Polish girls?" Mum's eyes glazed over. "I thought that business was all over and done with, Amy. You can't possibly believe any of that's true. Not Caddy's father."

"I didn't want to believe it any more than you."

"Why would Gordon Paver be giving you money to leave the village when you're already in Aberdeen?"

I'd been wondering the same. Both cheques had arrived before I'd even spoken to Ania, so at first I hadn't been

276

able to figure out why he thought I was a threat. Then I remembered what Mike had said to Kay when he gave her a bundle of cash. "No one has to know." It wasn't compensation - it was hush money. Paver probably figured out what his son had told me, and he was terrified word would get out.

"Between them, they're buying my silence," I said. "Peter told me a lot of stuff the police don't know. Gordon could be the one who put the idea in Peter's head to wipe the village off the map in the first place. His house is still up for sale, so he's obviously had enough of Lochinver."

"So where does that leave you?" she asked. "About the money, I mean."

"It can sit in the bank for now. That's the best place for it until the police get involved, because they'll be round here asking questions again sooner or later."

Or I could have a wee chat with our local bobby, Greg Farrell. Put him in the picture and let events unfold. But then I'd have to give the money back, including the five thousand I'd loaned Leanne. And if Mike Neilson ended up in prison because of my big mouth, Matt would never speak to me again.

69

MATT knew the score. The last time he'd been interviewed under caution, his solicitor told him to let the police ask their questions but offer nothing in response.

"Don't incriminate yourself."

'No comment' was the safest option since he'd be more inclined to drop his guard once any conversation kicked off. He'd be more likely to stumble when elaborating on any of his replies; more likely to fill in the scripted silences with denials and excuses until every sentence made him sound guilty.

But the two detectives didn't look too bothered. They'd seen it all before.

Matt wiped the sleep from his eyes. No doubt they had deliberately chosen to interview him when he'd be least resistant to their badgering - that bewildering hour of night when normal people were heading for their beds or already deep in slumber. He'd been at Dingwall for God knows how long. First in a holding cell while they took away his wet clothes and his mobile phone. Now in Interview Room No. 3. He felt cold to his bones, more from fatigue than anything. The overhead lighting and stale smell of cold coffee did little to make him feel more alert.

The two detectives on the opposite side of the table appeared to be as weary of the entire exercise. "You can

278

earn yourself a taxi ride home once you tell us what you were doing at Croft House Cottage yesterday morning."

"No comment."

"Let me put our cards on the table, Matt. You turned up at the crime scene with the murder weapon in your hand and the victim's blood on your clothing. It doesn't look good."

Silence.

"But we don't believe you killed the two people found in the car. You'd hardly be returning hours later to pull them out of the wreckage if that was the case."

Silence.

"But you knew Jenny Maclean, right? Because we have it on record you and Rick Tyler were good friends. We also know you stayed over in their flat a couple of nights when Rick was on the run."

Rick had never been on the run and the police knew that.

"No comment."

"It's on record you met up with Carl Tyler on more than one occasion."

What fucking record?

"The most recent being. . ." The detective shuffled the papers laid out in front of him, but Matt realised it was a cheap ploy to make him think they had a sizable dossier on him. "Tuesday the 16th of September. You met up at the Caley Hotel."

"If you already know all this shit why do you need me to confirm it?" Finally a chink in Matt's armour. The detective conducting the interview raised his head and stared into Matt's face, urging him to go on. But Matt sucked in the temptation to keep talking.

"We also have your mobile phone, Matt. A silver Blackberry Curve, model 9360. Can you confirm that you're the only person with access to make calls on this phone?"

"No comment."

"We've checked the records with your service provider. Jenny rang you shortly after she and Carl arrived back in the UK. You also made a number of calls to her number, but they were all of a short duration so I'm assuming you were unable to get through."

No question so no comment necessary.

"Moving forward a day or two, you made a call late on Saturday the 4th of October. The call was made to a land line registered as the home number of Cyrus O'Connor. Can you recall the night in question?"

Shit.

"No comment."

"We're well-acquainted with Mr O'Connor, Matt. In fact, our colleagues from Ullapool station have a warrant out for his arrest. Two of his associates are already in custody on suspicion of causing the deaths of Miss Maclean and Mr Tyler. I don't suppose you'd know anything about Mr O'Connor's line of business."

"He's a fisherman."

Silence dragging out again.

"He's got a boat, that's all I know," Matt added before clamming up again.

"That's correct. And we also have Mr O'Connor down as the registered keeper of a white 54-plate Peugeot van. Weren't you involved in an incident out at Ledmore a couple of months back?"

"No comment."

The other officer pulled out a printed page from the documents on the table and showed his colleague one of the items listed.

"Going back to the morning you were discovered outside Croft House Cottage, Matt. You'd been quite chatty the previous night. Isn't that so?"

280

"No comment."

"You made a call to Cyrus O'Connor at. . . 23:17. Then two and a half hours later, at 01:58 to be precise, you made a call to an Aberdeen number. Would you care to tell us who you rang at such an unsociable hour?"

"No comment."

"Let me jog your memory." He scanned the papers again. "According to our records, the number you called is listed under the name Brendan Michael Metcalf. Mr Metcalf is an uncle to Amy Metcalf. And you and Amy Metcalf go back a long way, Matt. Am I correct?"

"No comment."

"So we're left wondering why. What was so pressing a matter that you had to telephone the poor girl at two o'clock in the morning?"

"No comment."

"Then, of course, there's the alleged attack that took place at that same address less than nine hours later," the detective continued.

"An attack at Amy's flat?"

The detective ignored Matt's question. "Officers were called to an attempted break-in at 11:37 at an address in Wingate Place. One of the occupants, a female who identified herself as Amy Metcalf, reported being challenged by two men. Miss Metcalf managed to break free from one of her assailants who tried to gain access to the flat. When the police arrived, the two men had left the building. Ring any bells?"

"No comment."

"As you wish. But I'm wondering why you're being so uncooperative, Matt. If this business with Tyler and O'Connor has led to Amy's well-being being threatened, you need to consider who your silence is protecting. When the officers returned to the flat last night, at our request, there was no one home. And we're being told

281

that Mr Metcalf was due to rejoin his place of work on an oil platform in the North Sea today. But instead he's taken an unscheduled holiday at extremely short notice."

The urge to repeat the no comment mantra suddenly transformed to surrender. "I don't know anything about any of that. And it's got nothing to do with Carl and Jenny."

"So why did you phone Miss Metcalf?"

Matt stared at the surface of the table, desperate to control his breathing. "It was late. I'd had a few pints. I needed someone to talk to. Somebody I could trust."

"And that's the only reason you called Amy."

"Yeah."

"So what about the call to Cyrus O'Connor?"

Matt shook his head as if trying to dislodge an unpleasant image from his brain. "Wrong number. I've got his number on my contact list from when I used to do odd jobs for him. And it was nothing shady, before you ask."

"So you didn't actually speak with Mr O'Connor."

"No."

"Even though the call lasted one minute and seventeen seconds, according to your telephone records."

"No comment."

Technically speaking, Matt hadn't spoken to Slippy. Cindy's mother had answered the phone and Matt kept the message brief and to the point.

"That's fine. We're going to keep you here as an accessory to both crimes until our investigations prove otherwise. And for the record, a string of 'no comments' never looks good when we read your testimony out in court."

There it was. The threat of prison. Matt wasn't sure he could handle another spell inside, regardless of how well he'd coped at Peterhead.

"It's not what it looks like."

The officer straightened the documents and slid them into a manila folder. "It never is, Matt. But you're not giving us much room for manouevre. You're involved, somewhere along the line, and that's all that matters for now."

"I know."

"Forget about saving O'Connor's skin. Think of your friends and your family."

"That's what I'm trying to do here. My dad and Steff. Their life's not going to be worth living if it all comes out."

"Go on. We're listening."

70

GREG Farrell looked like he'd not slept for the last twenty-four hours. His eyes bloodshot, his face unshaven, and his uniform more creased than normal.

"Can I have a word, if you're not too busy?"

"It's been a long night, but come in. Take a seat."

I watched as he rearranged his paunch and removed an unopened packet of chocolate digestives from his in-tray and stored it inside one of the desk drawers. "You've been away, I hear."

"Yeah - at my uncle's in Aberdeen."

I let my gaze wander to the dog-eared posters on the office wall. A yellowing copy of an 'In the Event of an Accident' check card for hill walkers. A flyer for victims of domestic abuse along with a list of telephone numbers. Advertisements for Al-Anon and a helpline supporting Scottish families affected by alcohol and drugs. Hardly the glamorous crime-fighting job portrayed on TV but I felt safe in Farrell's company. He'd been the village bobby for as long as I could remember. He'd taken us through our cycling proficiency test at primary school. Dressed up as Santa for the Christmas Fare. Given us a friendly warning if ever a party got a little too rowdy.

"And how are things now? You're keeping well in yourself?"

I brushed away a stray hair. "I'm fine. It's taken a while

'cause there's always something that manages to bring it all back."

He raised his eyebrows. "You mean the business with Peter?"

"That's why I wanted to talk to you. You were here right at the start - when Caddy was killed and Kay Jepson was attacked. You know the whole story."

Farrell nodded. "Of course. I know what you've been through."

"That's why I wanted to talk to you," I repeated.

"So there's something still troubling you."

I didn't know where to start. Could I convince him I'd found one of the Polish girls who had been trafficked through here more than twelve months ago? Could I bring up the business of the cheques without incriminating Mike Neilson? Could I mention Gordon Paver's name without coming across as some obsessive, revenge-seeking freak?

"I heard about those two people who drowned yesterday morning."

He picked up a pen and began to tap it against the table top. "That's not something I can discuss with you right now, Amy. Not while there's an on-going investigation. The police are continuing their inquiries in connection with a related incident. Everything will come out in due time."

"OK. I was wondering what happened, that's all. Someone said it was Carl Tyler and Jenny Maclean that died."

"Listen," he said. "I know there's been history between your friend Caddy and Tyler's brother. But I still can't. . ."

I let out a gasp. "If it is Carl Tyler and Jenny Maclean, then there's something you should know. Something Matt Neilson told me in confidence. . ."

He cut me off mid-flow. "You're best speaking to the

285

SCD at Dingwall in that case. Let me give them a call."

He reached for his radio.

"There's no need." I pushed my chair back and got to my feet. "I've already been given the third degree by Mr Galleymore. He said he'd need to see me again, but I've not heard anything. I'd rather not stir things up."

It was hopeless.

"Listen, Amy. If you have information relevant to the case, I'd remind you it's your duty to tell the police. Withholding evidence is a serious offence."

"For God's sake, that's why I'm here. I thought it would be easier if I spoke to you face to face. Someone who knows what happened here without me having to go through the whole story again with a bunch of strangers."

He retrieved a pad from beneath a pile of papers. "Five minutes."

I sat down again and tried to compose myself while he scribbled something at the top of the blank pad.

"I'll take notes as you go through it all. Then we'll decide whether you need make an official statement or not. But I can't promise not to involve Dingwall once I've heard what you've got to say."

"I realise that."

"And take your time. Just tell me everything you know."

Where to begin?

71

"**I** was raped."

There it was. The sentence I hoped I'd never need to speak out loud. The word itself another punch in the guts as overpowering as *gwalt* - the Polish word for rape.

I'd lied to myself for such a long time that the truth didn't seem real any more. But it was clear Farrell believed me - leaning forward in his chair but saying nothing, as if waiting for me to elaborate. Presumably, he'd seen Matt's version of events in the Mail on Sunday.

"It was back in June." It felt as if a lump hammer was lodged in my throat, but at least I'd got Farrell's full attention. "Peter Paver and his pal raped me the night before he went on the rampage. I didn't report it because there was too much other stuff going on. It would have looked like I was trying to draw attention to myself; trying to get everyone to sympathise with me."

I sneaked a tissue out of my jacket pocket and blew my nose, then took the time to squeeze it up into a tight ball once I'd finished.

"Let me." He reached for the tissue and tossed it into the wastepaper basket next to his desk. "You're saying they both raped you."

At least he hadn't put his pen down and offered me a glass of water or a counselling session with a female police officer.

"Yeah."

"And the police investigating the aftermath were never told any of this?"

"It never seemed the right time, going back over everything. And once the interviewing officers found out we'd been having sex in Kay's flat they made their own minds up. Drugs, alcohol, sex. It was obvious I'd been up for it."

"That's not true, Amy."

"Whatever. I'd come to terms with how close I'd been to getting myself killed. My body hurt all over. All that fuss, getting me to hospital in the helicopter, then my sister and my mum turning up, wanting me to offload. I'd already locked the darkest stuff away in the back of my mind. I knew if I kept blanking everything out then it would be like it never even happened."

He stopped writing. "But now you're ready to make an official complaint."

"Not exactly," I tried to mask the revulsion I still felt for Paver and his soldier pal. "There's nothing the police or anyone else can do about Peter now, is there? I'm trying to establish where I'm coming from. Everybody thinks I'm still obsessed with his father. My mum. Matt Neilson. They've got no idea."

"So tell me more about Peter."

I took a deep breath. "You know what he did. Him and that Robbo. Well they got me drunk and gave me drugs. They were in party mode and it was obvious they were after a foursome with me and Kay."

"This was the night before Peter was killed."

"Yeah," I said.

"June 26th."

I couldn't focus on numbers and dates right now. I needed something to calm my nerves, but a spliff was out of the question.

"If you say so."

"Go on."

"Kay was already out of it when I got there." I let my eyes close and took in a deep breath. "Peter had stripped off her clothes and I could see what was coming next. She looked so helpless. I asked him to stop. I couldn't let Kay get hurt again. Not like that. So when he refused to leave her be, I offered to take Kay's place. I thought it would be over and done with in five or ten minutes. But it was nothing like that. They made me get undressed then took turns. I lost count."

I could hear my voice cracking. More deep breaths.

"You're doing fine, Amy. Take your time."

I wiped my nose again. "I could see it was getting light outside. My head was buzzing and I was sore down there. Things went quiet and they let me clean myself up. Then, as we were leaving Kay's flat, or maybe in the truck after we left, Peter began telling me stuff. Gloating, he was. How he'd got his dad's two Ukrainian buddies to attack Kay because she'd stolen the missing drugs. Said it was his business to put her straight. To break her."

"He was talking about the attack on Kay Jepson?"

"Yeah," I said. "Damo recorded everything they did to her on his mobile."

I let him absorb this information.

"Once Paver started he couldn't stop himself. Bragging how he was there on the bus when Caddy was killed. They originally thought she was the one who'd taken Rick's stash."

"Go on."

"Rick's money was missing as well as his drugs," I continued. "Money he owed the two Ukrainians. Money they were collecting on behalf of Slippy. You know Slippy, right?"

He nodded.

289

"The drugs were Peter's side of the operation. He told me he controlled the gear coming into the Lochinver area and his dad ran the human trafficking side."

"But there's no proof that will stand up in court, Amy. Whatever Peter told you is hearsay. Even if he'd survived, Peter wouldn't be the most reliable of witnesses, given his state of mind."

"I knew you'd say that." I tried to stifle a laugh. "But I've found someone else who was involved. One of the Polish girls."

"How do you mean 'involved'?"

"They came over on Paver's boat and were kept prisoner in the chalet park. Then the night before they were shipped to Aberdeen, she was taken to a party in Strathbeg House with the other girls. Gordon Paver and all his friends were there."

"She told you Gordon was there?"

"I showed her some photos taken at Caddy's funeral."

Farrell put down his pen and pulled the sleeves of his jacket down over both wrists. "You're not making a lot of sense now. Where can we find this girl?"

I took out the €5 banknote. "Her name's Ania. Read what she wrote."

He took it and glanced at the writing on both sides.

"Caddy found this in one of the bunkhouses at Strathbeg. It proves Ania was there and that she's telling the truth. Gordon Paver has always been involved with the Aberdeen side of the operation but the police let him get away with it."

Farrell handed back the banknote. "You've already shown this to the SCD - am I right?"

"Yeah."

"And they explained why it's not admissible as evidence."

"But they're wrong," I said.

"Caddy's not here, Amy. She can't corroborate where it was found. And this writing."

"It's Polish. . ."

"I realise that. But anyone could have written on this banknote long before Caddy found it at the chalet park."

"But Ania says. . ."

"There are no buts, Amy. The police found no evidence to tie Gordon Paver to any of these crimes."

"I know," I said. "But Ania's definitely the one who wrote it. She told me, and she left another note inside one of the cushion covers on Gordon Paver's sofa."

"And you believe her? This mystery girl that you suddenly found, God knows where."

"I know it sounds a bit far-fetched."

"Listen, Amy." He puffed out his cheeks before continuing. "Don't you think the police went over every inch of Strathbeg House when they arrested Mr Paver back in March? They conducted a second search after they discovered Peter had been staying there while his father was away and still found nothing incriminating."

Jan had told me pretty much the same thing when we'd been chatting about her course, weeks before. Forensics don't miss a trick. They'd even search a haystack for a single eyelash if they thought it might lead to a conviction.

"It was a scrunched up note." I put on my best pleading look. "Maybe they didn't realise. . ."

"They log everything and there was never any mention of a note. Are you sure this girl, Ania, is prepared to back up your story?"

"I don't know," I said. "She doesn't want to get involved."

He shook his head. "You should let this go, Amy. It's for your own good. The SCD found nothing to tie Gordon Paver to any of the goings on in Aberdeen. Apart from the Polish girls in the minibus, there was no trace of anyone being shipped through Lochinver. The operation appears to have been centred on Rosehall, and John Fleming and Stuart Coleman have already admitted to various offences. As far as the Crown Office are concerned it's case closed."

"Christ, you've no idea have you? Gordon Paver even filmed the goings on at Strathbeg House."

"Is that what this girl told you?"

"No. But you should speak to Mr Fleming and Mr Coleman again. Tell them what I've told you. You could get the prosecutors to make a deal and get them to tell you what Gordon Paver was up to."

"That's enough. You've been watching too many crime shows."

Shit. This was hopeless.

"What about Mike Neilson? Did anybody ever take him in for questioning? These drownings are connected to everything that went on here last year, long before Caddy was murdered."

Farrell looked me in the eye. "I can't spare you any more time, I'm sorry."

"So you don't believe me?" I said.

"Leave it with me for now. There's been another incident out near the harbour earlier today. Maybe something will come of that, but I can't say any more until we check further."

"What kind of incident?"

"I can't say, but I'd appreciate it if you stopped this vendetta of yours against Gordon Paver. I'm sorry you were attacked. It's not something you should have to deal with alone." He rummaged in his drawer and pulled out a faded leaflet headlined Rape Crisis Scotland. "If you don't want to make a formal complaint, I can still put you in touch with someone who'll offer professional support.

292

They're very good."

"I'm sure they are but I don't want to be treated like a victim. I'm trying to set the record straight about Gordon Paver, that's all."

"As you wish. I'm always here if you need to talk some more."

Yeah - whatever.

72

STEFF arrived to pick up Matt from the police station shortly after eight o'clock Tuesday morning, five hours after the police had terminated his interrogation and told him he was free to leave.

"God, you took your time," he said.

"Get in the car, Matt."

""I've been sitting in reception since half three. I'm freezing cold and I can't wait to get out of these clothes and grab a shower, but I'd kill for a decent cup of coffee." Matt leant back against the headrest.

"We'll need to run into Inverness first."

"What the hell for?"

Then Matt noticed the sickly pallor to Steff's skin. She kept staring into the rear-view mirror, screwing up both eyes whenever she blinked.

"It's your dad. Let me find somewhere to park. I'll try Lidl. I seem to remember there's a tea room down the next street."

"Dad?" It was unlikely the police had discovered the connection between Mike Neilson and Gordon Paver based on what he'd told them about Carl Tyler's attempts to blackmail Slippy. These things took time.

"He's in Raigmore hospital. He's alright, but they're keeping him in while they conduct more tests."

"Raigmore? Christ. What happened?"

"I'll tell you all about it once we have a hot drink and something to eat. I've been up since two o'clock this morning waiting for a telephone call. My nerves are in shreds."

The tea room was quiet. An elderly couple sat at one table sharing a pot of tea and a plate of scones and a young boy in school uniform slurped from a can of Coke while a woman in a hijab chatted with one of the counter staff.

Matt selected a table as far away from the action as possible while Steff ordered two coffees and a bacon sandwich. He got up to carry the tray to their table when he saw how frail she looked.

"Aren't you having anything?"

"This will do." Matt noticed the tremor as she raised the mug to her lips.

"So what's been going on with Dad?"

"Oh, God. Matt."

She burst into tears and reluctantly he took her hand. "Come on. I mean, you said he's going to be alright. Was it a heart attack?"

Steff dabbed at her eyes. "It's nothing like that. I got a telephone call at twenty past one this morning. Someone working at the harbour had found Mike sitting in his car next to the breakwater. The engine was running but there were no lights. That's why they went to look."

"Just sitting in the car?" Matt asked.

"He'd locked the doors. There was a hose pipe."

"Fuck."

"They're saying if they hadn't found him when they did - it doesn't bear thinking about."

"God." Matt shivered involuntarily and decided he could have done with something stronger than coffee.

"By the time the ambulance crew arrived, they'd managed to get Mike out of the car. They had to force open one of the doors."

Visions of Carl Tyler's vehicle.

"But they got him out so he'll be OK. Right?" Matt said.

"It's a miracle someone found him when they did."

"So, any idea why?"

Steff shook her head and wrapped the fingers of both hands around her mug. "There was an empty whisky bottle on the passenger seat. The paramedics couldn't wake him. They thought he might have taken something else as well. Tablets. But when they got him wired up in the back of the ambulance his pulse was OK and they got his breathing under control before they took him to Inverness."

"So who phoned you?"

"Greg Farrell. He said he had distressing news and the first thing I thought of was you." She began to weep again. "I thought he was going to tell me they'd charged you with something."

Matt drained his cup and began to roll the empty sugar sachet into a paper tube. "I told you, they've released me without charge. And if anybody asks, I was helping with their inquiries. Isn't that what the desk sergeant at Dingwall told you Sunday afternoon?"

"Yes. But your dad and I were thinking all sorts. It took so long."

"Yeah, well. I was first on the scene so they wanted to know all the ins and outs."

Steff rubbed her eyes as if trying to reassemble events in her head. "Mrs Hanley rang before I went to church. She's on the Ladies' Lifeboat Guild. We didn't know what to think."

"I was there when she rang the emergency services," Matt said. "We went across the road to her house and she let me dry myself in the kitchen before the cops turned up."

"I can't stop thinking about those poor people."

"I know."

"What were you doing there, Matt?"

"It's complicated. Jenny asked me to call round if ever I was passing. So, anyway. What's the score with Dad?"

"He'd been in a state all day Sunday."

"Because of me, you mean?"

"No," she said. "Somebody phoned him late Saturday night, before you got in. I think that shook him up, but he said nothing when he came to bed. Then he got another call next morning, and when I got in from church the car was gone."

"He left no note or anything."

"Nothing. I tried ringing but he must have switched his phone off."

"Weird."

"When Greg Farrell phoned I was expecting the worst news possible - that I'd lost you again."

"Don't be daft."

"He said I wasn't to worry. There'd been some kind of accident but Mike was fine."

"And Dad hasn't told anyone why he might have done it?"

Steff shook her head. "I didn't ask Greg, but I'm dreading what your dad's going to say when we walk in. I keep thinking I deserve an explanation, but if things are so bad that he tried to kill himself, I'm not sure I want to know."

Matt didn't need his dad to explain anything. He'd already worked that out for himself. The sooner the better they got home. Life was about to get very messy. Time to get cleaned up then get obliterated.

73

MATT made eye contact as soon as we walked into the Stag's Head.

I'd already heard the rumours - Mike Neilson passed out drunk in his car close to the breakwater, according to the story doing the rounds. Matt looked like he was on a similar mission. The way he propped himself against the bar then turned unsteadily to leer in our direction suggested he'd exceeded his quota for the week.

"Ames, Ames, Ames. Long time no see."

He got off his bar stool and wrapped an arm around my waist but I shrugged myself free and turned my attention to the menu board.

"Who's the ned?" Brendan asked.

I shook my head.

"That's Matthew," Mum replied on my behalf. "Matthew Neilson."

Matt raised his beer glass in a mock salute.

"So he's the one who's been giving you grief." Brendan turned to face Matt head-on, eyes hooded and his forehead looking as if it was about to explode.

"Leave it," I said. "We've come out for a nice meal. Don't let him spoil it."

"Oh, he'll no be spoiling anything on my watch," Brendan continued.

"You got a problem, Pops?" Matt said as he planted his

glass back on the bar and jutted his chin in Brendan's direction.

"I'm no your pop, Sonny Jim."

"Please, Brendan. Not here," Mum said.

I stepped in between the two rutting stags. "Matt, you're pissed. Do yourself a favour and go home."

He laughed. "What the fuck am I supposed to do there? Play happy families?"

"Whatever you want. Just stop being an arse," I said.

Mum guided me and Brendan into the restaurant area. We sat beside one of the large windows while someone brought our cutlery and serviettes and we watched a series of squalls head inland.

"Matt's always been an attention-seeker," I said. "It's better if you ignore him."

"Exactly. Matt and his dad never got on," Mum explained. "They're both as stubborn as mules."

"Aye. Mr Neilson and I had words," Brendan said. "He knows fine well what I think of his blessed son."

"It's Steff I feel sorry for," she continued. "They're both as bad as each other."

A sudden shower of hail battered the window panes and outside, in the beer garden, one of the habitual smokers turned up his collar and took a final drag at his cigarette before coming back into the pub.

"So are you still driving back to Aberdeen tomorrow morning?" Mum asked. "It's promised a hard frost tonight."

"Not sure. Me and Jan had a chat last night. I'm not due back on the rig until the 4th of November and she's away next weekend on a team-building exercise or some such nonsense. She said I should stay a wee bit longer and try a bit of hill-walking. All my gear's in the boot."

"That'd be great," I said. "Can I come as well?"

"Of course. It'll do us both good to blow away these

Aberdeen cobwebs."

"We could go Thursday. Make an early start."

"Any preference where?" he said.

I stared out to sea. There were so many amazing walks to choose from, but the days were growing shorter and the cold snap was forecast to bite hard over the next few days. "Quinag's my favourite. I love the walk across the slabs up onto Spidean Coinich then the narrow ridge down into the col."

The last time I'd followed that route had been with Matt. Sunburn in February, I'd told anyone who'd listen.

"Aye. But you'll need to carry an axe on the ridge this time of year."

"We could do Glas Bheinn," I said. "You can park close to the loch. Or there's the waterfall. Have you ever been there?"

"You mean the Chual Aluinn?"

"Yeah," I said. "There's not much of a path but you come out right at the top where the river drops over the edge and there's a fantastic view down into the glen. It's awesome."

That seemed like a plan. We ate our supper then after a few glasses of wine I let Brendan and Mum reminisce some more while I retreated to the bar to get the craic with Sara before she finished her shift.

"Did you see Matt? Pissed or what?"

"He'd been well on the way since we opened at two. Trouble at home, so he reckoned."

"Tosser," I said.

"You heard about his dad?"

"You mean falling asleep, drunk in his car?"

"They're saying he was trying to top himself," she said. "There was a pipe from the exhaust into the back of the car."

"No way!"

"That's why Matt's drowning his sorrows. He asked if he could come back to mine when I'm done. As if I'd let him through the door."

"You said no."

"My dad would have a fucking fit."

"So what time did he leave?" I asked.

She checked the clock on the wall. "About an hour ago. I refused to serve him. Told him he'd already had enough and I was giving him no more to drink, so he said something about going to the Caley. Said he'd be given a warmer welcome there."

"Shit." I felt my mobile vibrate inside my clutch bag. I pulled it out and Matt's number came up on the screen. "That's him now."

"Are you going to answer it?"

"Don't know." I stared at the phone again then pressed the green button. "Hello."

"Ames. I'm lost. Can you come and find me?"

I rolled my eyes and held the phone closer to my ear. "Where are you? I thought you were off to the Caley."

"I got waylaid." He gave a loud belch and I could hear the sound of raised voices and the thud-thud of music in the background. "I'm with Bob. Bob and Bob."

Fuck.

"You should go home. I'll speak to you in the morning once you've sobered up."

"No speak. I need to see you. My life's a fucking mess and I don't know what to do."

"It's always been a mess, Matt. I've heard about your dad. It's awful." The music got louder and I began to shout down the phone. "Steff needs you at home with her. I'll call and see you tomorrow."

"No. No. Steff doesn't want you there. You have to keep away, promise me."

I turned my attention to Sara and mouthed the words

301

'still pissed'.

"She found out you'd been sniffing around," he continued. "Stirring things up after the police had drawn a blank."

"Did you tell her?"

"No. Dad's confessed all," he said.

"Christ. So what does Steff say?"

"She's going to stick by him. She says it doesn't matter what he's done, as long as he comes clean to the police and admits he's done wrong."

"Shit she must love him."

"Him, the car, the house and the lifestyle. Just so you know, she always thought there had been something going on between you and Mike. As far as she's concerned, this is all your fault. And she went into meltdown when she found out I'm the one who dropped Dad in it with the police."

This was Matt all over.

"You went to the police after promising me you'd wait until we'd talked it through? Christ, you really are a piece of work."

"I didn't have a choice, Ames. You heard about Carl and Jenny? Well I was the one who found them. I ended up getting threatened. The cops were going to charge me with being an accessory before the fact, or whatever, unless I told them everything. It was that or prison."

"Didn't you explain this to Steff?"

"No, 'cause this whole mess is all our fault. Right? Yours and mine."

I let his drunken accusation sink in.

"It's too late to keep a lid on things so we need to talk. I didn't mention the money, not to the police or to Steff, so keep your knickers on. But we need to decide what we're going to do with it. It's still our secret, right?"

Our money. Our secret. Right.

74

CLACHAN, hidden away behind Jimmy Jump's former home at Luibeg, had been in darkness when Damo arrived. The rooms echoed empty when he opened the door, and boxes were stacked in the hallway and the main living area. The air was cold inside. No heat. No sound. No signs of recent activity.

'The armpit of Hell' he'd called the wetlands of Brackloch when Paver first showed the Danilenko brothers the cottage. And those first impressions hadn't changed during the two and a half years they spent in Lochinver. First working at one of the local fish farms out at Ardvar - both looking for something to occupy their time between dealing drugs and acting as Gordon Paver's enforcers out at Rosehall. Then as part-time couriers - delivering drugs and girls between Lochinver and the East coast or shunting the night shift crew from one of Paver's bunkhouses to the harbour.

Damo's younger brother, Barto, had always enjoyed a fight. But Paver's cash was the only reason they'd stuck it so long away from home. They earned more in a month at Strathbeg than in a year slaving away in Ukraine.

Then everything changed, following the night of the accident. Damo got away and had sworn to turn his back on the cursed place for good, regardless of Paver's promises. But now he was back to hunt down the girl with the red hair and to draw a line under his Scottish adventures for good. Gordon Paver's telephone call had been enough to spur him into action.

"You'll be glad to hear that little bitch who cracked your shins last Sunday is back home with Mama."

"That little cunt. Before your man shouts to me I already have her in my hands."

"Let's make sure we get her this time."

"So if I do this job, I do it alone," he said. "No more Alex or Jonno."

"Forget Aberdeen and get yourself over here," Gordon said. "It's turning into a shit-fest at this end. Slippy's taken off with the wife and kid like rats leaving a sinking ship."

"I meet you at the chalet park?"

"Christ, no. The local policeman has already been sniffing around, according to one of the nosy neighbours."

"So I come to the safe house in that case."

"I'll not be there, but yes. Leave your vehicle at the end of the road. The keys are under the loose slate above the porch. There's a guy from Inverness picking up all the packing cases at the end of the week. The papers for the cottage and the chalet park are already with my solicitor awaiting signatures. Then, after I tie up a few loose ends in Aberdeen, it's St Croix. Time to work on my golf."

"You have Neilson handling the sales?"

"The paperwork's completed for both properties," Paver said. "But Neilson's in hospital last I heard."

"And you have left the Remington?"

"It's behind a loose panel inside one of the wardrobes in the main bedroom."

"Ammunition?"

"There's two boxes of point-243 AccuTips," Paver replied. "That should be more than enough for you."

"What about the pretty boy, Neilson's son? Are you sure his father's not going to suspect something when I kill him and his girlfriend?"

"Neilson has plenty of reasons to keep his mouth shut. Girls as young as fourteen. His own daughter, drugged and blindfolded, giving blow jobs to her father's pals. He'll not want anyone finding my home-movie collection."

"Matt is also now in Lochinver?" Damo said.

"Yes. Make sure you shoot to kill. And once you get rid of young Matthew, I'm giving you carte blanche to do whatever you want with his little fuck buddy."

Sweet words. Damo had been watching as Amy left one of the local pubs and made her way along the sea front. This would be a good time to take her. But there were too many cars about. Too many prying eyes. He would wait.

He rubbed a leather-gloved hand against the back of his skull. The damage was superficial, and the pain was almost worth the pleasure he'd take in smashing the girl's cheekbones and eye sockets into a bloody pulp once he got his hands on her. Then he'd strip her naked and screw her until she screamed for mercy. But there would be no mercy, and he would keep screwing her until one of them stopped breathing.

75

AN uncanny silence woke me shortly after 07:00. No passing traffic along Kirk Road. No clatter of forklift trucks working the harbour across the bay directly opposite our house, or the shrill sounds of the village waking to a new day. I raised myself onto my pillow and stretched an arm to pull back the blinds. The window was sheened with condensation but I could sense the brightness outside. There was a tang to the air. The first snow of winter.

I crawled back under the duvet and folded my knees until I was jig-sawed against Matt's body, my front to his back. He was toasty warm and smelt of sweat. Not an unpleasant smell. I let the fingers of one hand stroke his head. His hair had grown back since his scalping in prison, but he still kept it short. His vest had ridden up above the waist-band of his boxers and I lowered the other hand deep under the bedding and let it trace the dip of his waist. Skin there as soft as a girl's. I dived deeper, stroking the fine hair on his belly. I could feel he was hard again and I held him there for a while. Not moving. Barely squeezing. The heat from his core went right through me. He didn't stir.

Mum slammed the front door as she left for work, an hour or so later, and I got up for a pee. She hadn't heard us come in, thank God. I wouldn't have been able to

306

explain what made me rescue Matt from the clutches of a potentially disastrous hangover in the early hours. He'd been way past drunk when I found him at the Two Bobs' flat sharing a spliff the size of a cigar with a collection of local degenerates.

"Ames, take a puff."

"No, Matt. We need to leave," I said.

"No. No. Don't be a party popper."

"You mean party pooper, and I'm not in the mood to party. You phoned me to come and find you. Don't you remember?"

I smuggled him into my bedroom and helped him undress for bed. Wrestling a live octopus might have been easier, but finally he lay on his stomach right next to me and fell asleep. That's when it all came back to me - the feelings I'd had for him since the first and only time we slept together and actually had sex.

God. How can you love and hate someone with such passion?

After my pee, I took off my nightshirt and climbed back between the sheets. I deserved a duvet day, and the thought of sharing it with a real, live body was too tempting to forego. Matt turned to face me and I slid lower into the bed so my head was under his chin and my breasts lay flattened against his ribcage. I could feel his heart beating. His lungs expanded and deflated with each breath.

When he finally woke and discovered a naked girl curled up next to him, I turned onto my side and crossed my arms against my chest. I was determined not to let him take advantage of the situation. This was meant to be Amy Time.

"Wow," he said.

I slapped his hand away from my belly.

"Are you sure you haven't told the police anything

307

about the cheques?" I said.

"Good morning to you, too."

"Matt, this is serious."

"Swear to God, I haven't."

He rolled onto his back and began to stroke the tops of my thighs.

"Leave it, Matt. We need to decide what we're going to do next."

"God, can't we talk later? You're getting me all worked up here. I never had you down for a tease."

"I know, but I'm trying to get your attention. No more funny business until you answer my questions."

"Fire away."

"You and Kaz. That's finished with, right?"

"Defo," he said. "It was never going to lead anywhere. She was there and. . ."

"OK. I don't need to hear the details. And all that stuff you said in the papers?"

"I know it was out of order, but I wanted the whole world to know you were the innocent party. You should have reported Peter to the police."

"None of your fucking business."

"OK. I'm sorry, Ames. So are we done?"

I reached for his roving hand and trapped his fingers in mine.

"This cash that's burning a hole in my bank account - how would you like to get away from all the shit that's been going on the last few months and come with me to New Zealand?"

76

MUM was home again when we surfaced, soon after 1.00. We'd showered together and Matt had watched as I went through the complicated process of moisturising my skin before getting dressed. It seemed weird, having some guy sitting on my bed, fingering my bra and panties and stockings before handing them across as if taking part in some elaborate, erotic ceremony.

"You're looking hot, Ames."

"Say it like you mean it," I said.

"You know you're gorgeous, right?"

"If you say so. But you need to put on some clothes. We're going to have to tell Mum what our plans are, and I know she'll be dead against it. Even the thought of us being together won't go down well."

But as it happened, she was fine. She barely blinked when we dashed into the kitchen, Matt trying to grab me by the waist as I pulled out the nearest dining chair. Mum had the portable tuned in to BBC News 24.

"Any coffee on the go?" I said.

"You'll both have to wait. There's something about Lochinver on the News."

"What's happened now?" Matt said.

"I'm trying to listen to it."

I signalled for Matt to shush and we sat down and watched the talking head on-screen.

'A tiny cottage, less than two miles outside the quiet, Highland village of Lochinver, is currently at the centre of a major police investigation involving human trafficking, prostitution and the supply of controlled substances.

A spokesperson from Police Scotland has, in the last hour, confirmed that raids have been carried out at two properties in Aberdeen as well as at this remote cottage on the North-West coast of Scotland. Unconfirmed sources suggest this is connected to the discovery on Sunday morning of two undentified bodies at a property five miles from here.'

The report switched to footage of police in full riot gear converging on one of the buildings in question.

'Acting on information, police called at the O-NYX nightclub on Bridge Street, Aberdeen, during the early hours of this morning. A number of prominent figures were escorted from the premises and are currently in police custody. In a separate incident, police have raided an apartment in the Rosemount neighbourhood of the city and several unidentified individuals were taken to the nearest police station for further questioning.'

Then the cameraman focussed on the cottage again.
"Anybody recognise that place?" Mum asked.
I'd been there. "That's Jimmy Jump's cottage."
"Luibeg?"
"Yeah."
But then the image changed to a second building tucked away at the far end of Jimmy's property.

'Intense activity continues as a team of investigators searches the remote cottage of Clachan for further evidence.'

"I thought Clachan had been empty since old Mrs Gregg passed away. Wasn't there something about the executors of the will having to wait for the land to be decrofted before they could sell it off."

"That wouldn't stop Paver putting in an offer," Matt said. "It's the perfect place, if you're looking to live off-radar. He probably paid someone over the odds to keep it all hush-hush."

"Hang on, Matt," I said. We watched as two men in suits were filmed on the steps outside Aberdeen Sherrif Court. "That's Fleming and Coleman."

'Police were unable to confirm whether or not this latest operation is linked to a recent court case involving two men from Sutherland who were sentenced to a total of eighteen years after being found guilty of human trafficking for sexual exploitation. A third person, local community councillor and business

consultant, Gordon Paver, was also
arrested in connection with the
original investigation earlier this
year but was subsequently released
without charge.'

A stock photograph of Paver filled the screen.
"Smug bastard," I said.

'The BBC have been informed that an
import-export agency operated by Mr
Paver is listed as the registered
owner of Clachan cottage. Mr Paver
also owns a local chalet park along
with a four-bedroom house which stands
at the entrance to the park. The
Police spokesman was unable to confirm
the identities of those taken into
custody during the raids, but the BBC
believes a warrant has been issued for
Mr Paver's arrest.

Keith Beresford, BBC News, Lochinver'

"Christ. About fucking time," Matt said.
The three of us had tears in our eyes. "Oh, Amy," Mum
said.
"I know." I turned to face Matt. "Has this got anything
to do with your dad?"
His face was grey with tension. "It looks like he's told
them everything."
That meant the police knew about the money. The
thought of seeing Paver behind bars was tempered by the
lost opportunity to get away. Matt had already committed
to escaping with me to the other side of the world, but

now our shared euphoria had come to a grinding halt.

"We can forget about New Zealand," I said.

"New Zealand?"

"It's OK, Mum. Just something we were talking about earlier this morning. It's unlikely to happen now the cat's out of the bag as far as the money's concerned."

She got up from her stool, stood behind me and began to comb a patch of wet hair at the nape of my neck. "You're going to catch cold."

"Leave it!"

"Maybe it would be for the best," she continued.

"Maybe what?"

"You leaving here. I hate the thought of losing you again, but it won't be forever, will it?"

I turned in my chair and buried my face against her breast.

"I've had your uncle Brendan on the phone while you were asleep. He says he'll pick you up in the morning at 08:00."

"You going back to Aberdeen already?" Matt said.

"No. We said we'd go for a walk in the hills while he's here. Glas Bheinn maybe - or out as far as the waterfall."

"Who's we?" Matt said.

"Me and Brendan, but you're welcome to join us."

"Forget it. He'd probably throw me from the top of the falls, seeing as he's not exactly my number one fan."

"He'll come round if he cares about me as much as he says he does. He'll be more than happy that I'm happy."

"So you're saying you're happy?" Matt asked,

"Happier than I've ever been. Who needs money?"

77

BRENDAN had joined us in our celebration supper as we watched events unfold on TV. Gordon Paver was apprehended at Edinburgh airport shortly after passing through Security on his way to Amsterdam.

Result!

And following the raid on Clachan, details emerged suggesting that Paver had been in the habit of organising illicit sex parties involving underage girls, as well as making a living from a number of shady escort agencies in Aberdeen.

Footage of the local reporter standing next to Jimmy's cottage, coupled with a mug shot of Paver, played in an endless loop on News 24 as further information became available.

"So Paver had a secret hidey-hole right under everybody's noses," Matt said.

"Looks like it." I thought back to Ania's story. The chances were, the police would find her SOS in Clachan.

"What about your dad? What d'you think'll happen to him?"

Matt didn't respond. I rested my hand on his thigh but he didn't take the five-fingered bait. Instead, he switched on his laptop and the four of us watched the videos he'd made of Suilven and Stoer Beach weeks earlier. Anything to take his mind off the cloud of flak about to envelop his family.

"You could fly it along the burn right to where it drops over the edge of the waterfall then whoosh - imagine filming the huge drop into the glen as the ground disappears."

"Cool," I said.

"If you're sure you want me with you. But I'll need to go home and pick up all my gear from the garage. There's my android as well as the drone."

"I can run you there after supper," Brendan said.

"OK. Steff's probably still at the hospital, but there'll be reporters everywhere."

"No problem. I've got my ice axe in the boot."

Even Mum managed to raise a smile.

"You'll have to show me how it works," Brendan continued. "We can to do the same kind of stuff once we get to New Zealand. Drones are all the rage down there - people posting videos and sharing them on YouTube."

"What d'you mean 'we'?" I said.

"I've already been on the phone to Jan. She's got friends out there. A place called Havelock, right at the top of South Island. We'd been talking about going over for Christmas. I've got at least six weeks' holidays owing and she says we can stay with them as long as we want."

"That's going to be brilliant," Matt said.

"The four of us could leave in the next couple of weeks and Jan can join us as soon as she finishes her next module."

"I can't believe my luck." I said. "Even if I have to pay back all the money, Paver's going to be locked up for good and we're going off on our jollies to New Zealand. Woohoo."

My good spirits weren't dampened next morning. Lashing rainstorms had followed weeks of summer drought and

315

I'd expected us to be knee-deep in bog along most of the track. But there had been a frost overnight. The ground was hard as cast iron and the tops were blanketed in thick snow.

08:15 and the roads were empty apart from a couple of fish wagons heading towards the harbour and a solitary car trailing a long way behind us. Once we turned left at Skiag Bridge, we lost sight of it. The parking space alongside the loch was empty. No tyre tracks in the snow. No footprints heading in the direction of the falls. We'd have the entire, magical day to ourselves.

78

SUMMER had done its best to scar the lower slopes of Glas Bheinn. An unseasonable drought, followed by torrential rain in the wake of Hurrican Bertha, had leached away much of the topsoil until it resembled a war zone. Gullies along the Southern shore of the frozen loch made progress slow, and there was little ground cover to mask Damo's movements as he tracked the three walkers. But this was how he liked it.

Two police cars had turned up at the end of the track to Clachan shortly after he arrived. He'd seen the lights and heard the crackle of their radios as they explored the outbuildings attached to Luibeg. By the time they reached the safe house, Damo was already away on foot. He'd telephoned Mr Paver, but the call went unanswered. He was on his own now, but no matter. If this was a set-up, he was still one step ahead of the authorities. He'd spent Wednesday night in his car, hidden amongst the abandoned, rusting wrecks at the back of the Coach House. He could play hunter and hunted. Both roles suited him fine.

Damo had always taken pride in how well he prepared himself for the kill. Today would be no different. He'd often gone hunting wild boar and deer in the forested ravines close to Kaharlyk, but hunters there paid good money to stalk and shoot from towers. That wasn't

Damo's idea of sport.

He'd woken early Wednesday, driven to the breakwater, and sat with binoculars watching for signs of life in the bungalow across the water. The mother left after first light and returned three hours later. The blinds covering the girl's bedroom window remained shut until midday. When she opened them he saw she had company. The boy they'd tried to drown at sea eight months earlier had obviously spent the night with her. He felt himself grow hard at the mere thought of what Matt and Amy might have been up to.

Then as it began to get dark again, a strange car pulled up and he saw a tall, well-built man go into the house. In the gloom it was difficult to make out his features, but Damo was certain it was the same man he'd seen entering the block of flats in Aberdeen the morning he and Alex drove away empty-handed. The same man now led the party of walkers along the rocky path on the opposite side of the loch.

Damo raised the rifle sights to his right eye and focussed. His target wore a bright red, woolly cap and a green- and white-striped scarf. The cross-hairs centred on his face. There was a slight breeze from the West, but that would make little difference with the target so close. One squeeze of the trigger and he'd be blown away. One down, two to go. But the lay-out of the terrain was deceptive. The path tracing the opposite shore dipped several times causing all three walkers to disappear from sight as they followed the banks towards the loch's outflow.

Damo cursed before packing the rifle back in its case. He slung it around his shoulder along with the loop of heavy duty wire he'd stolen from one of the outbuildings next to the scrapyard. Even though traffic had been non-existent, he was certain they hadn't spotted his car as he followed their tracks to the empty, gravel pull-in at the side of the road, twenty-two kilometres from the village. The road had been spackled in hailstones and patches of black ice, and it was easy to see where they'd turned left at Skiag Bridge. Then he waited until they collected their gear and locked the car before leaving his own vehicle at the side of the road some distance away and heading for the shore of the frozen loch.

All three were dressed in climbing gear and carried rucksacks. The boy also carried a large, white object strapped to his back. Damo had no map, but he could tell they were heading into the wilds. He couldn't figure out why anyone would choose to visit such a remote area in temperatures close to freezing. But he relished the opportunity to eliminate all three targets without witnesses. It was as if someone up above had answered his prayer.

He continued along the shore of the loch, then followed the riverbank until he found stepping stones and water shallow enough to walk across the outflow. There were boot prints in the frozen ground on the opposite bank. Someone had discarded the wrapper of a chewing gum stick. He picked it up and sniffed. It was all a game, but Damo still felt the thrill of the chase ignite a primitive spark inside him. He continued to follow the tracks along the uneven path as it approached a narrow ravine. Water crashed into its dark throat with a deafening roar, the only sound to break the silence.

In the distance he could clearly pick out the white line of path descending through the jumble of rocks before twisting out of sight again. He began to trot along the track, frozen clods cracking beneath his feet as he ate up the ground. He could smell the chill on the air. The scent of water and ice and the imperceptible tinge of scent. Maybe something Amy was wearing next to her skin.

The path continued to descend steeply now. The river on his right swinging further away then closer. Shadows from across the opposite side of the glen stretching ahead, then breaking as a shaft of sunlight pierced the gloom. Voices up ahead.

Damo crouched down. They were standing in the lee of a large boulder. The girl had unstrapped her rucksack and was pulling out a flask. The man helped the boy position something on the ground. Then Damo heard the high-pitched whirr of a motor and saw the drone rise into the air. He recognised the sound. Drones had been deployed during the Donbass conflict six months earlier. It continued to rise unsteadily before levelling off thirty or forty metres above the ground.

He unsheathed his rifle and checked the safety catch, then raised the stock to his shoulder. No breeze here. Just the cold making him shudder for an instant. He took in a breath then raised the barrel until the sights were lined up on his target. The man turned his back on Damo and watched the drone as it circled then came to ground again at the side of the path. Damo centred the cross-hairs on the back of the man's head. Another inhale. Breath on hold he closed his right eye, caressed the trigger then squeezed.

79

I didn't hear the air crack until a split second later. Brendan gave a gasp as if he was about to sneeze then he collapsed face-first onto the ground.

"God, are you OK?"

I knelt alongside him to touch his shoulder, but Matt had already reached out a hand to drag me away into the scrubby undergrowth. "Keep down. There's somebody shooting."

"What?"

"That was a rifle shot," he said.

I turned my gaze back to Brendan. There was no sign of a bullet hole or anything as dramatic. I couldn't see any blood pooling under his head, but it was clear he had been hurt.

"Didn't they see we were here?" I said.

"Don't know."

"Hey!" I called out. "Stop shooting."

"What are you doing?"

I'd got down onto my belly and begun to crawl towards Brendan. "We can't just leave him like that. Have you got your phone with you?"

Matt fumbled in his pocket before taking it out and studying the screen. "No bars."

"Shit. Help me turn him over."

He scrabbled across the ground and together we took

hold of Brendan's arms.

"Fuck, no. Please God, no." I pulled off my gloves and ran my hands across Brendan's chest, trying to work out where all the blood that soaked his jacket was coming from.

"Ames." Matt got to his feet and pulled me away. "It's too late."

"It can't be."

"Look at his eyes."

I heard the second shot. It was followed by the zing of metal on rock as the shell struck one of the boulders next to where we were standing.

"Fuck, get down," Matt yelled.

Everything went white like a washed out photograph. White hot. I fought for breath. Calming down. Brendan couldn't be dead, not just like that. He couldn't be. I lay beside him and took off one of his gloves. I needed to find a pulse. Something to help me take charge of this dreadful situation and stop such horrible thoughts swirling inside my head.

My Uncle Brendan dead?

Matt crawled next to me and pulled me lower. "We can't stay out here in the open."

"But I can't leave him. Not like this."

"You have to. There's nothing more we can do. There's a maniac with a gun out there, and he's not stalking deer."

"I don't understand."

"Do what I say, yeah?"

He wrapped his arms around me and we waited. My insides turned to mush as I watched Brendan's body grow cold. "Can't we at least phone for help."

He picked up his drone and crept behind the next outcrop of grey rock.

"Follow me. We'll head towards the top edge of the glen. There might be a signal there. But keep your head

322

down."

That made sense. "So you think someone's trying to kill us?"

"I'd put money on it," Matt said.

"Like who?"

"I'd rather not hang around to find out."

We picked our way through the difficult terrain, but whoever was tracking us seemed to have given up. There were no more gunshots. No sounds of being chased. No one calling after us or stumbling along the rocky ground on our tails.

"It's here." Matt held out a hand to slow me down. "Watch you don't trip 'cause it's a hell of a drop."

The falls were spectacular. The burn fell over the lip of rock in a cascade of white foaming froth before disappearing into space. Then, far below us, I could make out gravel bars and ribbons of water, weaving and interweaving across the floor of the glen to form the main river draining into the sea loch.

Matt took out his phone again and held it out in front of his face.

"Anything?"

He dropped it and I screamed as he spun and tumbled in a single movement onto the ground. Another shot sliced through the still air like a blade of cold steel.

I couldn't even move. I watched as Matt tried to haul himself upright. He raised the upper half of his body from the ground and propped it on both elbows. Then he turned to look in my direction. A patch of blood blossomed on the front of his fleece, and I could see a look of incomprehension cross his face.

"Matt!" I screeched.

He jerked his head to the right. "He's still shooting."

That's when I saw the guy with the gun step out from between the rocks to our right - the Ukrainian who'd

323

grabbed me outside Brendan's flat, days earlier. He ignored Matt. Instead he pointed the rifle at me and the grin on his pock-marked face grew wider. I was expecting to hear the shot, but he didn't fire.

"Come to me, nice and slow."

There was no way. I nodded as if I understood I had no chance of escaping. The rock forming the sides of the waterfall were slick with black ice where the spray had frozen on contact. Even if the rock had been dry, I'd have been taking my life in my hands trying to lower myself over the edge.

"I'm waiting."

I could see Matt moving behind the Ukrainian. He struggled to turn onto his side and he seemed to be searching the ground for something. His phone maybe, or a weapon of some sort. But the boggy terrain was frozen solid and there would be no loose rocks at hand.

I got to my feet unsteadily and looked down again. The drop was slightly less than the eight hundred feet Dad had sailed through on the way to his death, but it was still a long way to fall.

"Come now, Amy. Don't try anything stupid." He held the rifle down at his waist now. The look on his unshaven face as he slowly drew closer made me want to lash out at him. His maggot-eaten face. That unnatural gleam in his eye. Tongue licking his lips as he uncoiled a length of wire cable from his shoulder. One end was looped into a noose large enough to slip over my head. The arrogant tone of his voice suggested I had no choice.

"To me."

I saw the swagger as he stepped closer and reached out for me. Then he lassoed the wire and I felt it settle over my shoulders. I didn't give it another second's thought. I rolled onto my front and let my legs slide down over the lip of the rocky shelf into oblivion. The wire tightened around both arms, high above my elbows and across my chest, as he bore my full weight. I couldn't get a grip on anything. He kept pulling. My feet slipped over the frozen rock then the ground gave way. I heard him shout my name and I was falling.

I landed on my haunches four or five metres below the lip of rock, and the rest of the wire he'd been holding whipped past me. The impact as I hit the ground drove an arrow of pain along my spine and into my jaw. Breath spurted out of me. I lay on my side and tried to discount how close I was to the edge of the chasm. I could see the river tumbling over greasy, black rock an arm's length away from my face. Closer at hand I saw a spray of fern that had somehow gained a hold in one of the crevices.

I managed to worm one of my arms free of the cable loop and tested the ground on either side of my body with my bare fingers. The rock was slick with ice and cold, wet moss. My feet seemed to be wedged inside a crack between two boulders, but the rest of my body was perched on the narrowest of ledges sloping away from the mountainside. I dared not move.

Somewhere above me I heard someone call out again.

"Keep still. I'll help you."

It was the Ukrainian. He seemed to tower above me as he settled himself onto the rocks forming the lip of the falls. Then he held out something for me to grip. I recognized Brendan's ice axe.

"You bastard," I screeched.

"If you want to die, I can let you die. But it is better you let me help."

"So you can shoot me dead?"

He grinned again. "No, Amy. I don't mean to kill you today. It is too soon."

I tried to make myself smaller as he manoeuvred the tip of the axe into the loose loop of cable that still encircled my chest. It was no use. I felt an increase in pressure as he began to tug and suddenly I was being pulled back up the slippery rock face, the wire biting into me tighter than ever.

"Nice and slow," he said.

As he continued to pull he rose to his feet and backed away from the edge.

Finally he stopped tugging. I lay on the ground at his feet, staring into his face, safe from harm for the moment.

"Now we find somewhere warm," he continued.

I tried to roll out of reach but it was hopeless. He held me like a salmon on a line. He toyed with me a moment or two, snatching the cable so it dug into my sides, then he stooped to unfasten the noose. I could see Matt tapping away at his tablet. Then the drone rose from behind the rocks and the Ukrainian must have heard the whirr of rotors. He turned, and by the time I'd registered what was happening he'd let go of the wire, both hands raised in front of his face. The rotating fins of the drone struck him at eye level. He spun away instinctively before disappearing over the edge of the falls.

NOVEMBER

80

658 feet or 200 metres separated the lip of the Eas a'Chual Aluinn waterfall from the floor of the glen. That equated to roughly six and a half seconds before impact. I'd already researched online the physics of falling bodies and acceleration.

The literature recorded this particular drop as 440 feet - a mere 134 metres.

Shit.

It all came down to this moment. A summer obsession to end all obsessions. One step into oblivion and it would be over. I craned my neck to look at the gap between my bare feet. Matt caught my eye, as if pleading with me to step away from the edge. But my mind was made up. I'd already started the countdown in my head long before today.

I don't remember if I screamed or not. The chances were I did, but the sound got lost in the adrenalin rush as I plunged head first towards the broad ribbon of river far below. Eight seconds according to the video we were given afterwards. The shortest eight seconds of my entire life, but also the most memorable.

After I stopped bouncing up and down on the bungy

rope for a minute or so, they began to haul me back up. Two Kiwi guys - both about the same age as me. I felt like a fish on a line as I was finally dragged back into the pod, feet first.

I could barely catch my breath.

"Amazing," I heard someone shout as the next customer in line, strapped up ready for his jump, gazed down at the space beneath the launch platform.

"You OK?" Matt stood next to me, reaching with both hands to help me to my feet.

"I'm fine." Not even a single wobble as I straightened up and drank in the smiling faces all around me. Then I turned to face him and held onto his hug for an age before we were steered out to the gondola.

"Ready to go?" he said.

"Yeah." I was ready to go.

-

AUTHOR'S NOTE

You know the score by now. BLACK ICE is a work of fiction.

But I'd still like to remind my readers that both characters and plot are purely imaginary. Any locations or addresses portrayed within these pages are based on my own recollections, and where altered or enhanced have been fictionalised to suit the story. I'm at pains to reassure the communities of Assynt and Lochinver that this has always been the case. The very idea of this unspoilt corner of Scotland doubling as the crime capital of the North-West is closer to fantasy than reality. Likewise, all names and incidents are the product of my twisted imagination, and any resemblance to an actual person, living or dead is pure coincidence.

But several people have helped in shaping this book, and keeping my writing on track. In particular, I owe a huge debt of gratitude to Patrycja Rutowska for all things Polish, and to Nigel Sibbett and Michael Marnier for taking the time and trouble to scrutinise the final manuscript in search of errors and inconsistencies.

Many of the enhancements are down to them. Any retained flaws are entirely my own fault.

Finally thanks to you for reading. If you enjoyed BLACK ICE please consider leaving a short review on Amazon. It would be greatly appreciated.

C B

email: cyanbrodie@yahoo.co.uk

By the same author and available on Kindle and in paperback:

DARK SKY (Book #1 of the Lochinver Trilogy)

*When schoolgirl Caddy Neilson is found strangled in a remote
Scottish village the police are quick to establish both murderer
and motive.*
But those closest to Caddy suspect they've got it wrong.
*Best friend Amy and part-time student/small-time drugs dealer,
Matt, uncover evidence linking the young girl to a major crime.
But the search for the truth not only jeopardises their growing
relationship. It also places their lives in peril.*

and

WHITE SHORE (Book #2 in the Lochinver Trilogy)

*When seventeen-year-old Amy Metcalf's best friend is
murdered Amy's world changes overnight. The tiny fishing
village of Lochinver is no longer the safe haven of their
childhood.*

*While her on-off boyfriend, Matt Neilson, is in prison Amy is
forced to rebuild her life. Matt has adapted well to his new
surroundings and when he falls in with a bad crowd Amy finds
herself becoming increasingly isolated.*

*A face from their past declares war and Amy is forced to
accept an offer of support from an unlikely source. But when
this new relationship develops into something more than
friendship, events escalate into an uncontrollable explosion of
misplaced jealousy and revenge.*

-

Also available:

DREAMGIRL
(published by Red Telephone Books)

and for younger readers

TOAD IN THE HOLE AND TOLEY BAGS

-

And writing as Phil Jones:

80 HILLS IN NORTH-WESTERN SNOWDONIA
(published by Gwasg Garreg Gwalch)
available only in paperback.

Available on Kindle and in paperback:

80 POEMS (poetry collection)

and

SUMMERTIME BLUES (short story collection)

You can contact me at

cyanbrodie@gmail.com